To Bill ～

Najljepše želje ˇ!

best wishes!

Barbara Ziegler

July 2008

Also by Barbara Degler

THE CLAWS OF THE EAGLE
THE SEARCH FOR KATIE MULDOON

BOSNIA MOSAIC

by

Barbara Degler

This is a work of fiction. Historical incidents that are based on actual events are, to the best of my knowledge, represented accurately. Any errors are solely mine. I have made every effort to depict responsibly the circumstances of persons who lived through the 1992-1995 war in Bosnia and in the periods just before and after it. All situations involving the main characters are fictionalized. I trust that readers will understand that my intention is to offer, set against a background of war, a story of two families, told with compassion and hope.

Bosnia-Hercegovina, as the country is correctly known, is referred to simply as Bosnia since none of the story takes place in Hercegovina [also spelled Herzegovina].

Layout and cover design by Peggy Bjarno

ISBN 978-1-4357-0662-0

DEDICATION

To the memory of Mersiha Muratagić, my beautiful, intelligent, and dedicated interpreter in Bosnia in September 1998. She was 17 then, devoted to family, friends, and peace. Mersiha died four years later in an automobile accident.

U sjećanje na Mersihu Muratagić, moju lijepu, inteligentnu i vrijednu prevoditeljicu u Bosni tokom septembra 1998. Tada, sa 17 godina, bila je posvećena porodici, prijateljima i miru. Četiri godine kasnije Mersiha je poginula u saobraćajnoj nesreći.

She is sorely missed.
Neizmjerno nam nedostaje.

PRONUNCIATION GUIDE

a	ah, as in Ah, yes!
e	eh, as in best
i	ee, as in needs
o	oh, as in okay
u	oo, as in June

- some words omit the vowel; e.g., Brčko (Berch-koh)

c	ts, as in cats
ć	soft ch, as in teach
č	hard ch, as in chart
đ	dj, as in judge
j	y, as in yellow
lj	ly, as in million
nj	ny, as in canyon
r	rolled sound
s	s, as in seat
š	sh, as in sheet
z	z, as in zip
ž	zh, as in pleasure

Arkanovci	Ahr-kahn-ov-tsee
Balija	Bah-lee-jah
Bijeljina	Bee-yeh-lyee-na
Đavo	djah-voh
Hodža	hoh-djah
Krajina	Krah-yeena
Naranđasti	nah-rahn-djahs-tee
Republika Srpska	Reh-poo-blee-kah Serp-skah
Miloš	Mee-lohsh
Sanja	Sahn-yah
Sejo	Say-oh
Sirnica	seer-neet-sah
Šljivovica	shlyee-voh-vee-tsa
Tuzla	Tooz-lah
Višegrad	Vee-sheh-grad

GLOSSARY

Andrić, Ivo	1961 Nobel Prize winner for *The Bridge on the Drina*
Apoteka	apothecary or druggist; pharmacy
Arkan	pseudonym of a Serb paramilitary commander
Arkanovci	militia forces under the command of Arkan
Baka	grandmother (baka as a relation; Baka as a name)
Balija	a slur against Muslims
Chetnik, Ćetnik	Serbs formerly loyal to the monarchy; used by some as a slur against Serbs
Ćevapćići, ćevapi	spicy meat rolls on a bun
Dayton Accords	Peace agreement ending military action in December 1995
Đavo	demon, devil
Dimije	baggy trousers worn by some Muslim women
Federation of Bosnia	one of Bosnia's two entities, established by Dayton Accords
Hodža	Islamic teacher
IEBL	Inter-entity Boundary Line, established by Dayton Accords
IPTF	International Police Task Force
Krajina	Kraj means edge; the strongly contested western frontier settled by Austria-Hungary with Orthodox Serbs as a defensive barrier against the Ottoman Turks
Naranđasti	adjective for the color orange (as in Orange Demon)
NGO	non-governmental organization
OSCE	56-nation Organization for Security and Cooperation in Europe
Republika Srpska, RS	Republic of Serbia, one of Bosnia's two entities, established by the Dayton Accords
Sarma	stuffed cabbage rolls
SFOR	NATO's Stabilization Force
Sirnica	flaky cheese-filled pastry (sir means cheese)
Šljivovica	plum brandy
"Turk"	Derived from rule of Turkish Ottoman Empire; used as a slur against Muslims

BOSNIA-HERCEGOVINA

Note: Map is a composite of 1995 and 1998;
since August 1995, Krajina has been part of Croatia.

Prologue
Bosnia-Hercegovina
1992-1995

In Bosnia's mountains, valleys, and forests, the spirits whisper—not silenced by cracks of gunfire and the roar of explosives. In summer, their sighs drift through supple greenery; in autumn, they rustle dry leaves; in winter, they slip through naked branches. In the lush springtime, the stench of gunpowder and rot mingle with the sweet fragrances of lipa and plum blossoms as weeks roll into months and months into years.

Along the Drina Valley, thousands of husbands, fathers, and brothers are missing or dead. The spirits are saddened as new stories of slaughter, rape, and massacre are added to ancient ones.

In a bizarre combination of medieval and modern warfare, tanks creak along beside mule-drawn carts loaded with ammunition while deep in the mountains, militia forces prepare to surge down a steep hillside to attack a village. The charge begins in inky darkness, sharp bursts from assault weapons blending with screams and shouts as villagers flee.

The mountains tremble under the footsteps of disheartened refugees, carrying what they can, abandoning bits of their lives that become too burdensome. They leave behind them farms and villages that have been plundered and burned. The spirits drift amid the ruined houses where only stubs of walls remain, soon host to vines and weeds. There are no longer any people—no dogs, no chickens. In the rubble, a scorched picture frame, a child's shoe.

On the mountains, bone-weary soldiers, horses, and pack mules sweat in the blazing sun of August. In winter, tanks sit useless in deep snow, their crews shivering in blue-lipped numbness.

Day after day in Sarajevo, fire-blackened trams are idle. People hasten past them, intent on getting jugs of water, while on the hills, snipers track their passage in the crosshairs of Kalashnikovs. The library is consumed by fire, its priceless collections of literature, gathered over centuries, reduced to ashes.

The venerable stones of Mostar's treasured bridge tumble into the Neretva River, victims of relentless shelling.

In a town to the north, the spirits cringe when soldiers brutally rout the population, confiscating their small bundles of personal items. Near war's end, those who arrived to occupy the vacant houses are, in turn, evicted.

However, in the early spring of 1992, in Bijeljina—soon to be the first town savaged by the war—the spirits hint at future events that are inconceivable to innocent young people who sit on branches amid the fragrant blossoms of a plum tree.

1992~1993

CHAPTER
1

Pain shot down Sanja's arm as she was slammed against the open classroom door. She dropped her books, scattering them across the sill. As she bent to pick them up, she glanced up at the boy in the blue shirt who had shoved her. Why did he do that? All she'd done was smile at him. He glared at her and spat out a single bitter word.

"Chetnik!"

Sanja stared at him, amazed. She couldn't believe someone would shove her on purpose. She didn't know his name; didn't know anything about him. But he seemed to know her, at least enough to try to insult her. *Chetnik*, she huffed. She wasn't a Chetnik, even if she was a Serb. And since when was *that* a crime?

In her next class, she massaged her shoulder. It no longer hurt, but her feelings did. After school she'd tell Amela about it. Sanja could also tell Amela about the perfect grade she had earned on her English test, an achievement that took her one step closer to university … even if that *was* six years away.

After the last class, she rushed to Amela's classroom. "Hurry up!" she said. "There's a fight!"

"So?" Amela's wide mouth curved in a smile as she continued to gather up her books. She didn't get excited about schoolyard brawls like Sanja did.

"So let's go watch it. Hurry up!" Sanja had forgotten rude boys and English tests. This was much more exciting.

"Okay. I'm coming."

In the yard outside, two boys were punching and wrestling. The one in the blue shirt was the one who had slammed into Sanja earlier. When he fell, the boy in the brown shirt was immediately on top of him. They rolled in the dirt, their fists pounding each other's faces.

"What are they fighting about?" asked Amela. The crowd of onlookers was growing, and others were asking the same question.

The boy standing next to Amela shrugged and said, "I don't know. One yelled, 'You dirty Chetnik,' and the other yelled back, 'You filthy Balija scum.'"

Amela winced when she heard the cruel names for Serbs and Muslims. The second one might as well have been aimed straight at her. When Sanja heard *Chetnik*, she groaned.

Ivana, standing next to Sanja, chimed in. "Can you believe they're neighbors? The father of the guy in the blue shirt cuts the hair of the guy in the brown shirt."

"With sharp scissors?" Sanja said. "I think I'd change barbers." Everyone around her laughed.

The boys managed to get in a few well-aimed blows before two teachers rushed from the building and dragged them apart. Sanja's attacker had a bloody nose, and the area around the other boy's eye was swelling. The crowd began to disperse.

Ivana walked a little way with Amela and Sanja. "Name calling is nasty," she said. "I don't like it." She turned toward the bridge over the canal and gave a sigh. "Yesterday at the market I heard a man say something cruel like that. It didn't used to be that way. Bijeljina's always been a nice place to live." She sighed again, then waved good-bye and walked toward the center of town.

As Amela and Sanja walked home together, Amela asked, "Do you think Bijeljina has changed?"

"I don't know," Sanja admitted. "Maybe everything's changing in Yugoslavia. There's stuff on TV news, but I don't listen to it. I figure there's nothing I can do about it."

"My parents don't let me watch the bad stuff," said Amela. "But I hear them talk. It's all about politics, and I don't understand it."

They had reached the corner of Amela's street and were standing in front of a small market.

"Wanna get a soda?" asked Amela.

"Sounds good." Sanja checked to see that she had some money with her.

Joining three other customers inside made the store feel crowded. The girls each bought a soda and stepped back outside.

Sanja took a drink from her bottle, then said, "You know, that guy … the one in the blue shirt?"

"The one whose father cuts hair."

"Yeah."

"I know who he is," said Amela. "His father and mine went to mosque together last week. My father doesn't go very often, but the man came by to invite him."

"Well," said Sanja, "that kid bumped into me in school."

"So? What's wrong with bumping into somebody at school?"

Sanja shook her head impatiently. "I don't mean happening-to-meet-each-other bumping. I mean *bumping*. Like he deliberately rammed his shoulder into mine and shoved me against the door."

Amela smiled. "Maybe he likes you."

"No," Sanja insisted. "It was an I-can't-stand-your-guts kind of bumping. And he called me a Chetnik. If he does it again, *I'm* gonna be the one who gives him a bloody nose."

"You're not a Chetnik."

Sanja shrugged. "Of course not. My father's an army officer, but he's not … like, you know … political." She scowled and continued, "Personally, I don't care who's Serb or Chetnik or Muslim or Orthodox or if they quack or oink! Your family's Muslim. So what? My family's Orthodox, but we don't go to church. So what's the big deal?" She reached for Amela's hand. "Listen, let's never let anything like that pull us apart."

"Of course not, Sani. We've been friends all our lives—twelve whole years." Amela gave her friend's hand a squeeze.

"Almost thirteen. Here's to us!" said Sanja, raising her soda bottle in a grand gesture.

"I have an idea," said Amela. "Let's go to my house and my mother can braid your hair."

"Can't," said Sanja, "My mother's taking me shopping for clothes. I know we won't agree on anything. I'll like something red and she'll like something pink."

"Don't get pink. It's not your color. So, I'll see you tomorrow morning. It's Saturday, so I'm sleeping late. Let's meet at my house at about eleven."

"Right."

The next day Sanja arrived eager for action. "Let's do something fun," she said. "What about your sister? Dina's always a good subject for a practical joke. She's so 'I'm seventeen. I'm *so* superior.'"

"Oh, especially now. She's all mushy-gushy about her new boyfriend, and she's making me sick." Amela fluffed her honey-blonde curls, a shade darker than Dina's, and mimicked her sister's simpering tone. "She goes, 'Oh, Satko, Satko. You're sooooo wonderful.' It's disgusting. She made a big show of the box of chocolates he gave her last week and then only let me have one. She says maybe I can have two this week 'cause he'll give her a box every week—to celebrate their anniversary. Yuk! I felt like ramming every piece down her throat, one at a time."

"No, silly. It's *chocolate.* As much as you love it, you should shove every piece down *your* throat! You'd be in chocolate heaven!" Sanja was laughing.

Amela was laughing, too, until she felt Sanja's grip on her arm. "Oh-oh. What are you thinking up, Sani?" She'd seen that look before.

The information about Dina had given Sanja the skeleton of an idea, and now she was about to put meat on the bones. She was always the one with plans, daring Amela to go along with them. Amela didn't think things up, but she enjoyed a little mischief when it was presented to her.

"What day's their 'anniversary'?" Sanja asked.

Amela thought for a second. "Um, today! He came over this morning early and gave her the chocolates. He's coming back this afternoon to take her somewhere."

"Okay, here's what we'll do. You get hold of the new box of candy as soon as you can. I'll gather up a bag full of dead bugs, and we'll replace the chocolates with them."

Amela's eyes flew wide open. So did her mouth. "Oh, Sani, do you really think we should?"

"Well, of course we should!" Sanja knew just how to lure Amela into the plan. "I dare you."

Amela thought it over, then grinned and agreed. This time the dare was irresistible since the target was her annoying sister.

In less than an hour, Sanja was back with a small bag. Amela showed her the candy box on the kitchen table.

"I can't believe she left it there," said Sanja. Then she added with a giggle, "Little does she know it's going to have a magical transformation." Sanja had brought a remarkable collection of insects. No two were alike. The chocolates made their way into the stomachs of the two girls, except for the one they saved for Dina, now nicknamed "Anniversary Girl."

When Dina came into the kitchen, Amela and Sanja were well hidden, crouched behind the end of the sofa in the sitting room where they had a good view. They weren't disappointed. Dina filled the air with ear-splitting shrieks. She flung the box into the corner. "Amela! Amela! I'll get you! I will!" she screamed as she rushed to the sink where she scrubbed her hands raw.

When she spotted her sister and Sanja rolling on the floor, smug in their success, she picked up a breadbasket and threw it at them. Amela ducked. It hit the wall. Dina turned in a fury and left the house, slamming the front door behind her.

Sanja wanted to stay to gloat over their success, but her mother had plans. The girls agreed to meet the next afternoon in their special place.

"I'll get Mama to bake sesame seed buns," Amela promised.

The special place was a large backyard on the end of the block between their streets. The old woman who lived there—they called her The Old Crone—would chase them with her broom unless Sanja had come to buy šlivovica for her father. He said the old woman made the best plum brandy west of the Drina in the still in her living room.

The next day, after checking to be sure the woman wasn't at home, Sanja climbed one of the many plum trees in the big yard. That day at the end of March, the air was mild and the blossoms on the plum trees were soft white and pale purple. Sanja was glad she had only a tee shirt under her light denim jacket. She settled in to wait, tapping her finger impatiently. Amela was late. Amela was always late.

"I thought you'd never get here," Sanja scolded when her

friend climbed up and perched on a limb across from her. "How's Dina?"

"She had to forgive me because she wanted to borrow my yellow blouse."

"Ah, good," said Sanja. "I'm starving. Did you bring the buns?"

"Of course. *You're* the one who always forgets things. And don't fuss at me. Not today. I'm too upset."

"What is it? What are you upset about?" asked Sanja, immediately sympathetic. "It can't be about the math test. You always get good grades. Not that boy in your …"

"No, no. Nothing like that," said Amela with a quick shake of her head.

As they perched on the tree limbs, swinging their legs and wolfing down sesame seed buns, Amela told Sanja what was bothering her. "I'm afraid I'll be sent away." Her voice quivered as she told of the conversation she had overheard between her mother and father.

"My father's such a quiet man, but his voice was rough like sandpaper when he said, '*Hanifa, I want you and the children to leave. It's getting dangerous in Bijeljina.*'"

Sanja frowned as she licked sesame seeds off her fingers. Her gesture was slow, but her heart was racing.

"My mother said that the stories about war starting in Bosnia were just rumors," Amela went on. "She told Papa that he should know how easy it was for rumors to spread, but if there was really any danger, then he should come with us."

Sanja thought she knew what his answer would be. "He said he can't leave his patients, right?"

"Exactly," said Amela. "So then he said my mother should at least take us kids—Dina and Sejo and me—to Tuzla."

"To your aunt's house?" said Sanja, feeling the tightness growing in her chest.

Amela answered with a heavy sigh. "He said he wanted to know we were safe."

"But if there's a war, why would you be safer in Tuzla than here in Bijeljina?"

"I don't know, but he was sure there was gonna be trouble in Bijeljina. Mama didn't answer right away, and I held my breath. Surely she wouldn't do such a thing! Make us leave our town, our house? Make me leave you, Sani?" Amela brushed her hand across her cheek, wiping away the tear that had started to slide down it.

Sanja was listening intently, her eyes wide with concern. "You can't go, Amela. You can't! What did she say?"

"She said '*Well, …*' like she was actually considering it, and I wanted to yell at her, *Don't give in. Don't!* Then she said she'd call my Aunt Biserka. I was miserable."

Sanja pulled off a plum blossom and crushed it. She wanted explanations and didn't know where to get them. "Well, maybe your father's spooked by that explosion at the Café Istanbul last night," she said.

"A few people were hurt. My father treated them," Amela added.

"I heard about it from my brother and his buddy Ranko," said Sanja. "They were near there and they heard the explosion. They said it was a rocket aimed at Muslims inside. A couple Serb guys they talked to later said Muslims had threatened them."

"Why would they do that, Sani? It's not like there's a war. Wouldn't your father know if there was a war?"

"I'm sure he would, but he's away with his army unit, and we don't hear from him very often." Sanja missed her father. She liked it when he talked to her like she was a grownup. He answered her questions and explained things, not like her mother who had her own opinions and didn't care what anybody else thought. When her mother and father disagreed, it seemed to Sanja that her father was sensible and right.

Sanja swung onto a lower branch, then jumped to the ground. "Well, this morning," she went on, "the man on the news said Muslim militiamen were setting up roadblocks in town."

Amela slowly followed Sanja out of the tree. She reached over to whisk away blossoms from Sanja's jacket. "I heard my father say that things like that give Serbia an excuse to take over. He said Bosnia voted last month to be independent—just like Slovenia and Croatia."

"My mother says Serbia won't let Bosnia go."

Amela gathered up the paper and crumbs, all that was left of their snack. "It's politics," she said, her brown eyes troubled. "It's all so confusing. Well, I don't care! I won't leave, Sanja! I won't!"

But Sanja knew that if Amela's father said go, they would have to go.

"Well, just in case, we should do a blood oath. All we have to do is stick our palms with a sharp knife and mix our blood."

Amela's reaction was swift. "Oh, ick!"

"I saw it on TV. It looked cool." Sanja mimicked the actor's deep voice, saying, "'*Mingling our blood will ensure our friendship forever*,'" and then she giggled.

Amela shook her head and rolled her eyes. "That's revolting," she said, "and anyway, we don't need some silly ritual. Besides, it's all politics," she added testily. "It has nothing to do with us."

But she was wrong.

CHAPTER
2

Late Wednesday night, Sanja's brother Goran ran into the house summoning his mother and sister with his shouts. Being fifteen, he had access to more information than Sanja did, a fact that rankled her.

"I was over at the army barracks," he said, panting as he tried to catch his breath. "We heard shooting, and somebody came running in saying Arkan's guys are coming in on buses."

"Mama?" Sanja gave her mother an anxious look. "Who are they?"

"They're paramilitary forces, not regular army like your father. Arkan is their commander."

Sanja thought back to a conversation she had overheard. Her father had talked about Arkan saying he was a ruthless thug.

Goran was excited and continued his story. "I saw them on the other side of the canal. They had machine guns and they started shooting and one of them tossed a hand grenade into a shop."

"My God," said Stefana. "You children go down to the cellar. We don't know what to expect. I'm going to get some blankets and food."

Was this war? Sanja wondered. Maybe if she and Amela had done the blood oath … Oh, what a stupid thought! As if that would stop people from shooting each other if they were determined to do it.

"How long will we stay in the cellar?" Sanja asked her mother, but Stefana had no more idea what to expect than her children.

"We have nothing to fear," she kept assuring them, "because we're Serbs as are the soldiers."

"Papa's a soldier," Sanja insisted, "but he's not out there shooting. Is he?"

"No, of course not. He's away."

"If those guys aren't after us, then why are we hiding?" asked Goran. Sanja guessed he was scared, too, though he would never admit it. Neither of them could imagine how it felt to be struck by a bullet or blown to bits by a grenade. They thought their father's being an army officer was heroic and brave, but danger had always seemed unreal and far away.

"Being down there is just a precaution," said Stefana. "It's just until the shooting's stopped, and that won't be long."

Hiding in their cellar, confused and scared, Sanja shivered. It was dark and clammy. The cement walls gave off a foul, musty odor. The only furniture was three kitchen chairs they had carried down. The only light was a couple of candles her mother had set on a shelf in the canned foods closet. And there were mice. Sanja hated mice.

Stefana started up the stairs. "I'm going to go up to our bedrooms and get us some warm clothes. I'll see if I can find another flashlight."

"Sanja!" Goran's voice sounded tight coming to her through the dim light. When he spoke again, he was beside her. "Sanja, I'm going to sneak out and see what's going on. I won't be gone long."

Sanja gasped. "You're crazy! You could get shot!"

"No I won't. You heard Mama say they're not targeting us."

"Then who *are* they targeting?" asked Sanja, frustrated.

"The Turks, of course."

"Turks? You mean the Muslims? Goran! Don't call them Turks."

"All right, then. The Muslims."

A wave of terror washed over Sanja as she said, "No! I don't understand! Amela's Muslim."

Goran dismissed Sanja's concern with an impatient wave of his hand. "You're too young to understand," he said, his condescending tone doing nothing to calm her fears.

"I'm going with you," she said. "I've got to get to Amela's house to see that she's all right."

"That's crazy," he answered.

"*That's* crazy? At least I have a reason to go, not just stupid curiosity."

"Listen, we can argue later. If we're going, we've got to do it now before Mama comes back downstairs."

As they climbed the steps, Sanja reached for Goran's hand. He might be crazy and condescending, but he was all she had for comfort, and the thought of going outside was curling her insides.

They paused at the front door to listen and heard their mother moving about on the floor above. Goran opened the door a crack. With only faint moonlight to guide them, he led the way across the small yard, through the gate, and out to the street. Although the sharp popping of gunfire was loud outside, there was nobody on their street as they made their way to the end of the block. However, Sanja noticed an orangish glow in the sky across the canal. Was there a fire on the other side of town? They passed the house of The Old Crone and kept going. The nearer they came to Amela's street, the more activity there was. They turned the corner and paused.

"What's going on?" Goran murmured.

The street was filled with people and trucks. Some men wore camouflage uniforms, not the spit-and-polish Sanja was used to seeing her father wear. They were wearing masks and gesturing with their guns, barking orders. The wailing she'd heard as they approached the street was now at high pitch, women's voices crying and pleading. It was a ghostly sound that raised the hair on the back of her neck.

"Let's go home," said Goran with an urgency that Sanja felt, too. When she heard machine-gun fire nearby, she jumped and covered her ears, as if what she couldn't hear wouldn't harm her.

"No," she said. No matter how scared she might be, she was straining to see halfway down the block to Amela's house where she could make out a little knot of people. Was that Amela, her mother, her sister, and her brother huddled together by their front gate? Where was Amela's father? She pulled her hand away from Goran's.

"Sanja, don't!" he whispered, and turned to leave, then turned back. "You've got to come with me."

But Sanja was already two steps ahead, staring wide-eyed at her goal, and increasing her pace as she recognized her best friend. Then suddenly she swerved, going through the gate of the corner house, and almost losing Goran.

"Where are you going?" he called softly, trying not to attract attention.

"Through the backyards," she tossed over her shoulder. She counted the houses as they moved toward Amela's house, then they cut through the narrow alleyway to the front yard and the gate to the street. They were just a few feet away when Amela turned toward them. Sanja flew to her friend and flung her arms around her.

"What are they doing?" Sanja asked, nodding toward the truck. She wiped the tears from Amela's cheeks.

"I don't know." Amela couldn't stop crying. "They ordered us out of the house, and they put my father in that truck. Where are they taking him?" she pleaded, but Sanja had no more information than Amela did.

"They'll just ask him some questions and then let him go," said Goran.

Amela looked at him in surprise. She hadn't known he was there. "I hope so," she said. "But you'd both better go home. Everything's a mess. Sanja, meet me in the plum tree tomorrow morning and we'll talk."

"Amela, come here!" Her mother's command cut sharply through the cries of the other women.

As Amela turned to go, Sanja gripped her wrist. "Here," she said, thrusting into Amela's palm the birthstone ring she always wore. "Keep this tonight for good luck and bring it with you tomorrow."

Amela took the ring. It was too tight for her finger, so she slid it into the pocket of her jeans.

"Sanja, come *on*," Goran muttered through clenched teeth.

"Wait." Amela slipped her own ring off her finger and gave it to Sanja. "Good luck for you, too. Oh, and I have little Siva in my backpack," she said. Her toy animal looked exactly like Sanja's cat, only smaller.

Goran tugged at Sanja's jacket and they sneaked away through the backyards, coming back onto the street near the corner. Sanja was in the lead, her brother at her heels, when she heard him cry out. She turned to see him in the grip of a man who was wearing a camouflage uniform and a black ski mask. Sanja wondered what kind of soldier would wear a mask.

"Where do you think you're going?" the man asked, raising his rifle. He gave Goran a shake as he looked pointedly at Sanja. The smell of whiskey on his breath made her gag. Her scalp prickled with fear. Inside the mask she could see his eyes looking her up and down like he wanted to strip her naked. She tried to move away, but he let go of Goran and gripped her chin, turning her head this way and that. His fingers were rough. She wanted to run, but all she could do was stand there shaking.

"Let go of my sister! We're just ..." Goran began.

"Shut up. You're just nothing. Come with me." He grabbed Sanja's sleeve and poked Goran in the ribs with his gun. "Over by that truck," he ordered.

Then Sanja felt a hand on her shoulder. Panic tightened her throat. She squeezed her eyes shut. With relief she heard the person speak and knew that the hand belonged to Dragan Dušanović, a pharmacist and Amela's father's best friend.

"Let her go," she heard him say.

Behind his mask, the soldier's eyes narrowed as he swung his gun toward the pharmacist, then waved it toward the truck. "Get over there," he snapped.

"My ID," said Dragan calmly. He handed over some papers. "I've been sent to give medical assistance."

It didn't sound truthful to Sanja, but the soldier seemed to believe it. He scanned the papers, grunted, then said, "Stand over there out of the way. You, kid," he said nodding at Goran, "you get over there by the truck."

"No," said Goran. "We're Serbs and our father's an army officer."

The soldier laughed, then he swore as he gave Goran a shove.

"These young people are with me," said Dragan, standing

firmly beside Goran, his hand still gripping Sanja's shoulder.

The soldier put his hand on the back of Sanja's neck and started to pull her closer to him. "All right," he said, "you can take him, but leave the girl with me."

Sanja went cold. What was he going to do to her?

"No!" shouted Goran.

Dragan eased between Sanja and her tormenter. "She's my charge," he said firmly. "I'm taking her home, then I'll be back for that medical assistance."

The soldier hesitated, then said gruffly, "Take her then. I can find better entertainment on this street." He left them and walked toward the truck.

Dragan stared after the soldier, then whipped around to face Sanja and Goran. He looked grim, and Sanja expected a furious chewing out.

"What are you two doing here?" Dragan demanded. "This is a very dangerous place."

"My friend Amela ..." Sanja began.

"Yes, I know your friend," he said, "but there's nothing you can do. I'm here to try to help them and you two will only get in the way. Go home and let me do what I can! For all I know I may not even live through this cursed night!"

"But ..." Sanja's protest faded.

Goran started to leave, then turned back, saying, "The soldiers won't really hurt Serbs will they? I mean, like you and me and Sanja? That's what Mama said."

"On a night like this, anything can happen. Take your sister home. I'll offer your friends refuge, but we can't be sure of anything with Arkanovci shooting up the town."

Arkanovci.

Sanja tried to remember again what her father had said about the militiamen—Arkan's Tigers, he'd called them—merciless, cold-blooded thugs. She raised her eyes to the heavens. She was not used to praying, but she prayed now. She prayed that Amela would be safe.

Back inside their house, creeping silently to the dismal basement, Sanja and Goran hoped their mother had not missed them. But she had.

"There you are!" she snapped when she saw them. "I've been worried sick. I can't believe you were stupid enough to go outside!"

"We went to the corner," Goran said. "There was no one there."

Sanja's jaw dropped and she started to protest. She hated lying, but what he had said wasn't a lie. Exactly.

Goran lifted his chin defiantly. "You said the soldiers wouldn't hurt Serbs."

"Goran! A stray bullet won't know or care *what* you are! Nor will a drunken soldier!" shouted Stefana. "You two will not—do you hear me? *not*—leave this house again until I say it's all right. The soldiers will deal with the Muslim threat, and then life will be normal again."

Sanja was dazed. She couldn't imagine what kind of threat her mother was talking about, but she knew she would have to obey even though she was in agony. There hadn't been time for Amela to go to Tuzla, to be safe, as her father had wanted. Sanja would have to wait in anguished impatience for her mother to let her leave the house.

Four days later, the armed men had moved on down the Drina Valley, and permission was finally given. Sanja raced to Amela's house, stopping short as she watched a couple of scruffy-looking men carting away the television set. After they had gone, she crept to the door and, finding it open, ventured inside. It was empty. Most of the contents were gone. All of the people were gone.

Sanja went back later that day, but it was the same empty house. Amela wasn't there.

Each day for the next week, Sanja returned every chance she got, and then one day she saw a different family moving in. It made her feel empty and lost.

Amela was gone. What had happened to her on that dreadful night?

CHAPTER
3

Amela had climbed into bed that Wednesday night eager to finish the book she was reading. The story was about a girl on a holiday at the seashore, and it brought back delicious memories of her own sunny, sandy days on the Adriatic coast. She was starting a new chapter when she heard gunshots. A wedding celebration, she thought, not so common on a weeknight, but never mind. Dina, in the other bed, stretched and turned over.

Then Amela heard explosions and the rat-a-tat-a-tat of machine guns. Startled, she dropped her book. This was no celebration! She was alarmed when she heard pounding on the front door. She ran into the hall and part way down the stairs in time to see her father opening the door. Her mother was beside him in the entry. Sejo came up behind Amela. At seven, he had even less idea than she about what might be happening. His eyes were wide with questions. She put her arms around him and could feel his heart thudding beneath his thin pajama top. Her own heart was thudding, too, as she saw a man in the doorway wearing a black ski mask.

The man yelled, "Everyone in this house—you have five minutes to gather your belongings, then outside!"

Amela swallowed hard. She felt Sejo's shoulders go rigid. Their mother glanced up at them, her eyes dark in an ashen face, and Amela could tell that she was scared, too. Sejo started to pull away, to go downstairs, but their father looked up and shook his head hard at him. Sejo shrank back, waiting as his parents started toward the steps.

Amela ran back into her bedroom. Dina was sitting up in bed, clutching the sheet to her chin. Their mother rushed in, shoving past Amela. Hanifa never behaved rudely.

"The men downstairs ..." Hanifa said.

The color drained from Dina's face. "Are they soldiers?"

"Paramilitary. That's worse than regular army. A few were at the bus station and the hospital earlier today." Even as she replied, Hanifa was pulling clothes out of the wardrobe. "Here, wear these," she said, tossing dingy, shapeless items on Dina's bed. "And, Dina, pile your hair up. Stuff it under this cap. You understand."

"Yes," said Dina.

Amela didn't understand, but there was no time to ask questions. Hanifa helped Amela and Dina as fast as her hands could fly. Amela guessed her father was with Sejo, packing a bag for him, too, but as she was cramming things into her backpack, Sejo came into the bedroom alone. He was dressed, and he was crying.

"Where's Papa?" she asked, an anxious lump in her throat.

"Come now," said their mother. Amela picked up the backpack she had hastily stuffed. She could hear loud voices and scuffling downstairs in the entry. She seldom had thoughts about Allah, but they came now without effort. *Please protect us!* she prayed.

In just a few minutes, Amela, Dina, Sejo, and their mother were at the top of the stairs. Hanifa had filled a pillowcase and one small satchel. She motioned to her daughters to carry the satchel, then put her arm around Sejo and started down. Amela followed with Dina, who had the cap on her head and her chin tucked into a bulky sweater. Hanifa detoured into the kitchen to throw some food into the pillowcase, then they moved to the doorway as if glued together. Amela looked for her father, but he wasn't there.

One hooded soldier stood by the door, stern like a guard, motioning impatiently with his gun. Amela and the others barely had time to shove their feet into their shoes and grab their coats from the hooks above. As they were hustled outside, three men carrying guns and wearing black ski masks that flattened their noses surged past them into the house. Behind the masks their eyes burned fiercely, as if they hated the people they were evicting. But why? Amela wondered.

The four of them hurried down the short walk and through the wrought iron gate to the sidewalk. Amela saw her father in the middle of the street with other men from the neighborhood. The soldiers shouted at the men to stay together. Just then an open-back truck rounded the corner. It stopped in the middle of the block. The men—Amela's father, too—were herded toward it.

"Papa!" she screamed, but her cry was lost in a chorus of wailing and screaming from the women clustered in small groups. Sounds of explosions from nearby streets and from other parts of town added to the surreal situation.

All the women were crying—Amela, too. She looked back at her house where things had been so peaceful just a short time ago. Her face was streaming with tears, and then she rubbed her eyes hard because she couldn't believe what she was seeing. Sanja was coming through the front yard! Amela flung herself at her friend and fell into her comforting arms.

Sanja looked around nervously. "What are they doing?" she asked.

Amela explained about being ordered out of the house and

about her father being shoved onto a truck. "I don't know where they're taking him."

Then Goran spoke up. "They'll just ask him some questions, that's all."

Amela hoped fervently that he was right. "You'd both better go home," she said, though desperately wanting them to stay. She and Sanja exchanged rings, then she watched them leave, melting into the darkness. She rubbed Sanja's ring for comfort, then slipped it into her pocket.

Hearing Dina's cry, she turned back to her family. Dina's boyfriend Satko and two of his friends were running toward them from the end of the street. Dina called to them to stay away, but even if they could have heard her, it was too late. They came abreast of the soldiers who pointed their guns at them and pushed them, moving them together into a small group. A second truck pulled up behind the first, and more men were shoved into it, prodded with the guns until the last one was crammed aboard.

Amela had lost sight of her father, then spotted him behind the cab on the first truck. The truck started to move, and he leaned forward to wave good-bye as if he were going off for a day in the country. Surely Goran was right, Amela thought. Her father would be back soon. The roar of the truck engine was not enough to drown out the screams of the women and children. There was so much confusion, and she was so afraid. She saw all too clearly the taillights of the truck as it moved away down the street, taking her father away. She could hear her mother moaning and saying his name softly, over and over, "Kemal, Kemal, Kemal."

Beside Amela, the girl who lived next door was screaming hysterically. She had only been married a month. Suddenly she bolted toward the remaining truck at the same time as her husband jumped out of it and started running toward her. A soldier lashed out savagely with the butt of his gun. The young man fell, his face bashed and bloody. Another soldier struck a blow to the woman's head with such brutal force it sent her sprawling into the gutter. Satko and one of his friends charged at the soldiers. Then the guns chattered and men started falling. Satko dropped to the pavement. His body was kicked, then dragged over to lie next to the woman in the gutter.

"No!" Dina cried, springing forward, but her mother jerked her back, clinging determinedly to her and to Sejo. Dina kept screaming as she leaned against Amela, her body heaving, her wet face pressed against her mother's shoulder. Amela patted her sister's arm, the only thing she knew to do. Such a useless gesture.

No more chocolates, thought Amela, then was sickened that her immediate thought had so casually dismissed a boy's life. She was lost in a tide of remorse and regret. It might have been a hundred seconds or a hundred years that they stood there as the soldiers kicked and clubbed the fallen. They sounded triumphant as they pronounced Satko dead. One of the wounded men moved. More shots were fired. Then he was pronounced, "Balija scum." And dead.

The soldiers shut the back gate of the second truck and it started to roll. Amela watched terrified as the soldiers strode past, their masked heads swinging from side to side scouring the street for anyone they had missed.

"Mama." Amela spoke so softly she wasn't sure her mother could hear her. "Are they only taking the men? Will they put us in a truck, too?"

Her mother, half listening, answered, "Just the men, child." Amela wasn't sure whether that answer was true or just said to calm her, but she hadn't seen any women gathered up so far.

Only three soldiers were left, clustered together and passing a bottle around. A depressed hush settled like a quilt over the street, pierced from time to time by a forlorn cry. Some of the women and children stood holding each other. Some drifted away, back to their homes or to the homes of others, their muffled weeping a reminder of how wretched they all felt.

Fear flashed through Amela when she heard a man's voice beside her, then it faded in relief as she recognized Dragan, a pharmacist and her father's dearest friend.

"Hanifa," Dragan said, "someone will be coming for the bodies soon. I don't know what's going to happen after that. You and the children can't go back inside the house. Arkan's militia is looting."

From inside her house, Amela could hear the sounds of glass breaking and metal clattering. Why were they destroying things?

"Wh … What can we do?" Hanifa could barely get the words out. "They killed those boys. And where have they taken Kemal?"

Dragan said, "You must go somewhere until this grisly business is over."

Hanifa was sobbing. "Go? Go where?"

"To Sanja's!" Amela said. Who better than her very best friend could comfort her and keep her safe? After all, Sanja had faced danger to come find her and give her the birthstone ring.

"No," Dragan said without a moment's hesitation. "My house is not far. If you can get there, my wife will let you in the back way. We'll hide you and as many others as we can. I promise I'll do my best to find Kemal."

Dragan left them to talk to another woman. Amela felt like they were each a tiny island in a sea of misery.

But it wasn't over yet. Three old men who had been left standing in the street nearby were gathered together. A soldier led them into a nearby yard. A woman fell to her knees, wailing and praying. Two other women tugged at the soldiers' sleeves, begging for information about their menfolk.

Amela pleaded with her mother to join them, but Hanifa said, "Tomorrow. Tomorrow I will go to the police. These thugs, these butchers, are not the ones to beg."

Hanifa drew her three children behind the low cement wall that separated their house from the street. Crouched there, they could see the street through the iron fence on top of the wall.

"I wish we could be invisible," Dina whimpered.

Sejo buried his face against his mother's coat. When they heard gunshots from behind a house, Amela and Dina flung their arms around each other. There were only two militiamen left and one of them radioed for another truck to take away the bodies.

Hanifa straightened; shook herself. "Come," she said, "We must make our way to Dragan's. Be quiet and be careful." She guided them past the side of their house. Like shadows they crept through backyards until they reached the main street. As they crossed the intersection, they would be exposed.

The four of them moved as a single body. There were fewer explosions in the nearby neighborhoods, but occasional cracks and bangs from across the canal, close to the center of town. Dark and deserted, the silence felt eerie compared with the recent commotion. The smoky air held a strange metallic flavor. The familiar street didn't feel familiar. Amela was fascinated by the sound their shoes made. Squish, squish, squish.

Then she heard a different sound. She barely had time to register that it was the thump of boots striking the pavement before she saw what she feared most. Two soldiers came toward them, swaggering, their guns raised. One had his mask rolled up, showing a thick black beard. Hanifa pushed her children behind her.

The hooded soldier lowered his gun, letting it hang by the strap around his shoulder so he could grab Hanifa's wrist. "Give me your money and jewelry." It was a gruff command. "And that wedding ring you're trying to hide behind your back, too, you low-life cow!" He yanked her right arm toward him and drew a knife out of his belt, touching her finger with the blade, drawing a few drops of blood. Amela gasped. Her heart sank as she watched her mother take off her ring and give it to him. She was glad Sanja's ring was in her jeans pocket. Oh, but what if the soldiers searched their clothes? Instead, the hooded man took their suitcase and the pillowcase and dumped everything out on the street. Neither one noticed Amela's backpack.

She thought things couldn't get any worse, but she was wrong again. The bearded soldier reached around Hanifa and flicked off Dina's cap. Her long blonde hair tumbled down.

"Ah ha ha … what a pretty *boy!*" the man said. The way he spoke had the feeling of a slimy gutter.

Four other soldiers had arrived and were breaking into a shop across the street. At a shouted order from one of them, Dina's tormentor put his mouth against her ear. "Don't go away, bitch," he said. "I have something very special for you." He patted his crotch, then the two men left them and disappeared into the building across the street.

Dina started making mewling sounds.

Hanifa said, "We've got to get to Dragan's house. Now!"

She hurried her children along without even a glance at their belongings lying in the street. Amela was shaking so much she didn't think her legs could hold her up as they went to the back of the house and knocked. She didn't know who opened the door or who led them into the house because her eyes had stopped focusing. She heard her mother murmur, "Bless you."

There were others crammed into the large room that served as a sitting room at one end and a dining room at the other. It was dark, with only the dim light from the upstairs hallway, and stifling with so many people there. Amela and her family had been there just a short time, sitting on the floor under a side window that was heavily curtained, when Dragan's wife drew aside the drapery and peeked out.

"Oh, my God," she said. "They're just a few houses away. They're searching for Muslims."

Everyone was hustled down to the cellar where they waited breathlessly for the knock that didn't come. No one thought it was a good idea to go back upstairs.

And so, Amela, Hanifa, Dina, and Sejo stayed through the night. It was cold. Even with the blankets they had been given, they felt the chilling damp that seeped up from the cement floor. Sejo, on Hanifa's lap, started to whimper. Dina murmured Satko's name, curled herself into a tight ball, and wept. The smell from so many sweating bodies made Amela queasy, but it was better than being on the street.

Amela had dozed off when she heard someone come down the stairs and saw the dark shapes of two women. One of them stumbled. They settled on the floor nearby—they seemed to be a mother and daughter. The younger one was sobbing and was bent over, as if in pain. She hid her face in her hands. Hanifa scooted around Amela to talk to them briefly.

When she moved back, Dina said in a quivery whisper, "Mama, that girl is in my class at school. What happened?"

Hanifa waved off the question, but Dina persisted.

"The hooded ones grabbed her on the street. They took her into a house," said Hanifa, "and after a little while, they sent her back out to her mother."

"Yes, and … tell me." Dina's breath came in little gasps.

Hanifa put a comforting arm around Dina as she said, "She was raped." Amela could sense her mother's helpless fury as she muttered, "The bastards."

Dina cried herself to sleep. After some fidgeting, Sejo slept, too. Amela slipped the toy kitten out of her backpack and cuddled it to her chest. They all slept in snatches, then would wake up, confused, until they remembered what had happened just a few hours before. For the rest of the night and the next day, people came, mostly women and children. They moaned and cried. They would creep, one or two at a time, upstairs to use the bathroom, then immediately scurry, quick as mice, back into their hole.

There was little room. The floor was cold. Amela learned that if you were tired enough, you could sleep sitting up. Over and over she told herself they were in a safe place. Or—as reality set in—as safe as any place could be for what was left of a Muslim family in Bijeljina.

She rubbed Sanja's ring, trying to crush the thought that they might not be meeting at the plum tree. How glad she was that her own ring was with Sanja.

Shooting went on throughout the day. It was hard to know whether people were being killed or the soldiers were drunkenly celebrating their victory. Amela heard someone say there was almost no resistance. Once when she dozed off, she dreamed that the attackers found them and took them out to be shot. Not just them, but Dragan and his family for sheltering them.

"Amela, I don't like it here," said Sejo, clinging to her arm.

"I don't either," she said soothingly, "but it's only for a little while."

The little children started to get restless. Amela passed the time worrying about her father or playing word games with Sejo. In the evening Dragan's wife brought some salami and bread, but food had to be rationed because no one knew when they could go out to buy more.

Late that evening, Amela went upstairs. On her way back past the kitchen, she heard Dragan talking with his wife. Amela listened, desperate to understand what was happening.

"Must you go out? Surely you aren't safe."

"That's true," he admitted, "but there are things I have to do. We've been able to get a few people out."

"Dragan, is it only Muslims who are in danger? Are we? Should *we* leave? Where would we go?"

"It appears that the forces are moving south along the Drina, but who can be sure? Some Serbs are leaving if they can, but I don't think we should. For now, you and our children must remain inside until I tell you otherwise."

Even with what she'd heard, Amela didn't understand. Forces? Why were forces going south? South to where? Who were the Serbs who were leaving? Wouldn't she and her family be able to go back to their house soon? There wasn't nearly as much shooting as before. Was her father at the house? Surely Dragan would have told them if that were so.

Amela had only been back in the cellar a few minutes when Dragan came down to talk to Hanifa. Amela listened closely.

"What is it like out there?" Hanifa asked.

"It's strange," said Dragan. "I notice not hearing the muezzin's calls to prayer. It's something we're used to, five times a day. The calls to prayer, the church bells. They make life feel normal. But," he went on, "the situation isn't good. Even if the militia leaves tonight, the town's in turmoil. Your people are not safe. They're being subjected to harassment and humiliation and worse."

Amela heard the sharp intake of her mother's breath. She didn't understand what Dragan meant by *your people*. She didn't hear what he said next, but she heard her mother's reply. "Then we can't stay here." Amela rubbed her sweaty palm on her jeans, waiting for him to say *of course* they could stay. But that was not what he said.

"Is there somewhere you *can* go? Almost any direction is dangerous, but west is likely to be better."

"Then to my sister's in Tuzla," Hanifa replied. "My husband …" She paused as the word caught in her throat. "My husband thought it would be safer there than in Bijeljina. He urged us to go before the soldiers came. But how would we get there?"

Dragan said, "I can get you out of town, then you'd be on your own. I don't know how long we …"

Hanifa waved her hand to interrupt him. "It would be better for us and for you if we go soon. We can go first to our weekend house. It's on the way to Tuzla. You've been there. It's very small, just two tiny rooms—just a place where we could relax in peaceful times, putter in the garden and tend to our fruit trees—but …" She let the sentence hang, and Amela felt like she was hanging, too. She loved to go to the little weekend house, but not like this. And how would Sanja know where they were?

A few hours later, after it got dark, Amela picked up her backpack. She followed her mother up the stairs where they were given a small bag of food. Then they left the house. As they walked to Dragan's car, Amela wondered if this could be the war her father had worried about.

This time she was more than just late getting to the plum tree.

She had not made it at all. Had Sanja? Would Sanja be worried? When would they meet there again, laughing, sharing stories, eating sesame seed buns? There was no way to let her father or Sanja know they were leaving or tell them where they were going or when they were coming back.

Goodbye, Bijeljina. Goodbye, Sanja.

CHAPTER
4

They left Bijeljina—they who had been robbed—sneaking away like thieves in the night. Besides the food Dragan's wife had given them, she had also lent Hanifa her identity papers in case they were stopped.

Usually Amela would be happy to be going to their weekend house, even though it was small and the bathroom was outdoors. As her mother had told Dragan, it was a nice place to relax, but this time there would be no relaxing. They could only hope it would be a safe place to stay until they could find a way to get to Tuzla. Or, even better, to go back to their house in town. Amela imagined the reunion with her father who would be waiting for them.

She and Dina climbed into the back seat of Dragan's car with Sejo scrunched down between them. Dina shoved her hair under a new cap she had been given and squeezed herself into the corner. Amela peered out the window.

"Now remember," Dragan cautioned them, "if anybody asks, you are my nieces and nephew."

Amela knew the route well, so she was puzzled when Dragan started off in the wrong direction. She sighed, telling herself she'd have to believe that the adults knew what they were doing. Dragan drove slowly. Amela hadn't seen any soldiers, but could still hear occasional shots and cries. There was an explosion off to their left and every few minutes the clatter of machine guns. Just at the outskirts of town, the sky glowed red. Soon they were on the Pantelinska Road. What a pity. If they could stay on it, they'd be in Tuzla in an hour.

Amela was beginning to feel secure when she heard Dragan say, "We're coming to a checkpoint. I've scouted the route. It's police, not military, so we should get through without a problem."

She shrank against the seat. She had never been at a checkpoint. What would happen there? Sejo reached for her hand and snuggled close to her. Dragan stopped the car, but left the engine idling.

"Hey, Marko, you lazy cop," he said. "What are you doing out here in the middle of the night? Why aren't you in a warm bar drinking brandy?"

The policeman laughed and patted his pocket. "All I'm lacking is the warm bar. Where are you headed, Dragan? I'm supposed to ask for papers."

"Eh, don't bother. I'm just going to the village down the road, delivering some medicine, and taking my sister and her children to stay with relatives."

The car started moving again.

"On second thought," the policeman said, "I'd better follow orders and take a look at your papers. I don't want to get in trouble."

"Not a problem," said Dragan.

Marko studied the papers Dragan gave him, peered across at Hanifa, and said, "Same name. Your sister?"

"My brother's wife," said Dragan.

The policeman nodded, scanning the faces of the passengers in the back seat. "Ages?"

"The oldest is just fifteen," Dragan lied. "No telling what identification we'll soon need, eh, Marko? There's a lot going on in Bijeljina."

"Damned right. We're getting rid of some undesirable elements, huh?"

"I could drink to that!" Dragan said.

The policeman and Dragan exchanged casual salutes, Dragan rolled up the window, and they drove on. Amela heard him say to Hanifa, "The undesirables I'd like to see go are Arkan's bullies."

Sejo's hand relaxed. Dina let out a long breath. Amela was glad to be past the checkpoint. At two more stops she tensed, but they proved to be no problem. Soon they turned off the highway and bumped along on the narrow dirt road to the house. It was a welcome sight.

Dragan got the family settled in, cautioning against the use of the wood stove even though it was chilly. Fortunately, there were narrow couches to sleep on and blankets to wrap themselves in. Dragan also said he would go first thing in the morning to find Kemal and bring him there. And so they tucked in to wait through the rest of the night.

The next day passed slowly. Hanifa wouldn't let the children go outside for fear of patrols, so they couldn't even walk down to the village after their food was gone. Amela rubbed Sanja's ring so often she was afraid she'd wear it out. It had become more than a token of good luck, it was a token of their loyalty. It meant they'd find a way to be together again.

It was dusk when they heard a car drive up, and Amela was frightened until she heard the signal Dragan had arranged. Then she raced to the door, bumping into Sejo and Dina who were also eager to greet their father. It was Dragan, and behind him, a strange man and woman. But not their father. In that moment the crack of despair in Amela's heart grew wider.

"What news?" her mother asked, clinging to Dragan's arm. Hanifa, the soul of hospitality, didn't even welcome the other visitors.

"Nothing yet, Hanifa. I've tried everything. The men were taken away. Nobody knows where."

The strange man caught Hanifa as she collapsed and laid her on the narrow bed. When she was sitting up and the family had stopped crying, the man, whose name was Hasan, said, "My wife and I are going over the mountain to Tuzla. We can take you with us."

They all gaped at him. Hanifa said, "Is it safe on the road?"

"We won't be driving. We plan to walk."

"Walk! But ..." Hanifa turned, pleading, to Dragan. "How can we leave without Kemal? And walk? Over Majevica Range?"

"No, Mama!" cried Dina. "I can't possibly walk that far!"

"Hanifa," said Dragan, "you must decide. We think the war has come. Many Muslims have left Bijeljina, and those who've stayed are being treated badly. It would be dangerous for you to return and probably just as dangerous to stay here, but I promise you, I will keep searching for Kemal and send him to you."

The man called Hasan put a comforting hand on Hanifa's shoulder as he said, "I've hunted in the forests between here and Tuzla and fished in the streams all my life. I'll guide you. We're refugees, like you."

Refugees? Is *that* what they were? *Refugees*? The word was like a knife in Amela's heart.

"We're refugees though we haven't left our own country," the man added bitterly.

Hanifa shook her head slowly. "Soon there will be no country left to leave."

She dropped her head. She was not used to making decisions for her family, but the decision-maker was not with them. At last she straightened her shoulders and said, "Only a few days ago,

Kemal demanded that I take the children to Tuzla. That is what he wished, so that is what I will do." Her eyes were troubled as she said to Dragan, "Let my husband know we are with my sister."

Hasan said, "We should be able to find refuge with my friends in a village a little way from here. I also have family farther along."

Dragan nodded. "We don't know where there might be patrols, so stay with Hasan. He'll guide you. I promise again, I'll do everything I can to locate Kemal."

After Dragan left to return to Bijeljina, they waited again until dark. Then they closed up the house and started out on foot, staying close to the trees between the road and a farm. The trees soon became thicker.

"I'm scared," whispered Sejo, reaching for Amela's hand.

She felt scared, too, surrounded by ghostly silence. Even the birds were sleeping. It was not at all like playing in the woods in the daytime. There was little moonlight. Hasan told them they couldn't risk any light or any talking. He led the way as his wife and Amela and her family followed. They moved along, stumbling over roots and stones. Amela's jeans and jacket were snagged by shrubs and low branches.

Where there weren't woods, there were cornfields. In the summer, the corn would be high enough to give them cover, but in early April the fields were flat. They dashed across the open spaces one at a time, Amela's turn coming after Sejo's. Her head hurt, her feet hurt, but she had to keep going. It was some distance to where Hasan's friends lived, and who knew what they'd find when they got there.

They stayed clear of the main road, every once in a while crossing a dirt lane or wading knee-deep through a stream. The farms were quiet and still as if they, like the people they belonged to, were holding their breath. Life was not going on as usual. For their little group, every step brought them to a new unknown. Sometimes Hasan thought they would be safe enough walking on the road. That took less effort, but there was the uneasy awareness that they could be seen. There was no regular traffic, but there might be soldiers in jeeps. The temptation to cry was great, but whenever Dina whined, Amela resolved that she would not complain.

After a while, Hasan directed them back into the woods. Amela whispered to her mother, "Was this walking to Tuzla a good idea?"

She realized her mother was crying when the answer came in a voice thickened by tears. "I don't know. I don't know."

Sejo was as brave as he could be, suffering from fatigue and hunger as they all were. Sometimes Hasan carried him; sometimes Amela let him ride piggyback. She and Dina began walking close together, for warmth, for comfort—for both.

Hasan had said he had friends in one place and a cousin in another. It was late afternoon when they came to the first, a simple farmhouse with a small barn attached, and he was told there was room for them in the barn.

"At least we can rest and get a bite to eat," he said. "They're heating the water in the bathroom. They said we could use the sink inside to wash up."

"Oh, yes," sighed Dina, sinking onto a bale of hay as far from the cow as she could get. Although there were some chickens in an enclosure outside the barn, the cow was their only roommate. Hasan said the cow and three chickens had been successfully hidden from marauding soldiers, but two sheep and a good many chickens had been stolen. Of course there were no pigs for them to steal at a Muslim farm, he added with a grin.

From the house, Hasan brought some bread, cheese, coffee, and tea and—oh, joy!—baklava, sweet with honey and almonds. When the water in the tank above the sink was heated, they took turns washing up in the tiny bathroom.

"I'd give my heart for a bath," said Dina, but she had to make do with the quick cleanup that was offered.

A few hours later after snatches of sleep, Hasan said, "I still want to travel when it's dark, so we'll be leaving soon. It's best if we get to my cousin's house before dawn. God forbid we should chance upon any soldiers, but if we did, at least they'd be hung over."

After they had walked for a couple of hours, the group skirted cautiously around a village. They had almost reached the road to the village where Hasan had relatives when they heard gunshots. A hunter, a drunken villager, soldiers? Hasan steered them off the road to a resting place while he went to investigate. Amela had started thinking of him as "The Optimist" because he never wavered in his belief that they would make it to Tuzla.

It was darker in among the trees, but they were glad to sit down even if the ground was damp and cold. Hanifa tore hunks of bread off the loaf they had been given and they gobbled them down.

"I'm saving the salami and cheese for tomorrow," she said.

Amela thought she should have named her "The Optimist." Her mother actually thought there would be a tomorrow. The thought cheered her.

Hanifa leaned against a tree trunk and held Dina close. Amela snuggled next to her with Sejo tucked between them. Hasan's wife was nearby, her eyes closed, but sitting erect and vigilant. No one spoke, partly because they didn't want to alert soldiers, but even more because they were numb. Numb in body and in mind. Sejo was shivering.

Dim moonlight filtered through the trees. Amela looked around. At the base of a nearby tree, she saw a bundle of rags. She pointed them out to her mother, then cautiously crawled over to them. They'd help keep them warmer while they waited for Hasan. On her hands and knees, Amela reached out. It was a large bundle, maybe abandoned by someone else who was fleeing. Bundles could be a burden on a long trek. She took hold of a bit of rag and pulled. It didn't budge. Maybe the rags were tied together, she thought. She yanked on it again, and the whole bundle suddenly rolled toward her. It stopped under her chin.

Amela was staring into the lifeless eyes of a man. Even in the dark of the forest, she could tell by his face, ashen and waxy, that he was dead. The vomit erupted before she knew it. She barely had time to turn her head, and almost threw up on him, a final disgrace. Hanifa scurried over and drew her away. Amela lay on the ground, trembling.

After a few minutes she felt calmer, but her teeth wouldn't stop chattering. When Hasan came back, he looked at the dead man and murmured, "He was shot. There's dried blood." Amela was horrified. She turned away when Hasan started to rifle through the dead man's clothing. She heard him say he'd found a little money and a Swiss Army knife that would be useful. Hasan also said he'd made contact with his cousin. Amela couldn't wait to move on.

CHAPTER
5

The family at whose house they stayed that night was nervous at having them as guests. Nevertheless they insisted that the travelers eat and gave them blankets. The floor she slept on was hard, but Amela was glad to rest her aching feet.

The group of houses was barely big enough to be called a village. The militia had already been through there once, they were told, so probably would not come back.

Moving so urgently from place to place had given Amela little chance to wonder why they were running and what they were running from. Of course she had been hearing about the mysterious Arkan and had come all too close to his not-so-mysterious Tigers, but she still didn't understand why they had taken her father away and why her family and others had to leave Bijeljina. Why was it that Muslims had been singled out?

It seemed a long time ago that she and Sanja had tried to talk about the coming trouble. She was worried about Sanja. Amela had thought about her during the long treks through woods. Was she in danger, too? It would be impossible for Amela to mention her worries to her mother, but maybe she could talk to Hasan. She found him at the back of the house cleaning a gun. She had not even known he had a gun. He had said he hunted, but this was not a hunting gun. It was too small.

"Hasan," she said timidly, "can you explain some things to me?"

He grunted, then shook his head. She was afraid she'd bothered him and started to turn around.

"Here, little Amela," he said, laying the gun on the table in front of him next to a bottle of beer. "Don't leave. It's not that I mind your asking, it's just that I'm not sure myself. Come and sit beside me. We'll talk."

Amela perched on a chair. "I know Yugoslavia is breaking up," she said. "But why?"

"Well, some people want it that way. Two parts of it are already established as new countries. Now the people of Bosnia, where we live, have declared their independence, but others claim it should be part of Serbia, partly because of the Serbs who live in it. Many Bosnians are afraid that would lead to discrimination because we're different from one another."

"How are we different, Hasan?"

"Well, different religions, for one thing—Catholic, Serbian Orthodox, Islamic."

"That's what I am," said Amela. "Islamic."

"Muslim, yes. I'm a Muslim who drinks alcohol," he admitted with a twisted smile as he reached for the bottle and took a drink. "Some people would call me a secular Muslim."

"Religion doesn't seem like anything to start a war about," Amela fretted. "Is it about politics, too?"

Hasan reached across the table and moved a plate of sliced bread closer. "Well, yes, politics, nationalism ... that and more ... money, greed, power." He patted her hand.

She frowned and said, "So it's not just because we're Muslim."

"No. No ... and yes." He shook his head. "You're no more

mixed up than most grownups, Amela."

She squirmed on her chair and reached for a piece of bread. "My friend Sanja's a Serb. She doesn't want a war."

"She's not a politician," Hasan said, smiling. "As for me, I like a country with people of different backgrounds. I voted for Bosnia to be independent."

"That's how I'd have voted, too," said Amela, trying to stifle a yawn.

Hasan grinned at her. "Get some sleep now," he said. "We'll have to leave soon."

She looked at the gun he'd finished cleaning and was now tucking inside his waistband. "Would you kill somebody, Hasan?"

"I would kill anyone who tries to hurt my wife or you or your family, little one."

Amela crept back to her blanket on the floor, but she couldn't sleep. She thought about what Hasan had said. Sanja's father wasn't a politician, but he was a soldier. Wherever he was, was he shooting? In all her twelve years Amela hadn't thought about differences, but she remembered the fight between the boys in the schoolyard. It was terribly confusing, and frightening, sort of like being swept into a whirlpool in the Drina River.

It was barely light when Hasan roused his fellow travelers and hurried them outside. A timid sun was trying to push away thick fog without much success. Somehow during the night Hasan had found a man who had an old truck and who was willing to drive the six of them. Amela had not met Hasan's cousins, hadn't even seen them, but she was grateful to them.

Hasan had acquired something else — information. He said the area was crawling with military, that the regulars were beginning to show up on the heels of the paramilitaries they had already seen.

Hasan told Hanifa about a schoolhouse in the Majevica foothills he had heard was being used as a refuge by fleeing Muslims. Amela wanted to listen, to understand. At the same time, she wanted to sleep. Her feet were sore and her tattered sneakers had rubbed blisters. She would be very glad to be riding.

The back of the truck was canvas-covered. They crawled inside, burrowing behind some boxes. The driver closed the flap and started the engine, which sputtered and whined as the six of them, his newest cargo, gritted their teeth and clung to one another.

Not more than five minutes back out to the main road they came across a patrol. Amela's weariness vanished, abruptly replaced by fear. Her heart was thumping wildly as they pulled over, but it turned out that this was the driver's route. He was good friends with the soldiers, who were locals. And, as Hasan had predicted, the soldiers were groggy from hangovers. The truck got through without being searched. It was a close call, and the driver knew it. He drove like a maniac, but Amela didn't care. The faster he drove, the sooner they'd get to wherever they were going. Safety, she hoped.

It was hard to judge the time, but when they pulled over, the driver said they were at a café and he wanted a coffee. Panic closed in as Amela wondered if he could be trusted, then she remembered he'd gotten them past the patrol.

But their problems weren't over. Information the driver got at the café was of fighting and troop movement on the other side of the mountain, between them and Tuzla. Even in the Serb villages, everybody was scared and hiding. He had heard of a nearby Muslim village that had been abandoned. The driver and Hasan figured that a deserted village might be a good place for them to stay while the driver scouted the situation ahead. They rode a little way until they came to what wasn't much more than a dirt track. Amela and the others got out of the truck. The driver said he'd come back when he could. They waved good-bye and limped toward the village.

The village was made up of about a dozen destroyed houses — houses with no roofs, no windows. The walls were riddled with bullet holes, and one had graffiti scrawled on it that read, "Welcome to Greater Serbia." Hasan left them to go check out a building a short way down the road. He came back smiling. Amela wondered what there could possibly be to smile about.

"Come along. There's a two-room school building," he explained.

To Amela's surprise, the building was full of refugees, lots of them. *Them.* No, she thought ruefully, not *them. Us.* There were about forty people, mostly women and children. Some had lived in the burned houses; others were from different places. The men had been shot or taken away.

Even in her temporary home, Amela did not feel safe. Fear, she decided, was like a great hungry beast that lived among them, a beast that could rear up at any time and devour them. Nevertheless, she and her family and Hasan and his wife settled in as best they could for a prolonged stay. It was the best they could do until the truck driver came back with information.

They joined the others, managing to get enough food to stay alive. People foraged in the woods; Hasan knew how to trap rabbits and squirrels. He said they could chance using the woodstoves in the corners of the schoolrooms as long as they did so only once every night. Smoke would not be visible at night and if they were quick about it, the smell of smoke wouldn't last long. Amela was glad that they could cook meat now and then, but she gazed longingly at the stoves. If they could have kept a fire going, she wouldn't be cold all the time.

There was an eleven-year-old there, a girl, and Amela found her pleasant enough, but they had little in common. She missed Sanja more than ever.

The time dragged. Amela thought the third day they were in the school must surely be the thirty-third. Curiosity overtook boredom. Rooting around behind some tables and chairs shoved against a wall, she found a ripped and worn English grammar book, then an English dictionary in slightly better condition. One of the women yelped with joy at the discovery. She had taught English. Amela had studied it the past year, so the teacher helped her learn more. Then together they started teaching others.

During the second week, Sejo found another way to ease their boredom. One of the women wound yarn around rocks to make balls. First he and Amela played toss, then they found a bucket that Hasan cut the bottom out of and mounted on a pole. Sejo claimed to be the Bosnian Michael Jordan and got together a couple smaller boys to throw hoops. It wasn't the Chicago Bulls, Sejo admitted, but it seemed like normal life.

Another activity was not for fun. Hasan pressed everyone twelve or older into round-the-clock guard duty in front and behind the building and by the main road. He put everybody through drills in which they practiced gathering up everything and scrambling up the wooded hillside behind the school. Each adult and older child took charge of a young child. Amela was surprised that so many people could move quickly and quietly, but everyone obeyed well. Even the old women and little children did their part.

And then, it wasn't a drill. The guard at the road signaled. After a collective gasp, they all sprang into action. Hanifa, Dina, and Amela grabbed their charges and the items they needed to carry with them. Sejo guided a three-year-old whose mother was the guard at the road. The eight of them started out together. Hanifa reached her assigned place behind a rhododendron bush, giving her children an anguished look as they struggled on. Dina and the child with her tucked into their spot. Hearing male voices at the bottom of the hill, Amela and Sejo quickened their pace. They reached the fallen tree trunk that Sejo and his charge would lie concealed behind. Amela pushed them down, nodding her head to encourage them to feel safe. Safe. What a flimsy word.

She continued, guiding her four-year-old through thick growth to their place farther up the slope. Near their destination, Amela tripped. She clutched at a low branch to keep from falling, but her knee struck a sharp rock. She cried out. It was just a tiny cry, but it wouldn't take more than that to alert the soldiers. Then they would search the hillside. If just one person was discovered, most—maybe all of them—would be. How could she have been so careless! Her pants were torn, her knee scraped and bleeding, but she continued, at last scrunching herself and the little girl into their niche. With the child on her lap, Amela listened anxiously for soldiers' shouts and women's screams, but she heard only the ripple of leaves stirred by a brisk breeze.

She was relieved to see the last of their group, the guards, move into their hiding places below. Then she caught her breath as Sejo's little boy stood up and started to go to his mother, the guard who had given the alert. Amela moved to set the child aside so she could go to help him, but Sejo pulled the boy back behind the trunk just as the enemy soldiers rounded the corner of the school at the base of the hill.

Amela wrapped her arms securely around the little girl. From their high perch, she could get a glimpse of the road into the village and the side of the school building. At least ten men were checking things out, poking around in the houses, scanning the wooded hillside. Finally satisfied, they sat on the ground. One lit a fire. Amela watched them eat and drink and laugh as if they were having a picnic. Even if they left by dark, she was sure Hasan would not cook that night, a condition her growling stomach found objectionable. As twilight deepened, one of the thugs gestured toward the school. Apparently they, the intruders, would camp there for the night while those who were temporarily evicted stayed cramped and shivering on the hillside.

Early the next morning, after a miserable night, Amela and the others saw the soldiers leave the school, stretch, eat a quick breakfast, and leave. When at last the signal was given that it was safe to return to the school, everyone climbed down the hill on stiff legs. They were soiled and chilled through.

In the two weeks that followed, there were two more alarms that proved to be false, but the possibility of discovery never let up. Amela was beginning to wonder which to expect – that she'd be shot or die of old age at the school. The driver had said he'd try to get back, but he had not, and she was losing hope.

Then one day, there he was. This time he had a bigger, newer truck with metal sides and a tailgate and canvas that closed off the back. He told Hasan that he could take them all the way to Tuzla. Amela thought her mother gave him some money. So into a truck they went, a half dozen others from the school as well, squeezed in behind large cartons. It was so hot and stuffy that Amela was sure they'd arrive suffocated. She didn't know what cargo they were carrying, but it was such foul smelling stuff it turned her stomach. Hasan said he thought the driver had it there for a reason, so everybody put up with it. They even joked that it didn't smell any worse than they did.

The first time they were ordered to stop, they hugged each

other good-bye. It was heartbreaking to have come so far, but everyone was sure there was no way they would not be found. Amela's heart lurched when she heard the flap whipped back and the tailgate lowered, but the soldiers had just started to poke when they were revolted by the odor. They yelled and cursed the driver. They pounded on the side of the truck, but that was it. No matter how much the *cargo* suffered, every time they were stopped and a search begun, it was ended quickly.

"We're starting to descend," said Hasan at last. "That means we've passed Stolice Peak. We will soon reach the valley."

Amela crawled to the rear of the truck, lifted a corner of the flap, and peeked out. What she saw was a road sign, bullet-riddled and half shot away. The writing was not in the Cyrillic alphabet sometimes used in Bijeljina, but in the Latin alphabet that was used in Tuzla. Fog, like thick layers of chiffon, hid the view, but soon the sun began to burn it off. As it became thinner, Amela could make out a wide valley.

Sejo slid over to join her. She put her arm around him, aware of how small he felt.

"Amela, you're very brave," he said.

She blinked back the hot tears that sprang into her eyes.

"I want to be brave, too," said Sejo. "I'm going to be. I'm the man in the family until Papa comes back. I'm going to take care of you and Mama and Dina."

Amela wanted to speak, to tell him she wasn't any braver than he was, but her throat ached and no words would come. She kissed the top of his head as a tear rolled down her cheek.

A little farther on, out of the mountains and on level ground, there were alarming sounds. Cracks of gunfire and a booming that Hasan told them was mortar shells. Amela covered her ears as their truck just kept rolling until they finally reached the city.

Her Aunt Biserka nearly fainted, whether from shock or relief or the way they stank, Amela didn't know.

Arriving safely in Tuzla after their three-week journey was something to celebrate, but telling the story of that grim night in Bijeljina brought back the horror and sadness. Even as she slipped into a bed for the first time in weeks, Amela couldn't shake off the thought that they had escaped, but others had not. Was her father all right? Was Sanja?

CHAPTER
6

Sanja couldn't stop worrying about Amela. Dragan had said that Amela's father was missing, and that she and her family had left Bijeljina, but he didn't know whether they had reached their destination, which was Tuzla.

Sanja missed her friend at school. She missed her whenever she passed The Old Crone's plum trees, their fruit long since harvested. Every time she heard Siva meow or felt the cat rub against her ankle she thought of its toy twin, the one Amela had with her.

Somewhere.

It wasn't only Amela she worried about. She was also anxious about her father off somewhere with the army and about her cousins in the Drina Valley. Although the fighting had moved on from Bijeljina after about four days, it was still raging there, to the south. According to Goran, when the Serbian army command took control of Bijeljina, its leaders had a plan to bring all of Bosnia under its control in just fifteen days. It had been six months.

There had been reports of massacres in and around the places where Sanja's cousins lived. Muslim forces had overrun towns in the Drina Valley, burning whole Serb villages and killing hundreds of civilians and soldiers. Sanja felt wretched. If only she could know that her cousins Miroslava, Franjo, and their sons, especially little Mirko, were safe.

In Bijeljina, people gathered in shops, cafés, and barbershops to share their anger and fears. Sanja overheard two men talking as they looked at hunting knives in a local shop.

"It's best to be prepared," said one.

"Our authorities are prepared, but you may be right. All it takes is a few Muslims sneaking in from the woods outside town."

But weeks went by. When nothing happened in Bijeljina, Sanja forgot the conversation. When her mother asked her to pick up some things at a farm a short distance outside of town, she recalled what she had overheard, but decided the men must have been exaggerating. Nevertheless she asked Goran to go with her.

He grabbed his cap, as delighted as she was to have a change of scene. When war tensions were high, they couldn't indulge in any of their favorite summer activities. They could not drive out to the country or go apple picking or go to the river. They loved the Drina's swift current and whirlpools, but it was their father who knew how to swim or raft there safely, and he had been away all summer. No one they knew had gone to the Drina for months. War made people nervous, even if it was not being waged in Bijeljina, and some, especially the older folks, refused to go outside their own neighborhoods.

The weather was glorious. It was an autumn-crisp day, made even better by a cloudless blue sky and the tempting fragrance of roasting chestnuts. Sanja and Goran stopped to buy the first bag the vendor prepared. They caught a local bus and made their way to the back seat, passing two women, the only other passengers. Concerns about attacks slipped to the back of Sanja's mind as the bus took them into the countryside. Early-rising farmers lined the roads hoping to sell their bags of onions and potatoes. Their donkeys stood patiently beside the carts.

"We'll need a donkey after we get everything on Mama's list," complained Sanja.

As the bus approached a side road, a woman ran toward it, waving and calling out. The bus driver pulled over. He stopped, opening the door so she could clamber aboard. Puffing and laughing, she told him that she was glad she'd made it because she didn't want to be late. He laughed with her as he put the bus in gear and started to pull back onto the main road.

Sanja reached into the bag for a chestnut just as the explosion tore through the front of the bus. It reared up like a spooked horse, and then came slamming down. Sanja was flung over the back of her seat and tumbled into the cramped back corner where she lay wedged. All she could see were tiny white dots floating in a sea of black. She tried to focus. Her ears were ringing. She smelled smoke. Someone was screaming.

As her vision began to clear, Sanja recognized the bus, but above her the roof was large squares of broken glass ... the windows. Beyond them was a clear blue sky. She realized that the bus was on its side and a small part of her brain registered *accident*. She reached out to take hold of a metal rod on the back of the seat, at the same time using her other hand to give herself a boost. She cried out in pain and saw that she had cut herself on a piece of glass. She carefully removed it. Her palm was bleeding. Her head was throbbing.

Goran! Where was Goran? She called his name, but heard no reply.

Sanja struggled to her feet, completely disoriented. What had been the bus floor was now the side. Somebody outside was pounding on the bus and shouting, but she ignored it. She had to find her brother.

"Goran!" Sanja cried. She was frantic. "Goran! Where are you? Answer me!"

She squeezed past the seat, trying to go toward the front. The rows of seats looked peculiar jutting out along the side. Ahead of her, the front of the bus was a twisted, blackened wreck. Sanja edged her way into what had been the bus roof. She saw Goran lying on his back at her feet.

He moaned and shifted. Sanja gasped. He lay on a shattered window, his cap askew but still on his head. She crouched down in the narrow space between seats. She wished the pounding would stop. It made her head hurt more.

Goran was pale. He squinted up at her, moving his head gingerly as if he was afraid it wasn't still connected to him.

Sanja gave an anxious cry. "Are you all right? Do you know who I am?" she pleaded.

"You're no angel, Sanja, so I must not be dead." Still squinting, he looked around, puzzled.

"The bus is on its side," she explained. Nervously she eyed a jagged piece of glass that clung precariously to the window frame above. She took off her jacket and gave it to Goran saying, "Hold this over your face." Then she climbed onto the arm of the seat, reached up and pulled the glass out, tossed it away, and climbed back down. She folded her jacket into a pillow that she eased under her brother's head. He tried to get up.

"Don't move!" Sanja ordered. "There's broken glass under you. Oh, God, are you hurt? You must be hurt!"

"My left leg," he said.

"Your left … ?" She looked at his bloody sneaker.

The woman who had been screaming was no longer screaming, but was instead calling for help. The other two women were silent. Someone was trying to pry open the back door. As Sanja moved toward it, it flew open. A man maneuvered his way into the bus, another man followed, and then a third.

"Oh, thank heaven!" Sanja gasped. "Please, please help my brother. He's hurt."

The first man worked his way toward the middle of the bus, edging past hanging seats, crunching broken glass underfoot to reach the women. The other two men bent down beside Goran. He told them his left leg hurt.

"We shouldn't move him," said one man.

The other agreed. "His leg might be broken. There's an ambulance coming."

"It's here," somebody leaning into the back called.

Several by-standers helped Sanja out and to a car parked nearby. She dropped gratefully onto the front seat, waiting for the medics to bring her brother out.

"Where's the bus driver?" she asked.

A man standing by the car door said, "He's dead. So are two women who were sitting up front."

Dead. How could that be? Sanja thought. "No. You're mistaken. We're going to the farm."

The man patted her shoulder. At that moment two policemen stopped to talk, and Sanja strained to overhear their conversation.

"Was it a mine?" said one.

"Yeah," said the other. "Looks like it was buried by the side of the road. The front tire hit it. Lucky it wasn't enough to take out the whole bus."

At that moment, Goran was handed down from the bus onto a stretcher that was taken to the waiting ambulance. His lips were pinched together. Even though he tried to look unconcerned, Sanja could tell he was suffering. There was a second stretcher with one of the women on it.

Sanja climbed in next to her brother. As the driver was helping her up, she noticed writing on the road, words that had been spray-painted there.

"What's that?" she asked.

The man read the message. " *'To avenge our Muslim brothers.'* " He spat on the painted words, then spat again. "Bloody monsters," he said fiercely. "They asked for anything they got."

Sanja's eyes narrowed. As she looked at the writing, the conversation of the men in the shop came back to her. *'All it takes is a few Muslims sneaking in from the woods outside town.'* She had not been afraid before, but now she was.

As they rode to the hospital, Sanja put her head in her hands. She was tired, so tired. And so cold.

At the hospital, sister and brother were thoroughly checked. Sanja had cuts and bruises and a sprained wrist. There was a knot on her forehead, but her ears had stopped ringing. Goran's leg was broken; he had a cracked rib and a cut on his neck.

After Sanja had been treated and was waiting for a nurse to take her to Goran, she had time to let her thoughts catch up with events. It was a nightmare, not something that should happen on a lovely October day. She looked up and down the hospital corridor wondering if she would see Amela's father. But of course he didn't live in Bijeljina anymore.

The nurse advised Sanja that her mother had been called, but apparently was not at home. She would try again. In the meantime, Sanja was glad when she was able to see her brother.

"So why didn't I land on top of you?" he asked Sanja. "Then maybe *you'd* have the broken leg."

"I notice your sense of humor didn't suffer," she replied tartly.

"Sani, what happened? Somebody said we hit a landmine."

"We did."

Goran looked stunned. He grew paler. "Who would do that?" he said. "Who would do that?" he repeated, his voice tight.

Sanja wished their father was there; he would know what to say. She told Goran about the conversation she'd overheard between the two men and the comments from the ambulance driver about the writing on the road.

He screwed up his face, then said, "Those people who planted the mine are crazy!" He was quiet for a few minutes, thinking. Then he said, "I guess we're lucky. At least we're alive."

Soon after that, their mother came for them. Sanja expected her to yell—at the men who laid the mine, at her children, at everyone in the world, but for a change Stefana was quiet. She carefully tucked them both in when they got home, as if they were little kids again.

Three months later, in January, a letter came from Sanja's cousin Miroslava. It was brought by a Serb refugee and was a month old. There was an attack by Muslim forces in September, Miroslava wrote, and the only reason she had survived was that she had been in a neighboring town helping a friend give birth. Her husband, Franjo, and their sons, including two-year-old Mirko, had stayed at home. They were massacred, their bodies mutilated.

As Sanja's mother read the letter, they both started to cry. Stefana reached for a tissue, blew her nose, and said, "Do you remember our last visit there? It was Mirko's first birthday."

Sanja remembered it well, and tears spilled down her cheeks as she thought of Franjo romping in the field with the kids, laughing and running, every bit as joyful as the little ones. His mother had cooked her special sarma, demanding that they *"Eat! Eat!"* Stefana picked up the letter and started reading aloud what her cousin had written.

> *Following the soldiers were the torbari—the "bag*
> *people"—thousands of them. They're scavengers who*
> *follow the Muslim soldiers. Those people are butchers.*
> *What unknown grievance drives their desire for revenge?*
> *They attacked with anything that could be used to kill*
> *— shooting, knifing, smashing. Our village was left*
> *empty. I shudder to think about it. My sons are gone. My*
> *Franjo is gone. It's so hard to write these things. I will*
> *stay here for the time being, but no place is safe.*

"Well, you see how this proves we have to protect ourselves from the Turks," said Sanja's mother, wiping her eyes. "And this isn't the first time either."

Sanja gritted her teeth. She hated it when Stefana started bringing up atrocities of the past. Sometimes she went all the way back to 1389 to relive the indignities that had come to her through generations of ancestors.

Sanja glared at her mother. "You know, I don't need to go back centuries for tragedy and sorrow. For me it's here and now."

Stefana ignored her. "Can we ever forget," she went on, slamming the letter down on the table, "that they joined with the Austrians to burn that village in 1914, and the hundreds of Serbs who were killed during the Second World War, or ... ?"

"Mama! Stop it!" Sanja shouted, grabbing the letter. "I don't care what happened in 1389 or in 1914! It's hard enough to deal with what's happening now. My father's off defending our homeland and could get shot. My cousins are getting killed. Goran was injured. And what if those bag people come here?"

Sanja felt like the world had turned inside out. Muslims attacked the bus; Muslims attacked her family. But Amela was Muslim and Amela thought hurting people was wrong. Every time Sanja started hating Muslims, her memories of Amela got in the way. She thought about Amela's father, a gentle man, a doctor who helped people and saved lives just like her father did. He *couldn't* be a terrible person who wanted to kill Serbs.

Ten months ago Sanja would have run to Amela's and found comfort. But now there was no Amela and there was no comfort. Was Amela even the person Sanja remembered or was she someone completely different? Ten months ago they had sworn to be friends forever. Was their friendship destroyed now along with everything else?

Sanja left the table and climbed the stairs to her room as fast as her devastated feelings allowed. She closed the door before bursting into tears. There was nothing she could do to help her cousins. She couldn't bring back her loved ones or take away the horror. She felt completely helpless.

Sanja crumpled the letter. She threw herself on her bed, sobbing until her eyes were swollen and her throat ached. She ignored a tap on her door until the tap got louder.

"Go away," she sniffed.

"Hey, it's me," Goran said, his voice muffled by the wooden door.

Her brother was the only person in the world she'd talk to in her present state. She opened the door. He came in looking concerned.

"Wow," he said softly. "Miroslava's letter hit you hard, didn't it? Can I read it?"

She lay back down on the bed as he sat down on the chair beside it.

Sanja handed him the balled-up paper. He smoothed it out, reading it slowly. Then he read it again. When he finished, he picked up a small wooden box from the nightstand and hurled it at the wall. "Damn, I hate them," he said and swore again.

Sanja was angry, too, and miserable. "At first I was crying for Miroslava and Franjo, the boys and … oh … for Mirko," she said. "Then I was missing Amela, too, and wondering where she is and how she is."

"Your chubby friend," said Goran.

"No, she's not! Well, maybe now she's thin because she doesn't have enough to eat. Maybe she's hurt. Maybe she's … no, never mind. I just wish she'd come back." Sanja sat up and fingered the chain with Amela's ring on it.

"That's a foolish wish, Sani. She wouldn't even have a place to stay since there's a family from Sarajevo living in her house now."

"I know. Oh, Goran! Will things ever be right again?"

"I don't know, but I keep hoping. Tell you what … Pick a date—any date in the future—and you and I will aim for it. The war will be over, everybody will have money and a great life. We'll take a trip. To Portugal."

"Portugal?"

"Anywhere," said Goran. "Egypt, America. You name it. When everything's good like it used to be."

"Better than it used to be!"

"Yes, better!"

"I wish we could go now," said Sanja. "Or in the summer. The war will be over by then."

"Of course. But we have to get ready. Let's start saving our money. Mama won't want to let us go, but by the time I'm nineteen and you're sixteen, it'll be harder for her to say no."

"Oh, Goran, if only …" Her voice reflected the hopelessness she felt.

"C'mon, Sani! Where's your spirit? I'll steal your favorite line—I dare you. When I'm nineteen and you're sixteen, we'll hit the road. Let's say in August 1995. Deal?"

He was working so hard to revive Sanja's spirits, she smiled and said, "Okay. Deal."

It would have taken a lot more imagination than either of them had to guess what "hitting the road" would mean in the summer of 1995.

1995〜1997

CHAPTER
7

Amela sighed and switched off the television as her aunt came into the kitchen.

"Soup smells good," said Biserka. She spooned a cupful of broth and sipped it standing at the sink.

Amela smiled. "Enough onions make up for a lack of meat."

"What's on the news?"

"They said maybe there'll be a peace agreement by summer's end." It was more than three years since that miserable night in Bijeljina—nearly thirty-eight months and counting. "The news from the Drina Valley's disheartening."

"Goražde and Srebrenica and Žepa? Yes," Biserka agreed. "Bosnian Serb forces are apparently trying to hold Muslims hostage." She rinsed the cup and set it on the drainboard, then left the room.

Peace could not come too soon, Amela thought. It would be a blessing if the killing and torture ended—but what then? It would take years to restore electric power, to rebuild factories, and get trains running again. How long would it take to find a father?

The whirlwind entrance of Jasmina interrupted that line of thinking, which, Amela thought, was probably a good thing.

"Look, look," Jasmina said eagerly, lifting her reddish-brown hair. "I found these neat earrings today for practically nothing. What do you think?"

"For practically nothing, they'll probably turn your ears green." Amela thought they were beautiful, but couldn't resist teasing her cousin. Jasmina was a year older than Amela, but seemed younger. Maybe tramping through woods and hiding out in schoolhouses aged a person.

"What a thing to say!" Jasmina scowled. "Have you forgotten your sixteenth birthday is just a week from now? Maybe I won't give you a present." But she could never hold a temper for long. Even as she pretended to stomp off in a huff, she couldn't quite hide a smile.

Amela chided herself for teasing her good-natured cousin. Be good, she thought. Think about what you *have* rather than what you don't have. Sure the Tuzla house was crowded, but everybody made do. Sure they didn't have much money, but they weren't starving.

And there was Adnan. Ah! The thought of him brought a happy smile to her face. She closed her eyes and imagined him sneaking up behind her, wrapping his arms around her waist, pulling her tight against him. She could feel his lips warm on the back of her neck.

Jasmina's voice broke into her daydream. "Hey, Amela!" she said. "Have you forgotten? It's Day of Youth and I'm meeting some kids at the Kapija. Are you coming?"

Amela *had* forgotten. In the boredom of wartime Tuzla, holidays didn't mean much to her, and Yugoslavia's late Premier Tito and his Day of Youth seemed out of date. Better there should be a *Day Off From the War* day. But she supposed anything to perk up their lives was welcome.

Later, as she slipped into her shoes, Amela asked, "Is your brother coming with us?"

"Ahmed's working."

"He got a job? Super!" said Amela.

"Yeah, he's a waiter. He's serving ćevapis instead of eating them ... well, probably eating them, too. It's near the bus station. He's working till ten, but he'll try to come later."

"A little more money will be welcome," Amela commented as they started down the hill toward the bridge. She knew he would contribute to the household.

"Yes," Jasmina agreed. "I don't know how my mother manages."

"I wish my mother and I could help more," sighed Amela. "If we could just sell more of our knitting and needlework ... but who is there to buy it?"

The cousins had not yet reached the bridge when Amela stopped suddenly. She looked at her shoe, its heel broken. "Well, you go ahead," she told Jasmina, "and save me a place."

"Okay. The others should already be there. I hope we can sit outside. Want me to order you a coffee?" asked Jasmina. When Amela nodded, she added, "Oh, and bring me another pack of cigarettes, will you? I think I dumped them in the mess on my bed."

Amela did a double take. "Where did you get cigarettes?"

"Not real ones—don't be silly," said Jasmina. She wrinkled her nose. "I rolled up grape leaves. Last week I came across some tea, and that was better."

"Give it up," said Amela.

"No way! Then I'd go to pieces when I hear a shell coming in."

"I'm glad you don't live in Sarajevo. You'd run out of grape leaves."

"So will you bring them?" asked Jasmina.

"All right."

When Amela returned to the house, she was surprised to see Adnan coming out. Her breath caught as it always did when she saw him. For months she had admired his broad shoulders; his thick, dark hair; and his eyes that twinkled with laughter. He was two years older, and she had thought he would not notice her. But two months ago, he had. He was so gentle and caring, easing her through moments of despair about her father.

"I thought you were at your aunt's," she said.

"I caught a ride. Came back early. I missed you." He slid his hand around her waist and drew her close.

"And I missed you," she said, raising her mouth to his kiss. Oh, how strong he was and how delicious he tasted! It was a gentle, lingering kiss; however, they were standing in full view of the neighbors, and Amela did not need their nosy inspection.

"Do you want to come in?" she asked.

"Actually, I thought we could go to the Kapija. Everybody's there. Later we can take the long way home."

"I'm on my way to meet Jasmina there. I just came back to change my shoes."

"I have to drop off some medicine with my mother, but that should just take a minute. Running an errand for her was the only way she'd let me leave my aunt's early. Amela, I have some news."

"About university?"

"I wish. No, I'll tell you later."

She hoped it wasn't about the army. She didn't want that kind of news. She wanted him to go to Sarajevo to study even though she would miss him. He was smart and funny. They could talk for hours, and he made her laugh.

"Well," she said, "why don't you go ahead, do what you need to do, then find Jasmina. I'll be along soon. You can tell me the news then."

"Okay," said Adnan, "but don't keep me waiting long. Every minute without you ..."

"Oh, now you're being silly," she said, giving him a playful shove. "Next you'll be writing me poetry!"

He grinned. "Your hair is like … butterscotch. Your eyes are like … milk chocolate. Your lips are like …"

Amela was giggling. "You make me sound like a candy store."

"Ah, yes. Perfect for nibbling." He laughed, then kissed her once again before he left for the Kapija.

Amela was about to go into the house when she saw her brother. "What are you doing here?" she asked.

"Spying," Sejo said with a chuckle.

Amela ignored his comment. "I thought you'd be at the square."

"Nah," he answered. "I'm getting my basketball. Some of the guys are gonna shoot hoops."

"Are they older than you? You're tall for ten, but I don't want you outclassed."

"Nobody can outclass me at basketball," Sejo boasted. "Well, maybe Michael Jordan."

Amela was still laughing as she rooted through Jasmina's jumble of clothes on her bed. Her cousin must have tried on everything she owned before she made the decision about what to wear. Good for her. Since Jasmina didn't own very much, she might as well wear something she liked. When Amela found the grape-leaf cigarettes, she started off again. It was getting late; she had taken longer than she'd meant to.

It was twilight. The sun had dipped below the horizon, but in late May the weather was pleasant for sitting outdoors at a café sipping coffee. And soon she would be with Adnan. Thinking of him made her tingle. Oh, wasn't love wonderful!

Amela crossed the bridge and walked along the street toward

the Kapija. There was new graffiti, *Tito Volimo Te*, on the wall of a building. "Tito We Love You" sentiments were appearing with increasing frequency around town as the Muslim people remembered how the former leader had elevated their status in Yugoslavia. She appreciated his efforts, so maybe she shouldn't be a spoilsport about the holiday. At least it was a good excuse, if anybody needed one, to gather with friends.

The high-pitched whistling brought her up short. A shell! But where?

The answer came in seconds. Three blocks ahead there was a roar like a thunderclap. The Kapija! No! It couldn't have hit the square! Amela's knees buckled. She reached out to the wall for support. Her breath came in jarring gasps. Then she started to run—not away from the blast, but toward it. Maybe the shell had landed on the hill. Maybe it had landed on the road. Oh, please, in a vacant lot. Anywhere, anywhere, but in that place where her friends were! She ran, her pulse drumming in her temples. She ran as if she could save somebody.

Others were running, too, some toward the Kapija and others away from it. They bumped into each other and kept going. The closer Amela got to the square, the louder the screams. Who was alive to scream? Were there survivors? As she reached the side of the café, she could smell smoke. She called out names over and over again—"Adnan! Adnan! Jasmina! Jasmina!"—like a shrill incantation, as if by some miracle calling for them would bring them out whole and unharmed.

There were people everywhere, shouting, screaming, wailing—some bleeding. Amela tried to get through, but the crowd kept pushing her back. She had only a glimpse of the smoldering scene. A policeman grabbed her arm and ordered her away, but she had seen more than she wanted. She clapped her hand over her mouth, then stumbled against a shop window as her stomach reacted with violent spasms. Police and rescue workers were already arriving. Amela was shoved aside so that a barricade could be put up.

A girl she knew staggered past the wooden barrier. She was coming from the Kapija, and her cheek was bloody. Amela grabbed her arm. "Did you see Adnan? Jasmina?" she begged.

The girl gave Amela a dazed look, jerked away, and then sank to the pavement. She covered her eyes, screaming. Amela looked frantically for someone else to question.

Nearby stood a woman holding her bleeding forehead and sobbing. "The … c … cobblestones," she stuttered, grabbing Amela's sleeve, "came … came down like … like …"

Amela took hold of the woman's shoulder and shook her. "How do you know about the cobblestones? Were you there? Did anyone else get out?"

"No. I don't … I don't know. I o-only …"

Amela wasn't learning anything. A man in some kind of uniform rushed past and ordered them away. The first stretchers were coming through. The wounded would be taken to the hospital. That was where Amela would find Adnan and Jasmina. That was where she should go. Her aunt was probably there already.

The hospital was nearly as chaotic as the Kapija, but Amela waited, pacing.

"The Serbs fired the shell from Mount Majevica," she heard someone say.

Amela only saw her aunt for a moment. Biserka was busy with the injured. At the same time, she was frantic about her own daughter.

It was hours before the news came. When it did, it was crushing. Adnan and Jasmina were dead.

At the urging of the town's families, the city authorities decided that all the bodies would be buried in the same place, on the hillside above the city. Through the night, men of the town turned out to dig graves in the grassy slope, and Amela went there to watch. She was numb. It couldn't be just a few hours ago that she had teased Jasmina about her new earrings and Adnan about his silly poem. The memories floated about her, then shattered.

One of the men digging grew weary, swayed, dropped his shovel. Amela reached for it.

"No, no," he protested. "You're a girl."

"People I loved are going to lie in these places," she replied brusquely. "I can help dig."

"Me, too," said Sejo. "I want to help."

Ahmed was nearby, digging along with the others.

The workers sweated in the rain and dark, with dim light only from a few spotlights hung in the trees and an occasional flash of lightning. Added to that, the growl of distant thunder gave the scene an otherworldly appearance that seemed somehow appropriate. Grave markers lay in stacks, waiting to be put on mounds of dirt—crosses of brown wood to mark Christian Serb and Croat graves, planks of emerald green for Muslims.

A couple hours later, Ahmed put his muddy arms around each cousin and said, "The digging is finished. Why don't you go home and get some rest. You must be worn out."

Amela and Sejo looked at each other and shook their heads. "After the coffins are in place," said Amela.

The night was half over when the coffins were handed up the hillside in what seemed to Amela like an endless stream. There was a double line of men that stretched from where she stood in the clearing to the darkness far below. She watched the men trying to keep their footing in the mud as they passed the heavy coffins up the slope. Death was humbling, reflecting a greater power that could not be controlled. Yet, here was compassion and mercy, and a common humanity in the face of it. For the moment Amela wasn't alone in her grief.

She left the makeshift graveyard and did what others did. She went to the hospital where she helped change dressings and empty bedpans. Sometimes she just held someone's hand. After a few hours she returned to the hillside.

To avoid possible shelling, it was decided that the mass ceremony would take place at four-thirty, in the dark of early morning. It had stopped raining. Perhaps, thought Amela, the sky could not shed any more tears. And neither could she.

The death count had climbed to nearly seventy. Hundreds of people gathered in an enormous circle. Both Jasmina's and Adnan's families were there along with other grieving families. Soldiers, townspeople, and foreigners all came to mourn. They listened in silence to the prayers by local dignitaries and priests of both Christian faiths. Amela tried to follow the prayer of the imam of her Islamic faith, but much of what he said was blocked by numbness. Then the coffins were lowered into the ground. The graves were filled.

Amela felt suffocated. Surrounded by weeping, drained by the disaster that had robbed her of Adnan and her family of their lovely Jasmina, she cursed the war. The futility of it was clear to her as she listened to the sobs of Serbs, Muslims, and Croats, convulsed together in their common loss.

She continued to work at the hospital, helping in whatever ways she could. Her mother, too, was helping. Hanifa took on additional tasks at home to give Biserka more time for her nursing duties. Hanifa also prepared food baskets and made visits to others who were grieving.

A few days later, on the third of June, her sixteenth birthday, Amela hiked up to the cemetery. It still had an unfinished look as if the people buried there had not yet accepted what had happened any more than she had. She found the graves she was looking for, as other people were finding graves of their loved ones. She saw that most women wore black; she heard their wailing; she saw their tears. She wasn't wearing black. She wasn't wailing. She couldn't shed a tear.

Amela had brought a photograph of Jasmina for her grave. Only three months earlier, they had gone to a friend who had been a photographer in better days. The picture was a present for Jasmina's mother. Amela gave a sigh that came from the depths of her heart as she recalled that it was presented to Biserka on Jasmina's seventeenth birthday. She had looked so young, even younger than seventeen. Or maybe it was just her innocence.

Amela walked steadfastly to Adnan's grave. His family had placed his photograph there. Amela stood there, her body like an empty shell. All feeling was gone. The future she had begun to glimpse was gone, too, tucked inside that wooden box with a boy she had loved.

It was painful to look around at all the graves of innocents. The youngest was a toddler. How unfair it was for them to die and she to have been spared by the stupidest coincidence.

Blindly, with no thought about where she was going or what she was doing, Amela wandered among the graves with their green and brown markers. She drifted aimlessly away to stand next to a tree nearby. She leaned against it, gulping back sorrow and anger. Then she exploded—exploded as if she were the shell in the Kapija. She yelled and shrieked at the people who had caused the war.

"You bastards!" Amela screamed. "You dirty cowards! Why? Why in the name of … of … all that's holy …" Her fury choked her, but she had to accuse them. In that moment, the trees became the people she hated. She swung her bare arms at them, flailing again and again. "How can you … how can you … laugh? Eat? Sleep?" Then the tears came. She swiped at them so that the bark embedded in her arms scratched her face, but she continued to shout, hurling each word like a stone. "Why – aren't – *you* – lying – cold – in the – ground?"

"Haven't you …" she gasped, " … killed enough boys yet? Tortured enough ... enough men ... raped enough women ... robbed enough old people? Stop the war!" She dropped to the ground, hugging herself, rolling over and over. Her voice became a whisper. "Stop it." She curled into a ball and sobbed.

Amela was not aware of the kind arms that lifted her. She wasn't aware of being driven to the hospital, nor of being gently placed in the care of her Aunt Biserka. When Amela awoke hours later, she wondered why her arms were bandaged. When her aunt told her—reminded her of her fury—she only felt empty. She had raged against the powerful, and she had lost.

CHAPTER
8

By July 1995, the war had taken a number of twists and turns. Sanja prayed that Miroslava and her other cousins down in the Drina Valley who had survived so far would be all right. In Bijeljina, the war was affecting people's wallets, making some skimpier and others very, very fat.

Meanwhile Sanja's father had resigned his commission, and the family was holding its collective breath, hoping it would not mean arrest. So far it was his good fortune that everyone in the army was distracted by efforts to secure as much territory as they could before a possible peace agreement ended the war. Stefana's anxiety level had reached new heights, and she and Sanja clashed constantly.

Like Amela, Sanja longed for peace. Goran had been called up for military service. At first, with the blessing of his father, he had managed to avoid going, but eventually he had no choice. Some of his friends, especially those in Belgrade, had found creative ways to go underground. Sanja missed Goran. The last time she had seen her brother, they had talked about the future.

"Do you remember our plans to travel this summer?" she asked him.

"There's plenty I'd like to forget about the last few years," he said, "but not that. Where shall we go, Sani, when this is over?

You know there might be a peace plan soon."

Her scornful look told him what she thought about the prospects of a peace plan, but she sighed and said, "Okay. Let's say there's a peace plan. Where should we go?"

"America!" he said. "A big city with everything there for us."

She shook her head. "Dream on. I'll be a very old woman before I go anywhere but outside of town to buy potatoes."

Later, after one such trip, Sanja dropped her purchases at home, then escaped from the house before she encountered her mother. She was at a café waiting for her pizza order when she sensed someone watching her.

"Rado!" she cried as he leaned down to kiss her on both cheeks.

"Ah, Sani. You've called me that since you were three years old and you're the only person who does."

"When did you get back?" she asked. "Are you out of the army? Did you see Goran?" Sanja had always liked Ranko because he was clever and funny and had a sense of adventure. He and Goran had been friends since childhood, much as she and Amela had been friends.

Ranko laughed and took the seat across from her. Before answering, he lit a cigarette, took a long drag, then blew out a stream of smoke. "To take your questions in order, beautiful lady, I got in last night, I have a bit of leave from the army, and I have not seen Goran because he's off serving God knows where."

"God may know," said Sanja, "but even my father doesn't."

The waiter brought Sanja's pizza, and Ranko ordered a large slice of the Mediterranean style.

"Last time I saw Goran, he told me about your father's resignation from the army. Did he really do that rather than serve under ... ?"

"No names, please," Sanja cautioned. "Well, that's the reason my father gives us. There are many people in the army he respects, but he raves that it used to be a place for professionals and lately its honor has been stained by too many ... what's the word he uses? ... miscreants."

"Who are they?" asked Ranko, taking a piece of salami from Sanja's pizza.

"Evil-doers," said Sanja, slapping his hand. "Like people who steal bits off of other people's pizzas."

"So, tell me Sani, what have you been up to lately? Have you graduated? Are you ready to marry me?"

Sanja laughed as she always did when Ranko flattered her. He was attractive, but she preferred to keep him at a friendly distance. She said, "I was sixteen in May and I'm still in school."

"That can't be!" he said, feigning shock. "You must be older than that!"

"Oh, give me a break," she said, knowing she would miss his teasing if he stopped. "As to what I'm up to ... Are you kidding? What is there to be up to unless you deal with the black market?" Sanja wasn't surprised that Ranko glanced around, like it was a reflex. "But seriously," she went on, thinking of the recent news from her grandmother, "I'm worried about my baka."

"Which one, your mother's mother? The one who lives in Krajina?" Ranko asked.

"Yes. Her neighbor got in touch with us through a ham operator saying that she was ill; she has no one to take care of her. She wants someone to come and get her to bring her to Bijeljina."

"Doesn't she know there's a war?"

"Ah, my question exactly. Of course when would Baka let something as insignificant as a war stop her?"

Ranko frowned. "How ill is she?"

"We don't know, and we don't know what's wrong with her. It's a big question whether she can even travel."

"Which would include avoiding battles and roads clogged with refugees," Ranko added. "The Croats want Krajina and lots of Serbs are leaving. It's not a safe place."

"That's all the more reason to get her out of there," said Sanja.

Ranko's pizza was delivered, and he asked for a bottle of ketchup to replace the empty one on the table. He seemed to be seriously considering Sanja's dilemma, and she said quickly, "Don't even think about it. You're not going to spend your leave on some fool's errand."

"Sanja," scolded Ranko. "Do not call your grandmother a fool."

"You know I didn't mean it that way."

While they finished their pizzas, they talked about local matters and friends in town. Although they knew many of the same people, those that Ranko hung out with were decidedly not the same ones Sanja spent time with except for Goran and her friend Ivana, who had nursed a crush on Ranko since second grade.

Ranko insisted on paying for Sanja's lunch. As they started to go in different directions, he turned back to ask, "What does your father say about your grandmother?"

"He hasn't heard about this. He went to Belgrade, and then he was supposed to go somewhere else. With phone service such a mess, we haven't been able to reach him."

"Okay. Stay loose. I'll be in touch," Ranko said. With a wave, he was off.

His comment left Sanja puzzled, but she decided not to worry about what Ranko might or might not be up to. Just before dawn the next morning, she found out what that was when he knocked at their door.

"Pack a small bag, the less stuff the better." He gestured to a somewhat battered taxi.

Sanja thought for only a second, then dressed quickly and threw some clothes into a backpack. "Don't worry," she told her shocked mother, and got into the passenger seat. She wasn't sure going with Ranko in a battered taxi he had acquired who-knew-how was a good idea, but it was for a worthy cause.

"We got another message from Baka's neighbor," she told him. "She's really ill, and there are rumors that Croatia's going to force Serbs out of Krajina. I don't know why Baka couldn't leave with people from her village, but maybe they don't want to be responsible for a sick old woman."

"We'll call this 'Operation Rescue'," said Ranko, flashing a rakish grin. He was obviously enjoying the adventure. He threw the stub of a cigarette out the window, and lit another.

"What's our route?" Sanja asked, pulling a map out of the glove box and opening it.

"First to where the owner of this taxi will meet us."

"Does the owner know you have it?" she asked him.

"Sure," he said. "Rasim's a good guy. Lives in Tuzla. Runs a little black market. He's a buddy. A bottle or two of whiskey and he's my *best* buddy." He grinned broadly and Sanja guessed there must be more. "He's also my uncle. My father's sister's husband."

"And he's ..."

"He's Muslim," said Ranko, "but don't let that worry you. His father is Muslim. His mother was a Serb."

Although Ranko seemed unconcerned, Sanja was uneasy.

Then, on second thought, she realized that Rasim would be better able to manage any problems in Muslim and Croatian areas. In any case, it added to the adventure.

In spite of its beat-up appearance, the taxi purred slowly through fog as thick as goat's milk.

"By the way," Ranko said, digging in his shirt pocket and pulling out an object, "put this ring on. In case you missed the ceremony, we're married. Sorry I didn't bring any confetti."

"What!" Sanja opened her mouth to make a stinging reply, then started laughing, anticipating Ivana's reaction when she told her about the ring. She decided to trust Ranko's reasons and slipped the ring on her finger.

Suddenly it dawned on Sanja that she was hitting the road, but certainly not in the way that she and Goran had in mind three years before. "We should be driving to Portugal," she said, amused when Ranko threw her a puzzled look. She explained about the plans she and Goran had made when they had innocently expected that the war would be over in weeks. "This very month and year," she told him. "Too bad Goran isn't here to appreciate the irony."

"Hey, why waste a good plan?" said Ranko. "We'll just honeymoon in Portugal and pick up your grandmother on the way back." He winked at her and laughed.

"You can forget the honeymoon," Sanja shot back. "But I'll take the holiday. Wouldn't a beach be grand?"

"A beach," Ranko echoed wistfully. "But, sorry. It's Tuzla. The trip usually takes about an hour, but there's some shelling so we're taking a detour. And we'll have delays at checkpoints." He had no sooner made the comment than a fuzzy light shone ahead. Ghostly forms emerged through the fog.

"As I said, checkpoint. Reach up above the windshield. You'll find a zipper along the side. It's pretty well hidden, so you may have to feel for it. Unzip the roof liner and take out a bottle."

Sanja found the zipper and pulled out the bottle. Ranko took it as he slowed the car.

Ordinarily she had no fear of soldiers—she'd been around them all her life—but these were not the spit-and-polish types from the army barracks in Bijeljina or her father's unit. These looked like a rag-tag bunch of militia. About a half dozen of them were lounging about with shaggy beards and in rumpled camouflage uniforms. Her father would call them unprofessional. She hoped they weren't also miscreants.

A soldier flagged them down. He carried an assault rifle and wore a bullet-filled bandolier across his chest. A knife was tucked into his belt. Sanja nervously twisted the ring on her finger.

Ranko stopped the car. He rolled down his window, but didn't turn off the engine. "Hey, how's it going?" he called to the man.

"Papers," the soldier snapped, then, "What's your business on this road?"

"Going back to my unit and dropping off my bride at her cousin's."

The soldier was gruff. "You're army? Show me your papers."

Ranko pulled out some folded papers and handed them over. Sanja noticed he tucked the bottle inside them. She scarcely breathed while the papers were scanned. She would have bet the soldier couldn't read them, but at least he wasn't paying any attention to her. Then as if she'd called his name, he peered across at her. She felt prickles on the back of her neck.

Ranko eased open his door. The guard walked around the front of the car, motioning for Sanja to lower her window. He spat on the ground, and leaned forward with a string of saliva on his thick beard. His breath nearly blew her away, reeking as it did of whiskey. She sat perfectly still, looking straight ahead, keeping her face blank. She didn't want to give him any reason to talk to her. Or do anything else. Memories of the soldier who had grabbed her in Bijeljina years before were all too vivid.

After staring at her for a minute, he walked back around the car to the driver's side. Ranko had gotten out. The two of them talked for a minute, then laughed. Sanja shuddered when she thought she heard the word "kiss" and the soldier looked directly at her. Ranko chuckled, and gave him a chummy pat on the shoulder. Then he took his papers and got back in the car. The guard motioned them on. As they pulled away, Ranko was cheerful as ever. Sanja's insides had turned to jelly.

"A bottle of booze is a cheap price," Ranko said. She didn't ask what would cost a higher price. She didn't want to know.

They managed two more such stops in the same way, although the soldiers were a bit less disgusting. She thought Ranko gave one some cash. There was almost no traffic as they began to wind their way up the Majevica Range. Ranko neatly maneuvered the steep curves while Sanja clasped her hands in white-knuckled suspense, imagining sheer drops she couldn't see. Trees lined the road, mere smudges in the fog. She wished she could offer to help with the driving, but her father had given her just one lesson, a brief one in town. Anyway, it would make her nervous to drive someone else's car. Which reminded her of the taxi driver.

"Rado, won't your best buddy want his taxi back?" she asked.

"Nope," he said. "He's gonna drive it—all the way to grandma's house."

Sanja was glad there would be another driver along. It could be an exhausting trip, and there was no telling what they'd encounter. Hunger, for one thing. She dug out two chocolate bars and handed one to Ranko. He thanked her with a nod.

"There's not much on this road," he said, "but we'll stop in a few minutes. I could use some coffee."

"Will there be any more soldiers?"

"At Priboj, no doubt," he answered, "where our army's line is, but we're taking a detour before that."

They were the only customers at the tiny café where they stopped for coffee. Ranko chatted with the owner who said there wasn't much fighting on their side of the mountain, but maybe some mortar rounds on the other side of Majevica. Now that there was serious talk of a peace agreement, troops were being concentrated in other places. Of course, he added, there was a real land grab to the west. The Serbs in Krajina were plenty nervous. Sanja wasn't cheered by that news.

"We're headed for Lopare," Ranko said to the café owner. "How're things in that direction?"

"Generally quiet. If that's your destination, fine, but beyond there you could run into trouble."

"What did that guy mean about trouble?" Sanja asked when they were back in the car. "And about the Krajina Serbs? Will we be able to get into Krajina? How dangerous is it? Should we turn around and go back?"

Ranko said, "Honey, I never thought it would easy, but that's all the more reason to get to your grandmother. If she's really on her own, she'll need help even if she weren't sick."

"You said Lopare. We *are* going to Tuzla, aren't we … where your uncle lives?"

"He's meeting us in Lopare. That's the detour," he answered.

When they made a right turn past the café, Sanja saw the name Lopare on a road sign, the part that had not been shot away. She hoped she hadn't made a mistake putting her trust in Ranko, but there was little point in worrying about that now. He'd promised to get her to her grandmother, and that was what she meant to do. What the café owner had said worried her.

"You know," she said, "I appreciate what you and your uncle are doing, but why would he get involved?"

Ranko smiled and shook his head. "He's a maverick. Does what he wants when he wants. I don't ask his reasons for anything. Anyway, we'll hook up with him soon and he'll take it from there. Nema problema, no problem."

"You *are* going with us?" she asked, regretting her suspicious thoughts.

"Sure. Nema problema," he said again.

They had been traveling for nearly three hours. The sun was still having trouble breaking through the fog, and Sanja, not used to starting her days at five o'clock, was having trouble staying awake. Ranko said she was being unsociable, and started to sing. She told him his imitation of Bruce Springsteen was terrible. When they got to Lopare, Ranko pulled off the road and stopped.

"Looks like Rasim's not here yet," he said. "Won't be long. He's reliable."

They sat for a few minutes in silence, then he shifted toward Sanja. He put his hand on her shoulder, massaging it gently. "You're tense," he said. "Relax."

She gave him a hesitant smile. His hand slid across her back and he started to pull her toward him.

"Uh-uh," she said firmly, pushing him away. "We're not doing that."

"Aw, Sani. We're just filling in the time while we wait for Rasim."

"Look, I appreciate your trying to help me, but ..." She stopped abruptly as a shadowy figure approached the car.

Ranko turned to look. "Ah. Here he is."

Rasim was in his mid-forties, slim and wiry. He welcomed them—first his car, and then Sanja and Ranko. His sharp eyes studied Sanja as he shook her hand vigorously. He had been changing license plates in the building nearby, he told them. Then Rasim handed Ranko an envelope.

"An assortment of fake ID's," he explained.

Rasim helped Sanja into the back seat, and took his rightful place behind the wheel as Ranko climbed in beside him.

"We were smart to meet here and avoid the other road," Rasim said. "There's too much happening there. Now it's over Majevica and into Tuzla." He explained that the identity papers would be checked, but they were not to worry even though the patrols would be of the Bosnian army.

"If they try to grab Ranko for military service," he added, "we'll convince them he's going to Tuzla to enlist."

"How hard could it be," mused Ranko, "to serve at the same time in opposing armies?"

Sanja knew he was joking, but his voice lacked its usual spirit. She wrapped Rasim's confidence around her like a blanket, but a blanket frayed with apprehension. They crested the mountain and took the winding descent to the valley and Tuzla.

On the approach to the town, they came to another checkpoint. As Rasim stopped the car, Sanja felt shaky. If she had to get out of the car, she was sure her legs would fold up under her.

At Rasim's direction, she pulled another bottle of whiskey out of another secret place in the back. Was he going to use it as a bribe or whack the soldier over the head with it? The soldier took it, scanned the label critically, then gave a grunt of approval before he motioned them on. They arrived in Tuzla as the sun appeared at last.

Sanja was uneasy in a strange place. Was Amela in this town? This was where her father had wanted to send her over three years ago. Would Sanja recognize her if she happened to see her on the street? And if she did, how awful to be so close and not be able to talk to her! Or if they could talk, what would they say to each other?

Soon Rasim pulled into his driveway. The stop was brief, then the three of them were off, heading west to the Krajina. Sanja had heard news on the radio, but it didn't tell her much. Rasim tried to fill them in.

"It doesn't look good for Serbs. There have already been thousands of refugees, and everyone is talking about what Croatia is planning."

Sanja groaned. "Can we get to my grandmother's?"

"Nema problema," said Rasim. He had a good-natured laugh. "We'll make it."

They might make it *there*, Sanja thought, but would they make it back to Bijeljina with a sick old woman? That, however, was a problem for another day.

It was normally about an hour's drive from Tuzla to the next large town, Doboj, Rasim said, but these were not normal times. He and Ranko debated whether to take the longer, safer route through the mountains or risk the more direct, shorter way with the possibility of running into fighting. Considering Baka's situation, they decided to take the shorter way, following the Spreća River and switching to roads with the least traffic whenever possible. Sanja would have joined in the debate, but she wasn't consulted. Anyway, she had no clue.

The heat was intense and she was getting drowsy again. She roused when she heard Rasim say, "The sooner we leave this river valley, the better I'll feel."

"Shouldn't be much activity past Doboj," Ranko agreed as Rasim turned left—west, away from the valley. They had only gone a short distance when Sanja heard rapid gunfire and plinking sounds against the side of the taxi.

"Down!" shouted Rasim, slamming on the brakes. Before Sanja could think or react, Ranko reached back and shoved her onto the floor.

"Sounds like a skirmish," he said. "They're not shooting at *us*—well, not exactly. But stay down."

Sanja wanted to be a bumblebee, tiny, and with wings to fly away. She wished the people shooting at each other would just shake hands and go home. The gunfire didn't stop, but grew fainter, moving back toward the river. Ranko and Rasim sat up and exchanged a quick look. Rasim gunned the engine, and they sped away.

"If that's not 'much activity,' your definitions need help," Sanja chided Ranko. She couldn't stop trembling. She gripped her fingers so tightly her knuckles ached.

Rasim waved his hand to the right, saying, "Doboj's that way. We don't want to go there."

Farther on, he gestured and said, "Banja Luka's that way. The sports center's overflowing with displaced people from everywhere. Last place we want to go."

Soon he gestured again, saying, "Prijedor's that way. No one wants to go there."

Sanja wondered if there was any place they *did* want to go.

Their faster speed didn't last long. Traffic increased, almost all of it going in the opposite direction. Rasim was adept at finding opportunities, but it was still slow going. They had obviously reached a point of exodus from Krajina. The road was crowded with cars, wagons, and throngs of people on foot plodding east.

Sanja's heart ached for a man carrying a cage with two chickens in it. It might be all he had left of a fine farm.

As soon as possible, they left the large road. Rasim was a genius at finding lanes cratered with tooth-jarring potholes. It was not fast or comfortable, but the traffic was much lighter there.

The sun was cruel. Sanja's clothes were soaked. They stopped only a few times to rest, and then only briefly. Conditions made it advisable to find narrow, rutted farm roads whenever they could. Checkpoints added hours to the trip. Every time they were stopped, Sanja's heart stopped too. She was sure she'd seen Ranko slip cash to a couple of guards in addition to the usual whiskey and cigarettes. After the skirmish, there were few encounters with troops, but more with police.

Through the night, the men switched drivers frequently, cat-napping as they could or stopping briefly. Sanja didn't share the driving, but she was too keyed up to sleep. Visibility was poor on mountain roads. In the morning, even on flatter stretches, it was difficult. Fog wrapped around the car like a shroud. There was always the possibility of mines, both on and off the road. According to Rasim, driving through villages could also be dangerous.

"Village people are suspicious of strange cars," he said. "They're traditionally tight-knit, and now more than ever with soldiers and looters prowling about."

Several hours later, a country road dumped them back onto a main road where they were stopped by police at a routine roadblock. Rasim did what he'd done at other roadblocks, laughed, joked, and bribed. But this time, it didn't work. He and Ranko were marched off to a white building nearby. Sanja was ordered to remain in the car. She wasn't sure whether she preferred that or staying together. In fact, she would have preferred to be driving on. She waited, trying not to invent awful scenarios, knowing there were worse ones than she could possibly think of. When a policeman approached and peered at her through the open window, she tensed. The pulse in her temple throbbed as she imagined him opening the door and dragging her out. When he turned away, she nearly fainted.

Almost two hours later, Ranko and Rasim sauntered back to the car. As they pulled away, she couldn't believe the cocky look on Ranko's face.

"Well," Sanja demanded. "Aren't you going to tell me what happened? What did they do to you in there?"

Ranko turned his smiling face toward her. "We played poker," he said.

"*Poker*?" Sanja repeated, incredulous.

Rasim tried to keep a straight face, but failed. "In poker, Sanja, there are winners and losers."

"Did you win a lot of money?" she asked.

Rasim tossed a grin over his shoulder. "We won something better. Our release."

They drove on, and even though Ranko and Rasim took turns driving, the older man still looked exhausted. After the fog cleared, the day was scorching hot. The evening was only a little better. They'd snacked a little, but had not taken time to eat, so they stopped and sat in the warm twilight with the doors open to get whatever air there was. Ranko got out and stretched, being careful to stay on the paved surface where there was less chance of mines. Sanja unloaded bread, sausage, and apples, and the brandy Rasim's wife had packed.

"Wouldn't it be nice if we could sit under those shade trees?" she said wistfully.

Ranko squinted at the grove of trees nearby. "Wouldn't it be nice if we got blown to smithereens by landmines?"

Sanja glared at him.

"Sorry. Just showing my romantic side." He grinned and patted her knee.

"How much farther?" she asked Rasim. It had been nearly forty hours since Ranko had pulled up in front of Sanja's house.

"Another hour, with luck," he said. "We'll continue to stay off the main roads. The countryside is laced with lanes, but I used to live near here, so I know how they connect farms and villages."

And then Sanja had a terrible thought. "My grandmother doesn't know we're coming! What if she's not there?"

Ranko shrugged and said, "Then we'll pick up …"

Rasim didn't miss a beat. " … somebody else's grandmother." He finished the thought with a chuckle.

Sanja rolled her eyes. "Oh, you're both so witty," she said.

A couple of hours later, she found that she needn't have worried. Baka opened the door. She was hunched over and her complexion was pewter-gray. Right away she was shaken by a rasping cough. There wasn't any question that she was sick, and she fell into Sanja's arms, limp as a rag doll, but with a look of gratitude that made Sanja very glad she had come.

CHAPTER
9

Sanja lay awake much of the night on the sofa listening anxiously to the sound of Baka's coughing in the next room. *In the morning,* she had thought wearily … In the morning she would talk to Baka's doctor, and then they could leave.

No matter how miserable Baka may have felt, when morning arrived she was the proper hostess, shuffling about, putting food on the table and insisting that her guests eat. She did seem a little stronger than she had the night before.

"Maybe our coming has helped her," Sanja said hopefully to Rasim.

"Maybe," he said. Then he looked at Ranko who had showered and dressed in his uniform. "Your young man is very upset because he has to leave you."

"He's not my … Leave me? What do you mean *leave* me? Rado?"

He had the good sense to look sheepish as he said, "I told you I had a bit of time off. Well, it's over and I have to get back to my unit."

"And I'm just finding this out *now*?" Sanja was shocked and she was mad, but most of all she was panicked. How would she ever get her grandmother across Bosnia on her own?

Ranko said, "Rasim will be with you. He can take much better care of you than I can."

"Rado! You can't leave me!" Sanja shrieked.

"I'm sorry, Sani. I know it's not fair, but if I don't get back to my unit, I'll be shot as a deserter."

"But … but … but …!" she stuttered.

"Shot, Sani. As a deserter. I'm not kidding," he said.

Then another thought occurred to her. Sanja said, "Wait a minute. How are you getting there? What about the car? You're not taking Rasim?"

Ranko looked uncomfortable, but he answered, "Only for a little while. He's coming back for you."

"I will," promised Rasim.

"We're going in the wrong direction," Ranko explained. "You don't want to go that way."

"You don't," echoed Rasim.

With a hollow feeling in her chest, Sanja reflected on her decision to make the trip. It had been rash, but she'd trusted Ranko.

He reached for her hand. "I'm sorry. The trip took longer than I expected."

"So you're just abandoning me." She took off the make-believe wedding ring and hurled it at him. "I thought you were my friend!"

"I'm a professional soldier. Your father would understand."

Sanja was not about to let the thought of her father divert her attention. She yelled, "You're a creep! You're a weasel! You might have warned me before we left Bijeljina."

"And what would you have done?"

The question stopped her cold. Beside her, her grandmother was shaking her head, looking confused and frail. Gazing at her, Sanja was close to tears. Suddenly subdued, she put her arm around her grandmother and said, "Oh, Baka, I would have come. Of course I would have come. I just think Ranko should have told me. And I don't think he should be deserting you either," she added, glaring at him.

Rasim looked from Sanja to Ranko, then back again. "Sanja, I will get you safely home. I'm going to drive Ranko to where he can hitch a ride to his unit, and I'll be back by noon."

Sanja shoved away panic. She put her hand on Rasim's arm. "And what do I do if you're not back? How long should I wait?" No matter how faithful and trustworthy Rasim might intend to be, anything could happen.

"I will be back today, and we will leave this afternoon." He sounded so reassuring. "But if you hear anything ... alarming ..."

"Alarming?" The word had a chilling effect. "Such as what?"

For the first time her grandmother spoke up. "Explosions," she said matter-of-factly. "Or gunfire." Baka had survived an earlier war.

"Consider every possibility and be prepared," Rasim advised.

"How am I supposed to do *that*? *You* were my preparation!"

"Sanja, I have every intention of being back by noon."

Sanja was in a state of shock as Ranko and Rasim left. She immediately turned on the radio for the latest news, and heard a man speaking from Croatia. He sounded official, saying that ordinary Serbs should remain in their homes and trust that their property and rights would be guaranteed.

Ordinary Serbs? Who were they? she wondered. Was her grandmother an ordinary Serb? It sounded like everything would be all right if they just stayed put. And there hadn't been any explosions.

She had to talk to the doctor. Baka said his house and office were at the far end of the main street. When Sanja knocked, the doctor himself answered.

"My nurses and assistants have left," he explained, "and many of the townspeople as well. My patients live in villages around here, and I'll stay as long as I can. I've been treating your grandmother for a severe respiratory infection."

He described the medicines he had prescribed. "You must make sure she takes them," he said, then he shook his head sadly. "Old hatreds have been stirred up for nationalistic purposes. You mustn't stay."

As usual, Sanja was more concerned about immediate problems than age-old hatreds. She thanked the doctor and said she'd do what she could to leave.

Trudging back along the one main street of the village, she hailed people in passing cars, but no one was willing or able to make room. Traffic had picked up since the day before. One car had a baby's pram strapped to the back, another a wheel chair. Some people were tramping along on foot, stooped under the weight of bundles. Such a heartbreaking sight!

Back at the house, Baka took her medicine and slept again. Although her fever was low grade, her breathing was labored.

Noon came. Rasim had not returned. Sanja began to pace. She checked again the items they would need to take. How they would go without Rasim, she had yet to figure out. Her grandmother didn't have a car, only a tractor. Sanja had even less experience with a tractor than she had with an automobile.

She tried neighbors, but those who were still there had their own problems. At a house down the road, the woman who answered her knock snarled, "Chetnik!" and slammed the door in her face. The word whipped Sanja back in time to school and the boy in the blue shirt. A different time, a different place, but the slur was no less vicious.

The afternoon wore on without a sign of Rasim. Sanja didn't think that he would deliberately desert them, but he had been gone the whole day, and she was beginning to suspect it would be impossible for him to get back.

She spent a sleepless night. Very early the next morning, she spoke with the doctor again. He was still determined to stay longer, but told her, "You should go as soon as you can. The offensive, 'Operation Storm,' has begun. There are hordes of refugees from the Glina area, not to mention our own retreating troops."

Sanja thanked him, though she was not feeling at all thankful. Walking back to her grandmother's, she thought about the tractor. She almost resolved to drive it, but she didn't know the roads and then she worried that it would run out of gas. Then what would they do? Maybe it would be better to stay. To stay or to go? To go or to stay? The question was driving her mad.

Sanja spotted a small car with four people in it. There were only two pieces of luggage on top. She planted herself firmly in front of it. The driver stopped and motioned her to his window.

"We can't give you a ride, m'dear," he said in English.

"Please," Sanja begged. "My grandmother is sick and ..." More English words failed her.

"Listen, we're British journalists. You don't want to go where we're going."

The man beside him said, "*We* don't even want to go where we're going."

Sanja hoped journalists could at least give her some information and advice. She said, "So many people leave, but on radio a man say … uh … say Serbs should stay. He say our rights will be …" She didn't know the English word for respected.

The woman behind the driver hooted and said, "You don't *have* any rights. Don't believe that drivel; it's for the home and world audiences. From what we've seen …"

"What have you seen?" asked Sanja.

The man answered. "Your army's in rout. Be careful you don't get run over by their tanks."

"It's mass expulsion by the new name," the woman continued. "Ethnic cleansing. People who don't leave are rounded up, sent to refugee centers if they're lucky. Others, especially the elderly, are shot or beaten. Their houses are looted. Their villages are burned. It's not pretty. Get out of here as soon as you can."

"Good luck," said the driver as he shifted gears and moved on.

Feeling frustrated, Sanja went back to Baka's house. She reached the walk, glad that the cruel neighbor was nowhere in sight. She went inside and paced, restless and undecided. She set her backpack, a small bag with her grandmother's possessions, and a bag of food by the front door. When she took her grandmother some juice, Baka gave her a weak smile.

As the minutes ticked by, Sanja listened, with one ear tuned to her grandmother's breathing, the other for sounds of battle. She could hear the hum of traffic from the main road, and with increasing frequency, she thought, on their little lane. She moved toward the door. She had to keep trying. As she passed the front window, she heard glass shatter. An object flew past her head. She looked at the broken windowpane and then at a brick on the floor. Sanja dropped into a chair, her heart beating wildly. As she stared at the brick, she knew the decision to leave immediately had just been made. But she still didn't know how.

A few minutes later there was a knock at the door. Rasim! Sanja leaped up and raced to open it. Or was it soldiers? Or the neighbor woman? Surely soldiers would not be so polite, nor would a brick-thrower. When she opened the door a crack, she was relieved to see the doctor.

"I'm taking a pregnant woman, a patient of mine, to Banja Luka." He gestured to his car outside. "I can make room for you and your grandmother."

Sanja clapped her hand over her mouth to hold back a flood of grateful tears.

Together she and the doctor helped Baka into the back seat beside a young woman who appeared ready to drop triplets. She said her name was Slavenka. She was pale and biting her lip. As they got underway, Slavenka told Sanja that her husband was a soldier with the Army's Fifth Corps to the west and south. She had heard they were moving to secure as much territory as possible before a peace treaty was signed.

The Fifth Corps? Sanja tried to remember what the man at the café had said about the Fifth Corps. She was pretty sure he'd said it was made up of Bosnian Muslims.

"But you're Serb ... or Croat," she said, puzzled.

Slavenka shook her head. "I'm a Bosnian. So is my husband. And so—if God allows it—will our baby be." Her last word was squeezed out by a contraction.

"I swear," Sanja said fretfully, "I don't understand the Yugoslavia I was born into."

Sanja kept an eye on both of the women in the back seat as the doctor did his best to maneuver through the jumble of traffic. He swung around a tractor. He edged past people pushing wheelbarrows and people with babies or with small children clinging to their backs.

It was another hot, dusty, sweaty day. It took them over an hour to reach a town that appeared to be a staging area with more than a dozen buses and trucks parked there. Sanja could see that her own army was trying to organize the evacuation of civilians, but frantic people were cramming into any space they could find.

At that moment, Slavenka cried out, and the doctor stopped the car. After he examined her, he turned to Sanja, saying, "The baby will come soon. Sanja, let's see if we can get you and your grandmother onto one of the buses."

Sanja was stunned. Leave the doctor? Now *she* was frantic. Then she heard Baka say to Slavenka, "You deliver a healthy baby, and may God bless you."

Sanja drew a deep breath and pulled herself together. She kissed Slavenka's cheeks, and said, "Come on, Baka, we're going to get a bus."

There wasn't a square inch of space on any bus, but Sanja managed to eke out room in the back corner of an open truck bed. The doctor gave her additional medication, sunscreen, and instructions before he rushed back to his other patient.

Sanja eyed the bus wistfully because it had seats and a roof. The sun that was already hot would be blazing later in the day. She stood next to her grandmother, using her body as a shield as more women and children pushed on board. The tailgate was closed with a snap. The truck was declared ready. Women lifted their children up or perched them on the sides so they wouldn't suffocate or be trampled.

As the truck ahead of them began to move, a woman in it screamed, "Stop! Oh, please! My child—my Nikola! He fell!"

The woman was struggling without success to get to a little boy about two years old who was lying in the road, crying. In an instant, Sanja scrambled over the tailgate of her truck and scooped up the child. She started toward the mother's truck, then watched, distraught, as it pulled away, tucking in ahead of a bus that was leaving.

The woman, trapped and panic-stricken, called out, "Refugee Center, Banja Luka."

Apparently that was where they were all going. Sanja was alarmed to hear her own truck's engine start up. She *couldn't* be left behind. Baka was on the truck! Sanja sprinted toward it. Hands reached for the boy and pulled him aboard. Others grabbed Sanja. She clambered back on as the truck began to roll.

None of the women in her truck wanted to take on an additional child, so now Sanja had two charges. "Does anybody know where we're going? The Center in Banja Luka?" she asked, hopefully.

Her question was met with silence. Then a woman said bitterly, "My great-great-great-great—and more greats—grandfathers are weeping in their graves."

The comment gave Sanja further reason to curse the war and the politicians who had promoted it, but it didn't answer her question.

As she helped a woman fasten a sheet to provide shade, the woman told her, "Our convoy's going to a refugee center in Banja Luka." Sanja remembered Rasim saying as they by-passed Banja Luka that it was the "last place we want to go." Well, now it was the first place Sanja wanted to go, and the sooner the better.

The caravan was the usual assortment with motorcycles and bicycles weaving in and out, sometimes missing by inches the people trudging in long lines along the edge of the road. Or sometimes not missing them.

Sanja picked up Nikola. Easing herself into a small space

beside Baka, she put him on her lap.

"Where's my Mama?" he asked.

She stroked his wet cheeks. "She's on the other truck," Sanja said, adding with more hope than certainty, "You'll be with her soon."

Baka was coughing again. The bags with clothes had gotten lost, but Sanja reached into the food bag that she had managed to carry on. Inside was a bottle of water, getting warmer in the increasing heat of the August day. But it was wet. She dampened a cloth and sponged her grandmother's face and neck. Ignoring her own thirst, Sanja tipped the bottle to her grandmother's cracked lips, and got her to swallow a pill. She regretted having to be stingy with the water, but she had no choice. She gave a sip to the little boy. There was no telling how long they would be on the road.

She tried to console herself by thinking of the bits of good luck they'd had, but their good luck had a way of running out. It did again. After only a few kilometers, the truck sputtered to a halt. The driver got out and gave it a savage kick. Despite his rage, the beast refused to rally and would become just another impediment on the road. Sanja watched with alarm as the truck a short distance ahead, the one with Nikola's mother aboard, traveled on.

Someone helped get Baka and Nikola out of the truck bed. What should they do now? Sanja once again tried flagging passing cars while Baka and Nikola waited, sitting side-by-side, leaning against the stricken vehicle. Sanja wrung her hands, feeling forlorn and helpless. The truck, useless as a conveyance, at first offered a pitiful amount of shade, but soon they were sweltering under a merciless sun, now directly overhead. Some of the other passengers had started walking, but no one wanted to take a two-year-old child along, so Sanja held him on her lap, stroking his hair. He was so like her little cousin. She hadn't been able to save Mirko, but she vowed she would save Nikola and get him back to his mother.

She looked at her grandmother, so gentle, yet so strong. She thought of her mother, Stefana, Baka's daughter, who had inherited the toughness, but not the gentleness. Sanja heard her own voice—thin with despair—saying, "I don't know what to do." She took the withered hand that patted her knee and held it to her cheek.

Baka's voice crackled as she said, "You've done a brave thing, my Sanja. Such bravery will surely be rewarded."

Sanja felt hot tears welling up. The last thing she felt was brave, and she could not believe she had earned any rewards.

CHAPTER
10

Vehicles edged past the crippled truck, then went resolutely on their way. Sanja sat for a minute, despondent and weary from her efforts to get a ride. Nikola seemed to sense her mood. His mouth puckered and he asked again about his mother.

"We'll be with her soon," Sanja told him, trying to sound positive.

She looked up in surprise when a black car with a dented front fender stopped beside them and the rear door opened. A woman leaned her head out of the passenger window. She said, "Get in. We'll make room for you." Sanja went weak with relief.

It was an old car, a large Mercedes. A mattress, a suitcase, and a chair were tied onto the top. In the back were a thin old man and three children of various ages. The floor and the shelf under the rear window were stuffed with boxes and sacks. In the front, a man was puffing nervously on a cigarette.

The woman got out, balancing an infant on her hip as she casually tossed out several sacks. She rearranged the children, taking the three-year-old up front and installing Sanja and Baka in the back, with Nikola on Sanja's lap. It was crowded, but Sanja didn't mind. It was better than sitting on hot pavement. When the woman got back into the car, she introduced herself and her husband whose name was Miloš. Her name was Vesna.

"They came to our village at dawn," Vesna said, "firing their rifles in the air, ordering us all out of our homes, then looting them, taking anything they could carry. Then they burned the houses. We're taking our children and their two cousins to Banja Luka." It was hot and stuffy in the car, and that was the last anyone spoke for a long while. Sanja gave a piece of fruit to each of them as well as to Nikola and to Baka. That was the end of her food supply, gratitude having won out over her survival instincts.

When Miloš turned onto a narrow dirt road, Sanja looked about with concern. Another car turned off, too, and one tractor that she could see. A motorcycle sped past. The car bounced along from one rut to the next.

One of the children begged for water, then the others joined in. Vesna handed them a bottle, cautioning one swallow for each. Sanja gave the same amount from their next-to-the-last bottle to Baka and Nikola. She blotted her grandmother's glistening forehead. Sanja's sweat-soaked shirt was plastered to her skin. Miloš turned onto a dirt lane, and Sanja wondered if he knew what he was doing. But when their progress could be measured in more than a few feet at a time, her level of trust rose. The car jolted sickeningly.

As if in answer to her worries, Miloš said, "We're taking back roads and lanes through the mountains. First we go south, then we go north. Any other time it would be ridiculous, but today, it's best."

Vesna was reassuring. "My husband grew up in this region and knows the roads well. We just hope not to come across any fighting."

"Fighting? Who's fighting here?" Sanja asked.

"Who isn't?" said Miloš.

They drove for some distance, mostly uphill. The heat made

everyone drowsy. Sanja was glad Nikola and Baka were able to sleep. She checked her grandmother's breathing. It was no better, no worse.

When they reached a narrow paved road, the traffic increased, but traveling was more comfortable. Sanja was just starting to doze off too when she heard gunshots. Alarmed, she scanned a wooded area to the right. Ordinarily she'd have thought it was hunters, but there was nothing ordinary about their situation, and Sanja remembered all too well an earlier skirmish. Drivers hit their accelerators, racing recklessly as if they were chased by demons, as perhaps they were. Climbing again, they were flung this way and that as Miloš maneuvered sharp curves. The road was so narrow it could not even be called two-lane. Sanja chewed her finger and clung tightly to Nikola as their car followed two others darting around a slow moving horse-drawn cart.

"Well, there's no more gunfire, but I wouldn't say we're safe," said Miloš as they came to a flat area. After a few more minutes, he said roughly, "Sanja, get down on the floor and have the children hide you. Children, move over."

Sanja could see that cars ahead were being stopped by men wearing camouflage uniforms and carrying guns. Some had heavy beards, reminding her of the scruffy soldier who had frightened her at the checkpoint on the trip over Majevica. She slid down and folded herself into the cramped space behind Vesna. The children covered her.

"Are they soldiers, Miloš?" she asked, her voice strained.

"Who knows? Militia. Bandits. These days they're all the same."

For a brief moment, she thought dying of suffocation on the floor might not be worth it, then she heard a man's voice, and guessed that Miloš's advice had been good.

"Ho, you shit-faced Chetniks! At last you're getting what you deserve! Who's in this car?"

Sanja felt Baka's hand pressing on her head. She heard the driver's door open, then scuffling sounds. There were shouts and Miloš cried out in pain. Vesna screamed, and Sanja feared that she had been pulled out of the car as well. It sounded like Miloš was being hit and kicked and kicked some more.

"Get their money, watches, jewelry," said a second voice. Apparently things were handed over because the men grunted and then slammed the door shut. Back in his seat, Miloš was moaning, but he got the car underway again. Sanja's moment of relief ended when they stopped again. If only she could unzip a hiding place in the roof and pull out liquor and cigarettes. The child above her whimpered. In the road behind them, women were screaming. Maybe liquor and cigarettes would not be enough.

Sanja curled herself tighter when Vesna said sharply, "Stay out of sight, Sanja."

Eventually Miloš drove on. The children scrambled back to their places. Sanja came up for air. Glancing back, she saw that some cars had been pulled over.

Soon they were back on S-curve roads, hugging a steep cliff on one side with a long drop on the other. Miloš did his best to manage the turns, but his steady groans were a worry. After a short distance, he found a place to pull over, and stopped the car.

"Sanja," he said through clenched teeth, "please, can you drive?"

Sanja swallowed hard, then said, "Uh, sure."

Why not Vesna, she wondered, but Miloš must have his reasons. Sanja was all too aware that her single driving experience had not prepared her for this kind of challenge, but, on the other hand, if Miloš passed out, they could end up hurtling to the bottom of a deep ravine. They all changed places, Vesna in the back with Miloš in the passenger seat. Sanja slid behind the wheel, summoned up her courage, and put the car in motion. *Heaven be merciful*, she thought.

Miloš spoke in short gasps; Sanja could barely hear him. "Any more ... soldiers," he said, "you hide ... again."

"That last time we were stopped," said Vesna, "girls in the cars behind us were dragged out and led away to be raped." She left no room for doubt.

With fear settling like a molten rock in her stomach, Sanja clutched the wheel and concentrated on driving. She prayed they'd seen the last of enemy soldiers. She glanced over at Miloš, and saw that he was asleep. Or unconscious.

Sanja gripped the steering wheel until her arms ached, fighting for control on a narrow mountain road with no guardrail. Even an experienced driver would not be relaxed. She wasn't experienced and she definitely wasn't relaxed.

It was a little easier when they reached a plateau. On either side there was cultivated land and small farms. There were still a few other cars. Now, given the opportunity, the drivers gunned their engines and sped on. Sanja gulped. She hit the accelerator. The car picked up speed. What a story to tell Goran. If she lived to tell it.

Just ahead, Sanja saw a woman standing beside two children. One of the children was holding up a sign. Intent on driving, Sanja didn't read it, but she was shocked to hear the children calling out, "Kill the Chetniks! Kill the Chetniks!" The littlest one made a slashing motion across his throat. She was so upset she almost ran off the road.

Vesna tapped her on the shoulder. "You saw the sign that

little one was holding?" she asked, her voice shaky. "Our symbol. The four letters in the crossbar. *Only Unity Can Save the Serbs.*" Vesna started crying. "The child spat on it, then threw it down and ground it under his bare foot. A child! What does he know?"

Sanja's skin crawled. Not for the first time, she wondered what she or her grandmother or Vesna or little Nikola had ever done to these people to cause such loathing? She thought of the letter from her cousin early in the war and told herself to keep driving. Just keep driving.

Some time later, Miloš woke, shifted uneasily, and lit a cigarette. The children in the back seat wailed and fought. Vesna tried to sing to them, but she could not. Instead she wept. The old man never spoke. One of Vesna's children wet herself. Sanja felt sorry for her, but there was no place they could stop. After awhile the smell of smoke and urine made Sanja feel sick.

When Miloš found what he thought was a suitable place, he had Sanja stop the car. He got a can of gasoline out of the trunk. Together, they filled the tank. Once again, Sanja admired Miloš's planning because they had passed many stranded cars and many people trudging wearily along. Though Miloš was walking, he still wasn't steady. He seemed to be in great pain, but by now Sanja felt sure she could handle the driving.

Underway again, Vesna said, "In Banja Luka they're taking in refugees." She blew her nose and added, "That's what we are now. Refugees."

Just after sunset, they stopped again. Sanja's sore arms and back were glad for the relief. She parked in a small grove of trees alongside three other cars. Apparently there were no landmines, or so she hoped. The break gave them all a much-needed chance to stretch. Sanja watched Baka anxiously. Her breathing was more labored. For a few minutes, she suffered a wracking cough. Sanja thought she seemed weaker.

Nikola hugged Sanja and whispered to her, "Will we find Mama soon?" She held him close, assuring him that they would. Then he went to play with the other children.

While they were stopped, Sanja had a chance to look more closely at Miloš. She was shocked to see how bruised and swollen his face was. He was hunched over, his arms pressed against his ribs. Vesna crooned over him and ministered to him as best she could.

The rest of the trip to Banja Luka took over two hours. As they got nearer, Sanja was glad that Miloš insisted on driving. He kept on doggedly smoking and driving until the exhausted group reached the outskirts of the crowded city. There was no electricity. The streets were illuminated by the headlights of stalled traffic. Miloš wound his way through side streets—dark, noisy, and chaotic. Jumpy flashlight beams made Sanja feel like they were in a science fiction story. It took almost an hour to get to the sports center where a generator was providing electricity.

The farewell there with Miloš, Vesna, and their children was tearful. "If there is a heaven," Sanja told them, "you have a place in it."

The sports center was packed. There was barely an inch of floor that didn't have people curled up together like litters of kittens. It was noisy and smelled of days-old sweat and other odors too mingled to define. Sanja nudged out a couple feet of floor space against a wall, enough to let Baka lie down. She squeezed in beside her grandmother, knees drawn up, with Nikola nestled against her. Baka and Nikola were asleep instantly. Sanja envied their being able to tune out their surroundings, but she needed to be alert. She listened to her grandmother's labored breathing and sighed. The two of them were her responsibility, but she didn't know what to do. She scanned the throng for Nikola's mother. How would she possibly find her in such a mob, assuming she was even there?

After a few minutes, Sanja slipped Nikola over to Baka and got up. She was stiff and exhausted, but her need to find Nikola's mother was much more important than sleep. She found her way to the middle of the large hall, stepping over bodies and stumbling over bundles. The woman had called out "sports center" from her truck—or had she said "refugee center"? Were they the same? Sanja pushed and shoved her way from room to room, aching at the sight of the refugees. Some were hysterical, some were crying softly. Others appeared numb, just staring, seeing nothing.

An hour later Sanja had failed in her search. She made her weary way back to the wall where Baka and Nikola lay as she had left them. She inched out a space beside them, sitting upright, leaning her head back, and closing her eyes. At least for the moment they were safe. Maybe she could allow herself a bit of rest. As she dozed off, recent experiences came to her in flashes.

She awoke with a start, swallowing the scream that was caught in her throat. A dream—it was only a dream, she told herself, but in it she had been wading ankle-deep in scarlet blood, frantically trying to reach ... Nikola? Yes, Nikola at first. But then the child had become her cousin Mirko, his face swollen, purple with bruises. He was reaching out to her, but moving farther and farther away. She had struggled to reach him, but could not.

Sanja wrenched herself upright. Nikola was beside her, sleeping, though fitfully. She took several deep breaths before getting up to start her search again. She had to ... she *had to* ... find Nikola's mother. Baka and Nikola were her responsibility. She had to figure out what to do.

A half hour later, two miracles occurred. Across the room

Sanja saw the woman she had been seeking. Not far from her, she saw Rasim. Both of them reached her at the same time, and for a few minutes it was happy mayhem with everyone talking at once.

After pointing the mother to where Nikola was huddled with Baka, Sanja turned to Rasim who took her hands in his.

"Oh, Sanja! I've been in agony. I went back for you, but by the time I got to your grandmother's house, you were gone. I could only hope you'd find your way to Banja Luka."

She squeezed his hands, then hugged him.

"Your grandmother …?" He left the question unfinished, his face showing how worried he was of the answer.

"She's hanging on, but she needs help. I can't tell you what it's been like."

"I've heard stories," Rasim said.

"Are you all right?" Sanja asked him, wondering how safe a Muslim would be in a room full of Serb refugees. "Nobody's bothered you here?"

"You know me, Sanja," he said with a grin. "I change license plates. I blend in."

"But now," she asked him urgently, "can we blend out? We can't possibly stay here. My grandmother will die in this place."

Rasim was ready with a plan. "Meet me outside that door in twenty minutes," he said. "We're going to Tuzla where I can get your grandmother into the hospital."

True to his word, Rasim was waiting for them in his beat-up taxi. Sanja's grandmother made a supreme effort to walk to the car, collapsing onto the back seat, her cough now a frightening, deep rattle. Sanja sat with her in the back, allowing Rasim to manage the drive, thankful that he knew roads that likely were not on any maps.

Baka murmured, "Are we going home now?"

Home? She no longer had a home. Sanja turned away, pressing her fist against her mouth as the scene outside became a tearful blur.

This time when they skirted Doboj there wasn't anybody shooting. At the few inevitable checkpoints, Rasim contrived to use his stash of bribes, and they got to Tuzla in a relatively short time. Nevertheless, it was late Sunday night, almost Monday, when Rasim's sister, a nurse, admitted Baka to the hospital.

The trip had been hard on Sanja's grandmother. The respiratory infection had turned to pneumonia, but she had always been a sturdy and stubborn woman. The doctor who examined her said he believed she would recover. Then Rasim found a ham radio operator who was able to get in touch with Sanja's mother.

"Mama," Sanja said briskly, "we don't have time for hysterics. I know you have questions about Baka and Krajina, but these calls have to be short."

"I don't know what to say," were Stefana's first words. "You should be grounded for the rest of your life pulling such a stunt!"

"But?" Sanja asked, knowing very well what the answer would be.

"But nothing! It was stupid. Your grandmother would have been fine if you'd left her in her home."

"Just say 'thank you,' Mama. But much of the credit goes to Rasim and Miloš." She hesitated, then added, "And Ranko."

"Rasim?" Sanja heard the catch in her mother's voice, and knew perfectly well it was because she recognized a Muslim name.

"Yes, Mama. Rasim. I'll tell you about it when I see you. We'll leave as soon as I'm sure Baka's doing well. Rasim will bring me back. Baka will stay longer ... with Rasim's sister."

Sanja was surprised that her mother was content with a simple, "Mm-hm."

Settled as a guest at Rasim's house, Sanja spent most of the three days at the hospital. When she walked there, she wondered about Amela. She was alive ... she *had* to be! She had relatives in Tuzla, but Sanja had forgotten their names and didn't know where they lived. One minute she hoped she might run into Amela; the next she was afraid she would. If they recognized each other, how would they greet each other? Or wouldn't they greet each other at all? It had been well over three years since Amela had gone away from Bijeljina. Now Sanja was the one who was running. Did that give them something in common or just make them more aware that they were on different sides of the war? The damned war.

Four days later, Sanja's grandmother was recovering well. Rasim had done whatever he needed to with license plates, counterfeit papers, and replenishing his stash of cigarettes and liquor, and was ready to make the trip—or run the gauntlet— back to Bjieljina. Sanja was glad they would be traveling at night. August continued to be hot. They could not get there soon enough for her, but, at the same time, she was glad she had made the trip. Baka was in good hands. Sanja took a grateful breath as she stepped into Rasim's taxi.

"We're going back a different way," he said, "to avoid checkpoints. Then we'll slip into Bijeljina."

"And home," sighed Sanja. "Bliss." Then she thought of her mother. Bliss might be a while in coming.

CHAPTER
11

On the way back to Bijeljina, Sanja slept. She woke twice at checkpoints, and again when Rasim pulled up to a café declaring a desperate need for coffee. At the café, they were told that the Krajina had been secured in just three days. It was expected that a peace agreement would soon end the fighting. And then … what next?

What next was the question on everyone's mind when in mid-December of 1995 the Bosnian war ended. The country was divided into two entities—Sanja's, the Republic of Serbia, and the other, the Federation of Bosnia. Sanja and everybody else wondered how the two entities could exist as one country when ethnic tensions, memories, and hatreds were still so raw.

Sanja hoped the peace agreement would mean more than just an end to people shooting each other. She wanted it to mean that her father would be reinstated by the army or that he'd get a good job. She wanted it to mean she could go to university. She hoped it would mean an end to what her mother called wartime deprivations since even ordinary things such as water, electricity, and coffee had become luxuries.

And what about Amela? Where had she spent the war years? It was only three months since Sanja had walked the streets of Tuzla wondering whether they might possibly run into one another.

Did Amela have bitter memories and harsh feelings? Was she like the little kids on the road who wanted to kill Chetniks? Now that the war was over, would she move back to Bijeljina? That was not likely. Maybe it was useless to wonder, but the questions nagged at Sanja like a cut that refused to heal.

Near the end of December, the helpful ham radio operator in Tuzla sent word from Rasim that Sanja's grandmother was gaining strength. Rasim had found her a room there with a capable Serbian woman. Every so often his sister checked on her and reported that her health was improving. She still wasn't happy about leaving her home, but she was comfortable enough.

When were Stefana and Sanja coming to see her, she asked? When indeed, thought Sanja. There might be a peace agreement, but travel was worse than difficult. It was dangerous to enter the Federation with license plates from the Republic of Serbia, and vice versa. Even bus travel was risky.

By May, when Sanja celebrated her seventeenth birthday, day-to-day life was only slightly better. Her father had found work that brought in a little income. Goran had completed his army service. He hoped he would be able to attend university in Belgrade, something Sanja had quit thinking about. She spent her time cleaning house, tending their small vegetable garden, hanging out with friends, reading, and watching English-language television, which was at least improving her language skills. A trip to Tuzla was still out of the question.

When Sanja's friend Ivana stopped by to deliver a birthday gift and to show off her latest hair color—Petunia Pink—Sanja vented her frustration.

"If things were confusing during the war, they're more confusing now. I don't know why we fought a war," she added moodily. "I'm not even sure what our capital is. Banja Luka, some people say Pale. Certainly not Sarajevo."

Ivana sighed. She dropped another lump of sugar into the coffee cup Sanja had placed in front of her. "You've got electricity," she marveled.

"For the moment. We get coffee sometimes."

"It's good." Ivana absentmindedly stirred hers, roiling the grounds that had floated to the top. "Everybody's leaving, going abroad. My boyfriend's talking to somebody about a carpentry job in Germany."

"I don't know, Ivana. I've tried to get a job. Anything. Selling buttons … stocking a trout farm. And I can't find anything. I think Goran's going to get into university in Belgrade, maybe this summer, which is good, but I feel …"

" … hopeless," Ivana finished, saying what they both felt.

"Ranko's out of the army and got a job," Sanja said.

"Really? Doing what?"

Sanja smiled. "I'm not sure. It's probably connected with the black market. You know Rado. Next thing, he'll be running for mayor."

"I'm tellin' ya, Sanja. I'm gonna marry that guy and live in a mansion."

"Go for it." Sanja was laughing as she said it. She was over her anger at his leaving her—there was too much else to be angry about—but he wasn't winning any points by implying to his buddies an intimate version of their so-called honeymoon.

Sanja passed Ivana the box of candy Ranko had insisted she take as an apology for abandoning her. It was not a gift she was likely to get often, and the least she could do was share with her friend.

"So, tell me about your grandmother," Ivana said.

"She tried to see if Ranko's uncle Rasim—the guy who drove

me to get her—was available, but he's living out of the country now."

"That guy," said Ivana, "isn't he Muslim?"

Sanja chuckled. "He's whatever works for him at any given moment," she said, remembering Rasim's maneuvering and his ample supply of license plates, liquor, and forged papers. "But you could ask him five hundred different ways and always get the same answer. Rasim is Bosnian."

"Aren't you scared of him?" Ivana's eyes widened even as she considered it.

"He's not like some others," Sanja said firmly, feeling the familiar flash of fury at the Muslims in the Drina Valley.

"But he's Muslim—like, you know, he's a *Turk*. Sanja!" Ivana straightened her shoulders, preparing her instructional voice. "Those people were determined to kill all Serbs and take over. That's why we fought! To defend ourselves."

How often had Sanja listened to her mother ranting about the four centuries of occupation by the Turkish Ottoman Empire? Stefana feared whatever influence it still held over Bosnia's Muslim population, even though that occupation had ended a century ago. Or had it? Sanja blinked away the image of a butchered Mirko and other cousins who had been killed during the war. She could not see how she'd ever get over her feelings of horror and loathing. Rasim, like so much else, was too complicated to explain.

"Well," said Sanja, choosing to close the subject, "I want to visit my grandmother, so if Rasim ever comes back, I'll take my chances."

It was more than a year before a solution presented itself. It came from Rasim. He was back in Tuzla, a driver for the United

Nations. The first of November he would be making several trips between Tuzla and Bijeljina. The UN worker had agreed to let Sanja hitch a ride each way.

Without fog and in an official car, the trip was much easier than Sanja's previous one. She would have a cot in her grandmother's room, but before going to the house, Rasim took her to the hospital where his sister was a nurse. Salena wanted to talk with her about her grandmother, whose health was better, but still an issue.

The town was as unfamiliar to Sanja as if she had never been there. Her vague memory of traveling there after leaving Banja Luka's sports center with its horde of refugees was not one she had tried to hold onto. She had no recollection of the hospital.

Rasim dropped her off at the front door. As she watched him drive away, she suffered an uneasy feeling. She was alone, a Serb in a Federation town. Knowing that some Serbs had lived there throughout the war didn't help at all. She could talk boldly to Ivana about crossing the inter-entity boundary line, but actually being on the other side was unnerving. Before, on the way to Krajina, she'd been with Ranko and Rasim. On the way back—well, her concerns about her grandmother had eclipsed all others.

Sanja watched as people went into the hospital and people came out. No one paid any attention to her. *I'm a Serb from Bijeljina* was not emblazoned across her forehead. She calmed herself and went inside where she followed Rasim's directions to find his sister.

Salena was sitting behind a counter at her desk at the nurses' station. She smiled a welcome. "Rasim's coming back soon," she said. "He'll take you to your baka. Let me tell you about her condition."

As Salena finished her briefing, she glanced over at someone behind Sanja. "Oh, hi, there," she said.

"Hello, Salena. I've brought this for my Aunt Biserka."

The girl who had spoken leaned past Sanja and placed a package on the desk.

Sanja stared at her. She was slender and pretty with a creamy complexion and brown eyes that had just a touch of the exotic. Her honey-blonde hair waved softly around her face and curled at her shoulders. Shorter and a bit heavier, she might be …

"Amela?" Sanja said.

The girl looked at her with a puzzled frown, then turned pale. She clapped one hand over her mouth and gripped the edge of the counter with the other. Salena hurried from behind it. Amela waved her away and stood straighter.

"Sanja. I never expected to see you here."

For all that Sanja had fantasized about meeting Amela in Tuzla, the reality was a shock. Memories flashed through her mind like shooting stars—Amela at four running in the park, at seven agreeing to dares, at nine eating sweets in the plum tree, at twelve exchanging rings on a dark street. That was Amela. But who was she now? Was this person the childhood friend or did she carry the seeds of hatred that drove the Muslim fanatics of the Drina Valley?

Then Salena took charge, ushering them across to a row of seats. She glanced from one to the other as they perched on chairs side-by-side, backs rigid, jaws set.

"Sanja's visiting her grandmother, Amela. Her grandmother lives in town," Salena said, her voice filling the void.

"Oh." After a long pause, Amela added, "Your mother's mother?"

Sanja's answer came slowly. "Yes."

She could tell that Amela was wondering how her grandmother came to be in Tuzla, but she had no intention of explaining. The girl she had known since she was born was beginning to look less like a stranger. Twelve then, she was eighteen now. Well, she was bound to have changed. Of course Sanja herself had changed, and not just in looks.

"You've gotten taller," said Amela, as if she were reading Sanja's thoughts. Then she lowered her head. "Of course you've gotten taller. You're not twelve anymore."

Sanja allowed herself a tiny smile. "You've lost weight," she said, then nervously clasped and unclasped her hands. That was stupid. Why did she have to sound so stupid?

"Listen," Salena interrupted, pulling some bills out of her pocket. "Why don't you two go get ćevapis down at the corner? Amela, you know the place. I'll meet you in about fifteen minutes when I get off duty."

Both girls stiffened again, wary at the thought of spending time alone together. What would they talk about?

"Go on," Salena urged, placing the money in Amela's hand. Amela hesitated, then agreed. It would be rude for them to refuse.

With a timid smile Sanja thanked the nurse, at the same time noticing that Amela wore no rings. Of course Sanja didn't have on Amela's birthstone ring, the one she had worn on a chain around her neck for a year. On the first anniversary of their last meeting, Sanja had given up hope. Solemnly she had placed the ring in its own special box, and it had been there ever since.

The first half of the walk to the café was in stilted silence. Where did you begin after over five years? At last Amela broke it by saying, "Your hair looks good short." Whenever she had thought of Sanja, it was as her twelve-year-old self. Was this eighteen-year-old Sanja at all the same or was she very, very different?

"Thanks," said Sanja. Hair seemed like a safe subject. "Yours is still wavy."

"Yes." Amela lapsed into silence.

When they found a table and a waiter came, Amela, who had taken Salena's money, ordered ćevapćićis. Then she asked, "Do you still eat ćevapis in ... ?" She had started to say *in Bijeljina*, but cut the question short. Discussing with Sanja the town she'd been run out of did not feel comfortable.

"Oh, yes." Sanja said, so tense she wondered how she could swallow the meat and bread. She could tell Amela that nothing much had changed, but one important thing had changed. A Serb family from Sarajevo was living in Amela's house.

Amela came to the rescue with a question. "How's your baka? Was she ill? Is that how Salena knows her?"

"Yes, that's how. When I ..." Sanja didn't want to go into the details. "When she came to the hospital she was very sick. Rasim, Salena's brother, found her a place to stay. She doesn't know I'm here yet."

"Your coming will be a nice surprise," said Amela. "Some surprises are nice."

"Yes, some are." Sanja thought of their meeting at the hospital as more of a shock than a surprise. She was glad the ćevapćićis were brought then, and both girls started eating in silence. Ordinarily they would have enjoyed the seasoned meat and the juice that soaked the big buns, but neither of them had much appetite.

Salena arrived in less than the fifteen minutes she'd promised, easing the conversation by talking briskly about local matters and events at the hospital. Then she said to Sanja, "You know Amela's aunt is also a nurse at the hospital."

"No." Sanja replied. "I didn't."

Aunt Biserka. The name jogged Sanja's memory and she knew

she'd been right to guess that Tuzla was where Amela had gone. It was what her father had wanted, Sanja thought, recalling their conversation in the plum tree.

"How long will you be staying, Sanja?" Salena asked.

"Till tomorrow. I just wanted to see that Baka's okay."

Salena again managed to steer the conversation along, then finished her tea. She looked up as Rasim entered the café. "Here's Rasim, Sanja. He'll take you to your grandmother now."

Rasim took in the situation at a glance. He said to Amela, "Why don't you give Sanja your address so you two can write now and then?"

A look of panic crossed Amela's face as if she wasn't sure she *wanted* Sanja to write now and then, but wasn't sure she *didn't* want her to. Impulsively she grabbed a napkin and scribbled her address.

"Here." She handed Sanja the napkin. "I know your address. I'm not promising ..."

"Me either," said Sanja. "But maybe now and then."

"Yes, maybe now and then," said Amela.

Sanja gently rubbed her palm where a scar might have been. She glanced at Amela, and sighed as she thought, War does terrible things to illusions ... and to friendships.

1998

CHAPTER 12

"They're back," Ivana said to Sanja. "Amela and her mother. In their old house." She popped the olive—all that remained of their pizza—into her mouth. "Didn't you know?"

Sanja shrugged. "I knew," she said casually. She hadn't. Apparently Amela, her *friend-for-life*, had returned almost six years to the day after she left and a little over five months after Sanja had seen her in Tuzla. Neither one had heard from the other.

Suddenly aware that Ivana was talking to her again, Sanja said, "Sorry. What?"

"I said it's 1998 now, not 1992, and I personally don't have any problem with them living here—I mean Amela and her mother—but there are people who don't want Muslims here in Bijeljina." She gave a meaningful nod toward a man at the next table.

"I guess you're right," said Sanja, only half listening.

"Hey, it's not even midnight yet," said Ivana. "Let's go down the street for a dessert and coffee. Maybe we'll run into some cute guys."

"I'll have dessert and coffee," said Sanja, "and leave the guys for you."

In her house on the other side of the canal, Amela was in bed. She had only been asleep a short while when she heard shouting. It came to her as a bad dream like so many she tried to ignore. Half awake, she rolled over on the narrow mattress, pulled her pillow over her head, and willed the dream to go away. But the mattress was lumpy and the blanket too thin and the voice too insistent. In the dream, her mother was yelling at Sejo in his room across the hall. Then Hanifa was hovering over Amela, tugging at the covers and shouting at her. Amela jerked awake.

"Get up! Get up!" prodded her mother. "We have to leave the house!"

Amela bolted out of bed. In that moment, time rewound. She was not eighteen, but twelve, the year her life had turned black. "Soldiers?" she cried. "Where's Papa?"

She heard her mother's quick gasp, then her more urgent cry. "It's not soldiers. Our house is on fire! Hurry!"

And then Amela could smell the smoke. Smoke? She jammed her legs into her jeans, leaving on the sweatshirt in which she'd been sleeping.

"Mama! Where's Sejo?" Then she saw him at the bottom of the stairs wearing his black leather jacket and holding hers out to her. Memory of that other time burst like an overripe melon, and it was all Amela could do to clear her head. This was a new emergency.

Smoke? How could that be? As she hurried down the steps, she could hear crackling. Glancing toward the kitchen, she saw a hazy orange glow. Smoke was rolling into the entry along the ceiling. It made her eyes sting. She grabbed her shoes and rushed toward the front door that Sejo was holding open.

"Come on. Hurry!" he cried. He was coughing.

As she stumbled into the yard, Amela blinked back tears. It was not the smoke. These were tears of despair. Then despair gave way to anger. As it surged through her, she cried out in protest. "No! This just isn't fair!"

Sejo was beside her, glancing back anxiously. Amela bit her lip. This *would* have to happen on his first weekend visit. Hadn't his life been hard enough? At thirteen, he was flirting with manhood, sometimes impatiently, sometimes reluctantly. Lately it was clear he wanted to take care of his mother and sister and chafed at having to stay in Tuzla.

"Hurry, hurry," Hanifa repeated. "Oh, where can we go? Who will put out the fire?"

"I'll go next door to phone," Amela said as she stepped off the narrow porch and into the small yard.

As Amela turned toward the house next door, her mother grabbed her shoulder. "No, no. Don't go next door. We don't know who ... or why ..." Hanifa's voice caught. "I heard glass break, but I thought it was outside."

Amela stopped abruptly. "What?"

What glass? A window? Did that mean the fire had been deliberately set? The thought was like being dunked in ice water. Amela shook off the question for the time being.

"Well, we can't just stand here. I'm going for help." Just then she saw their next-door neighbor.

"Hanifa?" he called out, tugging at his robe. "I've called the fire department. I looked out my window and saw the flames in your kitchen."

The man's wife came out of their house then, to join them on the sidewalk. She was in nightclothes and barefoot. "We called for help," she said, echoing her husband. "Are you all right?"

"You bloody Serbs!" shouted Sejo, charging at the man, shoving him with both hands. "Wasn't a war enough for you? Don't you ever stop hurting people?"

Taken by surprise, the man staggered back, but didn't fall. Hanifa gasped. Amela threw herself in front of her brother and grabbed his arms. She held onto him as the fire trucks arrived, and the firefighters dragged their hoses to the side of the house. Amela heard someone shout instructions. Then she heard the roar of water.

Sejo had settled down. She started to speak to him when she noticed a figure crossing the street. She groaned as she recognized the boy. He lived down the block and had been in her school, cocky and a bully even then. Now he swaggered up to them.

"Hey, you miserable Turk!" he yelled, punching Sejo on the shoulder. "You wanna fight somebody, you fight *me!*"

Sejo broke loose from Amela's grip, ready to charge. "Yeah, Chetnik, just ..."

Before he could go on, the older man intervened, speaking with such authority that everybody stopped. Amela had forgotten he was director of the high school, and probably used to breaking up fights.

Addressing her brother, the director said, "Calm down. Tomorrow you may speak to me about this, but you may not strike me again. Right now your mother and sister need you."

"And, you," he said with clenched teeth, turning to the young man whose look was murderous and whose hands were still balled into fists, "You—just go home."

The bully hesitated, then turned and slouched off, but not without throwing a menacing look over his shoulder. "Balija," he muttered, making sure that his voice carried to Amela and Sejo.

The row had temporarily distracted everybody from the fire,

but Amela turned back to look anxiously at the house. It seemed like hours since she had been roused out of bed. The couple from next door stayed with them, staring at the house as if hypnotized and making sympathetic sounds.

For Amela and her mother, sympathy was not enough. They were seeing the destruction of their hopes. Sejo, who was growing tall and strong, slipped a protective arm around each of them. They all knew that by morning their kitchen — perhaps their whole home — would be a blackened mess, the donated table and chairs charred and beyond use, the kitchen curtains Hanifa had made in Tuzla … ashes.

Sejo's voice was choked with contempt as he said, "You know, of course, they can't let the fire spread to the *Serbs'* houses."

"Shhhh," warned Amela. She didn't want the neighbors to overhear him. She understood very well why he was bitter, but under the circumstances they couldn't let a tactless comment add to their troubles.

Worries raced through her mind. Would the Norwegian relief organization that had given them furniture continue to help? Why should they be willing to donate more? If only she and Sejo could convince their mother to return to Tuzla! And what if the fire really *had* been set to force them to go away again? Should they? But wouldn't leaving be giving in?

She had been happy in Bijeljina as a child, but even in the few days they'd been back, every time she passed a policeman on the street, she tensed. Even now, she was nervous about talking to the firemen. Of course she was glad they were there putting out the fire, but her heart filled with dread at the thought of facing them, submitting to their interrogation, enduring their demeaning looks.

"I'm going to talk to them," Sejo said, and started toward the truck.

Amela took hold of his arm. The memory of six young men, shot to death in this very place, roared back in hideous detail. She felt dizzy.

"Amela?" Sejo was looking at her, his brow wrinkled with concern. "You're remembering what happened. So am I, but ..."

She took a deep breath. "Let's both go," she said.

Amela heard her mother timidly refuse the neighbor woman's offer of coffee. None of the others who had come out to watch approached them. If this was arson, could it also be a warning to their neighbors?

"Thank you for what you did," she told the neighbor. "We have a place to stay. We'll be fine." It was a lie, but a necessary one. They'd think of something.

Amela was surprised, but relieved, that the fireman who spoke with them was professional and courteous. The fire was mostly contained in the kitchen, he said, but there was smoke and water damage throughout. He had no idea how the fire had started, but he assured them that there would be an investigation. They shouldn't go back inside until conditions had been checked and any necessary repairs made.

When the truck finally pulled away, Sejo turned to her. "Investigation? Huh! Not damned likely!"

"No, of course not," she agreed. It would be just like the phone company that had no particular interest in providing service for Muslims who were returning.

"But," she said, "right now my concern is for Mama and for where we're going to go."

They walked in silence back to the wall by the street, and stopped in surprise as they saw Samir, a family friend, seated next to their mother, holding her hands in his big ones. Samir lived across the canal. He got up when he saw them coming and kissed them each on both cheeks. His face showed the same jumble of emotions that they were feeling. He, like them and a very few other Muslim families, had come back to rebuild their homes and their lives.

"Samir, why are you here?" Amela asked, grateful to share her responsibility.

"Just by chance. I don't sleep well at night, so I either walk around the town or take a drive into the country. I was returning from a drive."

Amela knew why Samir was out walking and driving at night. Being the first refugee to return, he felt a responsibility for those who followed.

"Samir, what should we do?" Amela glanced at her mother, whose eyes were vacant, staring at something the rest of them could not see. It was as if she had drifted away as she had done when they first arrived in Tuzla.

"Come," Samir said. "There will be nothing more tonight, but you can't go back inside. You'll be more comfortable with my family, away from this."

They helped Hanifa to her feet and into the back seat of Samir's car, parked at the curb. Amela got in beside her, with Sejo taking the front passenger seat.

"We talked to a firefighter," he told Samir. "He said there will be an investigation."

Samir gave a loud snort. "Investigation."

"We know there won't be," said Amela, resigned to the fact that the authorities wouldn't be concerned. "But we do have to talk with the Norwegians to see if they'll continue helping."

"It will be tomorrow before you can inspect the damage," he said. "Possibly someone from the Norwegian NGO will go with you. In the meantime, you're all welcome to stay at my house."

They turned at the corner, driving past closed and shuttered shops. Only a couple cafés were open along the street that led into the center of town. They passed three girls who were probably on their way home from an evening of fun. Amela blinked, not able to see them clearly, but she knew the one in the middle was Sanja.

She'd seen her only the one time, last November, when Sanja had been in Tuzla to visit her grandmother. For Amela, running into Sanja in Tuzla brought back the same furious battle she'd had with herself for years. While one part of her believed that what had happened wasn't Sanja's fault, another part, the angry part, wanted her to feel guilty. As they had calmly eaten ćevapčićis together, Amela had been tempted to say, *Did you know your fellow Serbs carried my father away and forced the rest of us to leave town? And … How do you think it felt to have the boy I loved ripped apart by a shell your Serb soldiers launched?* Oh, she could have gone on and on. But that day in Tuzla she had been coolly courteous, and so had Sanja. They'd even talked about writing to each other, but neither one had.

Seeing Sanja now—laughing with her current friends—was a shock, compressing the past six years into a deep black hole in which Amela had merely existed while Sanja had enjoyed her life, growing up normally in Bijeljina. Amela dropped her head, partly to hide the tears that were beginning to flow and partly because she dreaded looking at the face, once of a friend, now of the Serb enemy.

At Samir's house, his wife got up, made tea, and brought out some blankets.

"Has there been trouble in town?" Amela asked her.

"Just looks, comments, some graffiti, little things. We just can't be sure, so we're careful."

Samir nodded. "It only takes one or two aggrieved people ..." He left the rest unsaid.

His wife sighed, and said, "I'll find you some clothes, too. I don't mean to insult you, but you all reek of smoke."

Samir and his family had been back in Bijeljina long enough for their home to look settled. The first floor had an extra room with a cot for his father, who came from time to time to visit. Hanifa, still shaken, would sleep there while Amela would take the sitting room sofa. Sejo would be given a sleeping bag in the dining room.

Amela was grateful to see her mother reviving a bit as she sipped tea with Samir's wife. As Hanifa rose to go to her cot, she leaned over to say, "If only your father had been here this would not have happened." For a brief moment, Amela thought her mother had finally accepted her husband's fate, but as she continued, hope plummeted. "No, no. It's better he hasn't come back yet. We must fix the house before he comes back. I don't want him to be upset."

After the others had gone to their rooms, Sejo came into the living room and sat on the arm of the sofa, his dark eyes troubled. The adrenalin rush had let down. Amela clasped her hands to control their shaking.

"Is Mama getting worse?" Sejo asked.

"She's up and down. How I wish we hadn't come back! But she's determined and stubborn. I don't know how the fire will affect her."

Sejo rubbed his forehead, a gesture that had always betrayed his anxiety. "Are we wrong, Amela? Are we wrong not to make her understand that father is never coming back?"

"But, Sejo! How can we be sure if there's no proof he's dead?"

"Don't *you* think he's dead?"

"Yes." But Amela couldn't let the affirmation stand. "Or maybe I'm more like mother than I care to admit and want to have just a tiny bit of hope he's still alive."

"Then where is he?" Sejo insisted. "Why hasn't he come back? No, I'd rather not hope for the impossible," he said roughly. "Get some sleep, Amela. In the morning we'll see about the house."

"Okay."

Sejo bent down and kissed her cheek, and she felt a rush of pride at his courage. She pretended to cover a yawn so he would not notice her wiping away the tears spilling down her cheeks.

"Sleep if you can," she whispered.

Sleep if you can, thought Amela. She knew very well she would not get any more sleep this night. She lay awake, fending off old fears, tucked away, but not forgotten. After a few minutes, she got up and tiptoed to the dining room. Her brother was snoring softly, mercifully having found the rest that she could not. This night—unlike that other night—he didn't have to run, or hide, or be shot at. The war was not beginning. It was over. Wasn't it?

Amela wandered to the entry. She had not intended to take her jacket off the peg. She had not intended to slip into her boots. She had not intended to open the door and step out into the pre-dawn cold. It would be a thirty-minute walk to her house, but she had to go there.

CHAPTER
13

In a house three blocks away from Amela's, Sanja tried to sleep through the commotion downstairs, but the urgency in the men's voices made her curious. She slipped out of bed and opened her door a crack so she could hear what they were saying. Her mother was standing at the top of the steps, listening too, a worried look replacing her usual controlled expression. They both strained to hear as the voices shrank to a murmur.

"What is it?" Sanja asked. "What's going on in the middle of the night?"

"Go back to bed, girl," Stefana said. "It's men's business."

Men's business. For all of her eighteen years, Sanja had put up with men's business, and she was beginning to think it wasn't worth that much. She moved over to stand next to her mother. Sivi rubbed against her ankles.

"I won't feed you, if that's what you're after," Sanja whispered. She started to pick up her pet, but stopped to listen as the men moved into the entry.

"Well, I don't know anything about it. Goodnight," she heard her father say before the front door closed.

"Go back to sleep," said her mother, a stern edge to her voice. "They've just gone to see about the fire."

"What fire?"

"There's a house fire a couple blocks over," Stefana replied. "They think it's a house some returned Muslims are claiming."

Sanja felt a jolt of alarm. "Maybe Amela and her mother?"

"I don't know, Sanja. Maybe they should have stayed away."

"You liked Amela."

"Yes, she was a sweet child. But this town doesn't want Muslims. When they try to return, it upsets everyone. It would be in their own best interests to live somewhere else."

That was what Ivana had said, that some people in town did not want Muslims to come back.

Stefana continued, her tone curt. "Those people just don't understand that Bijeljina is a Serbian town now." She ended the discussion with an irritated gesture before she went into her bedroom and closed the door.

Sanja tried to go back to sleep, but thoughts of Amela and the war pestered her like a splinter she couldn't remove. She finally got up and went to the window. She squinted at her clock. It was just past two.

So now what? She didn't want to lie back down on her rumpled sheets. She was wide-awake with too many thoughts tumbling through her head. She pulled on socks and the jeans and tee shirt she had carelessly tossed on a chair, then tip-toed out, easing her door shut behind her. She crept past her parents' closed door, stopping at the end of the dark hall. Her hand on the wall guided her to the stairs. Her sock-clad feet made no noise on the cement as she cautiously moved down to the entry.

She slipped into her jacket and her shoes, then slowly opened the front door, choking back a scream at the sight of a man on the porch.

"Goran, you scared me to death!" she hissed. "I forgot you were home for the weekend. Are you coming or going?"

"Coming. You must be going."

Sanja slid through the cracked-open door and closed it quietly behind her. "Don't tell Mama."

"'Course not. So where are you going?"

"Did you hear about the house fire a couple blocks over?"

He tilted his head and studied her. "I heard the fire trucks earlier. Why?"

She avoided mentioning the talk she'd overheard, but said instead, "I'm curious to see whether it's the house Amela lives in."

"Amela? I heard she'd come back. Why would you go there?"

Sanja folded her arms and turned away, her mind suddenly abuzz with questions. Was it hearing of Amela's return that had stirred up memories of the war?

"Goran, what was it like in the army?" she asked.

He stared at his sister, bewildered. "What brought on *that* question?"

"Tell me," she demanded.

"Okay. Mostly boring. The war ended just after I got called up, so I was never in a battle. Good timing, huh?"

"Do you understand about the war?" Sanja asked.

"What's to understand? We had a life. We had a war. Now we don't have a life."

Sanja's shoulders dropped. "You're right," she agreed. "No trains. No university. No steady jobs. We don't even know what country we live in."

Goran opened his hands in a helpless gesture.

"Never mind," she said. "Go on in, but don't wake Mama. I don't want her to check and find I'm not here."

"You're going to that house."

"I'm going for a walk," she said.

Sanja traveled the short distance and stopped just inside the low wall that separated the house from the street. After Amela left, the house had looked as spiritless as a dead body. Sanja had often come to see it, longing for happier times. Now as she looked sadly at the soot, thick as paint on the window frames, memories picked at her mind—sirnica warm from the oven and fresh, sweet sesame seed buns. She touched her dark brown hair, now shoulder-length, remembering Amela's mother braiding it as they laughed together at dumb jokes.

Sanja moved past a broken window along the side of the house, and turned the corner into the tiny backyard. Smoke hung in the air, making her throat feel raw. She was appalled to see the grimy remains of a table and chairs stacked like kindling.

While Sanja was inspecting the house, Amela was moving stealthily through the deserted streets. Nervously, she pressed against a wall, checking in all directions before moving on. She felt like an alien in the town where she was born. Only one shopkeeper was pushing back the grating, an early-rising baker. It was the place where they had passed Sanja earlier.

Strange. They had once been so close. They had practically lived in each other's homes, had played and studied together, and giggled together about boys. And Sanja ...? Well, there was no point thinking about Sanja who was home in bed now, sleeping much better than Amela had slept this night.

As she turned the corner and headed to the middle of the block, Amela looked around. It would not be pleasant to run into the surly guy who had accosted Sejo earlier. Pausing in the shadows across the street, huddled inside her leather jacket, she felt a chill that had nothing to do with the night air.

She had not been outside at night since her return, loath to confront the memories that lingered there. Now as she stood there, she imagined the street populated by people ... or were they ghosts? She recognized them, though their shapes were blurry—soldiers wearing masks and carrying guns, young men, old men. She heard sounds, loud then, now muted in memory—the racket of machine guns, the cracks of single shots, the wailing of terrified women. And then—hazy, in slow motion—she saw her father, head held high, waving from the back of a truck, not knowing that for six long years it would be the last memory of him she would have.

And then she resolutely shut off the images, just as waking cancels them from a dream. She vowed, as she had so often before, to let the past be the past. She was in Bijeljina for her mother and for her father, to find out about him, and she couldn't do that by letting tragic memories tear her apart.

Amela walked slowly across to her home. Seeing it on the day they came back, she had been shocked. The front wall was riddled with bullet holes. Above, the wooden balcony railing was gone, maybe used for firewood. Her stomach lurched. No matter how often she had seen houses battered by war, they had not been *her* house.

She moved gingerly along the side to the back. In the corner was a heap of scorched debris, what had a few hours earlier been kitchen cabinets, table, and chairs. The rear door was charred and hanging by one hinge. She poked it and it swung open a few inches, startling her so that she jumped sideways. Glass from the door's window crunched under her feet. Behind her, someone coughed.

Terrified, she spun around ... and gasped. "Sanja! What the ...

What are you doing here?"

"Hello, Amela."

"What are you *doing* here?" she insisted.

"I heard that a … " Sanja paused. She couldn't let Amela know she'd heard talk of the fire at home. "I couldn't sleep, so I decided to take a walk."

"And you just happened by?" Amela asked, immediately suspicious.

"I was remembering how much I used to like coming to your house." The girls gazed silently at the rubble.

"What a terrible accident," said Sanja.

Amela whipped around, her eyes flashing. "Accident? This was no accident! Someone started the fire. Do you know who it was?"

"Are you crazy? I don't go around with people who torch houses. Anyway, nobody around here would do such a thing. It was an accident."

"Accident. Huh! There are people in Bijeljina who don't want refugees to come back."

Sanja stiffened. She had just heard that comment from Ivana and then from her mother. But nobody would do anything violent. Her eyes narrowed. She said indignantly, "Serbs don't burn down people's houses."

"Plenty of houses got burned during the war."

"That was war," said Sanja. "Things got destroyed. It happened everywhere. Besides, the war's over."

"For *you* maybe," Amela said fiercely. "Anyway, soldiers didn't burn this house. Vicious people did."

The conversation stalled, each standing with folded arms, wondering what the other was thinking. Sanja recalled the grim night six years ago when she had been so worried about Amela that she had taken terrible risks to go to her. Surely she could not just walk away from Amela's grief now.

She said, "I … uh … I heard that you don't know where your father is."

"You remember the truck, don't you?" Amela said dully. "I haven't seen him since it drove away six years ago." Then, hurting, she added spitefully, "So, now are you satisfied?"

Sanja jerked back as if she'd been punched. "Satisfied? What are you talking about? You sound as if you hate me! What did *I* do?"

They glared at each other until Amela felt suddenly deflated. Her righteous anger evaporated; she dropped her gaze. "I don't know, Sani," she said wearily. Amela had unconsciously used the familiar name. It weakened the barriers she was struggling to keep up.

The name had not escaped Sanja's attention either. There were no proper words, but she tried, hoping she would sound as sincere as she felt. "After you left, I cried and cried," she said. "I came here every day, hoping you'd come back, but you didn't, and I cried some more."

It wasn't enough. Amela needed to accuse her. "We swore eternal friendship, you may remember," she added, her tone laced with sarcasm.

"Of course I remember! At first I hoped you'd come back. But you didn't, and I didn't know where you were. Tuzla? But I couldn't send mail there, and I didn't know anybody to carry a letter. Last November when you gave me your aunt's address, I wrote to you."

"I never got a letter from you," Amela said.

Sanja shrugged. "The postal clerk took one look at the Tuzla address and threw it away. Paranoid, I guess."

"Nationalistic is more like it," said Amela bitterly.

Sanja gave Amela a scornful look. "Why blame me? You never wrote."

Amela kicked the debris on the ground sending up a shower of ashes. "It just seemed … useless," she said stubbornly.

"Why didn't you let me know you were back in town?" Sanja persisted.

Amela looked away. "Maybe I didn't want to. Maybe because you're the enemy."

"*What?*" Sanja's eyes widened. She couldn't believe what she was hearing. "I may be a Serb—one of those people you think burn houses—but I was your friend."

Sanja picked up a piece of wood and angrily heaved it at the pile of charred furniture. Then she slowly turned back, trying to calm herself. Amela wouldn't even *try* to understand.

"You seem to think you're the only one who's suffered," Sanja said. "Well, you're not."

Amela blinked, taken aback. What could possibly have happened to Sanja here in safe Bijeljina? She stared at the ground. "A lot's happened. A lot's changed. Nothing's like it was."

"Of course not," said Sanja. "You're taller … and slimmer."

A slight smile curved Amela's lips. "Definitely slimmer."

Sanja brushed her hand through her hair. She wasn't sure what to say. She wanted to stay there, to prolong this first real conversation in six years. "I'm sorry about the house," she said. "Do you have a place to stay?"

"With friends."

"What about your weekend house?"

"We don't have it. Something about proving property rights," said Amela.

"How much of the house is burned?"

"I don't know. Mostly the kitchen, I think."

"I imagine it'll be a big job. Repairing, I mean."

Amela felt caught between admitting they were accepting charity and letting Sanja think they had money for repairs. She settled for, "The Norwegians have an aid program."

Sanja nodded. "I've heard of it." She glanced at the house. "Let's go in."

Amela rolled her eyes. She couldn't help feeling amused. It was just like the dares Sanja used to make back in the old days.

Sanja smiled. "Let's go in the front; the back's sooty and maybe unsafe." She was talking herself into the scheme, and trying to talk Amela into it, too. "You have a key, right?"

"No, not unless ..." Amela fished in her jeans pocket. She certainly had not had time to think about keys when they hurried away, but there it was, left in her pocket from the day before. It wasn't likely the door was locked. It had been a hasty departure.

Sanja pulled a flashlight out of her jacket pocket. "Okay. Let's go."

Together they made their way to the front. Just one step up and three steps forward, Amela thought, and she'd be at her front door, but those steps were formidable. Not because she didn't know what to expect inside, but because she did. Sanja was behind her now, so Amela gathered her courage.

As she'd guessed, the key wasn't needed. The door swung open. She staggered back, bumping into Sanja. She squeezed her nostrils. There was a terrible stench, heavy, dank, reeking of water-soaked ashes. Sanja leaned forward and danced a beam of light around the entry. Amela took a few cautious steps. Sanja was close behind.

"Oh, my," Sanja said, eyeing the rug that squished under her feet.

They crept to the sitting room door. Even in the modest light, they could tell that a dreary gray pall lay over everything. The mohair sofa was covered with a dusky film. The back corner looked singed. It didn't take much imagination for Amela to picture the rest of the house. The walls would be dreary with splotchy, dark spots. The shelves in the kitchen would have gone up like a bundle of twigs. With every image, her chest tightened. Her breath came in labored gasps as she continued her tortured review. She backed up, motioning Sanja out. As the girls retreated onto the front stoop, Sanja heard Amela's deep sigh, and wondered if she was crying.

But Amela's sorrow had turned to white-hot rage. How could they do this—the same ones who had persecuted her family before? And how could she—how *could* she—be standing there talking to one of them!

She closed the door. She had to get back to Samir's house, back to her own people. She spun around, brushing roughly past Sanja, causing her to stumble backwards. Then she stopped, walked back, and deliberately locked the door. It wasn't much of a statement—but it said that this was her home and she would protect it.

CHAPTER 14

Sanja walked home, tears glistening on her cheeks. For years she had hoped that, given the chance, she and Amela could take up their friendship where they had left off. She never thought it would be easy to reclaim those lost years, but why not try? Yes, terrible things had happened, but Sanja had not expected Amela to blame *her*. They were children when the trouble began.

So what now? They were no longer four or eight or ten. Sanja could not just stop by Amela's house and invite her to come out and play. She could only hope they'd run into each other sometimes. Maybe it was crazy to care, but a special friendship had been stolen from them both.

Amela, too, was having troubled thoughts as she raced through the chilly streets. She had returned to Bijeljina reluctantly. She hadn't expected to be welcomed back, just to be left alone. She didn't want to be friends with Sanja again. She didn't.

When Amela got back to Samir's house, her mother was up. Hanifa caught her taking off her shoes.

"You went to our house," Hanifa said sternly. "You were very foolish to go there." She turned and went into the kitchen.

"So was it arson?" Amela asked her mother's retreating back.

"We'll talk about it later." But Amela knew they wouldn't.

"When can we move back to our house?"

Hanifa managed to busy herself at the sink.

"Mama ..."

"I don't know, Amela. Don't ask me things like that. I don't know."

Amela sat on the front steps, her jacket wrapped tightly around her. It wasn't the morning cold that made her shiver. It was seeing the burned house, and perhaps even more than that, her encounter with Sanja. Naturally Sanja would think Serbs were decent people. She was one of them. But Amela had a different story, and in it Muslims were the victims and Serbs had done evil things.

But Sanja? Surely Sanja had not done those things. So she couldn't hate Sanja, could she? Sanja was just naive. She didn't begin to know how violent war could be.

Amela sighed. She had enjoyed Sejo's weekend visit, glad that the new common license plates made travel safer. But the visit was ending. How she wished she could go back to Tuzla with him! Dina was in Tuzla and engaged. Hanifa was pleased. After all, she said, she had Amela with her in Bijeljina.

Of course her mother needed her, Amela fretted, but what about her own needs? She shoved that thought away. She couldn't worry about that. Not now. She was helpless in the face of her mother's determination and her own desire to find out about her father. It was unthinkable to leave her mother alone in Bijeljina. So they were there ... waiting.

"Oh, Papa, please, please, please come home," Amela murmured. And all the while the answer lay heavy on her heart— *he's never coming back.*

⟿

No matter what she preferred, Amela and her mother moved back into their house a week later. Some of their personal items were in usable condition and, thanks to the Norwegians, the house was cleaned, painted, and made livable. The Norwegian NGO also provided a small amount of food. When it was gone, Amela went shopping.

The stalls in the central market were busy. She looked longingly at a blouse she couldn't afford. She could also use a new pair of shoes, she thought, looking down at her shabby sneakers. Someday. Today it was food they needed.

She moved on to another stall where she chose two of the pale green paprikas that looked firm and were a good price. She could stuff them with rice and tomatoes. That would do for tonight's supper. Tomorrow, if the woman she did needlework for sold her embroidered tablecloth and napkins, Amela would buy a little meat. Money was scarce. As long as her mother didn't declare her father dead, Hanifa could not get a pension. The occasional pay Amela had earned as an election interpreter in Tuzla had gone for household expenses.

Amela bought the yarn she needed, and made her last purchase at the bakery. As she took her parcel and turned to leave, she stopped abruptly. The bully who had charged at Sejo the night of the fire was blocking the doorway. Even if she hadn't recognized his stringy hair and the stubble on his chin, there was no mistaking his smirk.

"Pardon me," she said, coolly. "I'd like to leave." She hoped her voice wouldn't betray her anxiety.

"What's your hurry, Turk?" he said, looking around with an insolent grin. "Where's your macho brother? I'd like to finish our fight … and I *mean* finish it."

It took a heroic effort not to wince at the term *Turk*. He'd used it deliberately, of course, as a way to insult her. She lifted her chin and looked him straight in the eye. She wanted to declare, "I'm Bosnian, you weasel, and proud of it!" But she knew it wouldn't faze him.

"Just get out of my way." Her words were brave, but her body was rigid and her hands were shaking. She was mad at herself for letting a Serb male reduce her to a quivering mass.

"I can get him to move," said a female voice behind him. "I've bought a new broom. Would you like to know what I can do with the handle?"

Amela's tormentor whipped around, then growling words she could barely hear, shoved his way past the girl on the sidewalk and stalked off up the street.

Amela blinked, surprised to find herself face-to-face with Sanja. She dipped her head in a stilted greeting, uncomfortably aware that they had not parted a week ago with friendly hugs.

"Jerk," muttered Sanja, staring after the bully.

"Where's your broom?" Amela asked.

"Clever bluff. If I'd had one I'd have used it."

Amela was immediately self-conscious. The clothes she was wearing were donations. She was grateful for what she'd been given, but, still, she was embarrassed.

Sanja entered the shop, and gave her order, then said, "Have you gone back to your house?"

Amela hesitated. It was an innocent question, and Sanja no doubt intended to be nice, so why did it bother her? "We're back," she said.

"How is it?" Sanja persisted. "I mean, is it cleaned up? Do you have furniture?"

"We're working on it," Amela replied.

Sanja didn't know whether to give up or keep trying. Not easily discouraged, she said, "It's such a nice house. Remember when we were little kids and I used to stay over? We drove Dina crazy. I remember the day we hid all her clothes in a dozen different places. Oh, she was mad!"

Amela couldn't help but smile at the memory. "Yes. It took her hours to find them."

Another customer entered, and the girls left the shop. They stood on the sidewalk, neither one knowing how to continue the conversation or how to end it.

"How's your grandmother?" Amela asked. "Is she still in Tuzla?"

"Oh, yes," said Sanja. "Of course she'd like to go home, but that's not possible. Very few people are going home." She stopped, suddenly realizing that Amela, like her own grandmother, had been a refugee and was now one of the very few who had returned to their homes.

"You know," said Sanja, "we used to talk so easily. Now I feel like I'm always saying the wrong thing." She glanced at Amela's net shopping bag. "You've bought yarn," she said. "Do you knit? I've tried, but I'm hopeless."

Amela didn't know how to respond. Did Sanja want her to knit something for her? Much as she needed money, she would never take any from Sanja. She was trying to figure it all out when Sanja's attention suddenly jumped to something else.

"Ooooohhh, no," she groaned, then smiled sheepishly.

Amela almost allowed herself a smile as the years fell away and they were kids again. She knew what had happened. "You forgot the bread."

"I did."

"Well," said Amela, "you were always forgetful and I was always late. But I'm better than I used to be."

"Me, too," said Sanja, then noticing the amused glance Amela couldn't hide, she added, "No, really. I am!"

Amela laughed. She couldn't help it, and it felt good to enjoy herself, if only for a minute. Still, she was relieved when Sanja started back to the bakery. Their meeting had been a wearying experience.

But Sanja turned and said, "I feel ... I feel so awkward. I'd like to talk to you, to know about your life since we've been apart. Do you remember the last time we were in the plum tree?"

Of course Amela remembered. She'd thought often of the silly blood oath idea, but she could not just jump across six years as if nothing had happened. A great deal had happened.

"Maybe you don't want to be friends again," said Sanja when the silence lengthened.

That was just it, Amela thought—she didn't and she did. There was a time when they had told each other everything, but now.... She was so lonely in Bijeljina; it would be wonderful to have someone to share things with. If she could only trust Sanja.

Meanwhile Sanja fidgeted, uncertain how to proceed. Even if they agreed to overcome their differences and try to renew their friendship, it would be difficult. Bijeljina was a small town. Spending time together in public was impossible. Hostile attitudes of many people toward returned refugees were too prevalent. Going to each other's houses was not an option. Sanja was leery of having Amela run into her mother, and who knew how Hanifa would react to Sanja.

With those problems in mind, Sanja came up with a plan. "You know that memorial in front of the elementary school? It's across from Granny Radmila's farm where I buy cheese and cherries and bread. It's private when the kids aren't in school. We could take the bus out there and talk."

Amela reluctantly agreed to the meeting place. She was more reluctant for them to ride the bus together, and relented only if they traveled separately or at least sat apart.

In the next month, the girls managed to execute Sanja's plan several times, being careful to keep their conversations to generalities—the weather, the price of food, music groups. The future was a dead-end topic. If they stumbled onto the subject of the recent past, it provoked arguments. In that case, neither girl admitted she'd lost; neither celebrated a clear victory. If an argument got too heated, they either changed the subject, or, a couple of times, stopped speaking for days. Sharing their experiences, their feelings and losses, was something they still feared doing.

"Sometimes I feel like we're getting nowhere," Amela complained. "Why even bother to try?"

But they did bother, and the fact that they did became their strongest bond.

One evening in June, they happened to meet again in the central market.

"I don't suppose you'd come to my house for coffee," said Sanja, "but I'd like for you to."

Amela was astonished. Her immediate reaction was *Certainly not*. Coming back to Bijeljina had been hard enough. Going to a Serb's house would be too much. Trying to resurrect the past—even the good parts—might be impossible. She was sure her feelings were too damaged to try.

Sanja wasn't easily discouraged, but how far should she go? Should she take Amela's silence as doubt or rejection?

"So, will you come for coffee?" She considered what might be an enticement, and said, "Come Saturday. On Saturdays my mother visits her aunt across town, and my brother is in Belgrade. Will that make you feel better? If they're not there?"

The information only confused Amela further. Of course Sanja's mother wouldn't want her there. Nor would her brother. Life was already complicated. Why make it worse?

Sanja was troubled. She was doing her best to figure out what Amela was thinking. At last she said, "I guess we can't just turn back time and erase all that's happened, can we? That was a different life, and now we're on opposite sides of a very high wall."

"I can't climb over that wall," said Amela firmly.

Sanja shook her head in a defiant gesture. "I don't know that I can either," she declared, "but I'm willing to try. Think about it and call me."

Amela gazed at her. Sanja was as stubborn and strong-willed as ever.

"I can't call you," said Amela. "We can't get phone service."

"Why not? I know people back from Sarajevo and in one day …" Her words trailed off.

Amela nodded. Sanja had proved the point. "So you see?" Amela said, feeling smug. "It depends on who the people are."

"I don't understand … " Sanja began.

Amela interrupted. "You're right. You don't. Just forget it, Sanja. You'll *never* understand."

"That's not fair!" Sanja snapped. "At least I'm making an effort! Listen, I'll make coffee Saturday at two. If you don't come, I'll just drink it myself." With a quick wave she walked off.

Amela stared after her, blinking away bitter tears. Who said the war was over? If Sanja didn't feel anger and hatred, it was a miracle. If Amela didn't feel anger and hatred — it was betrayal.

CHAPTER
15

Saturday arrived, and Amela walked to the central market under a dark cloud of doubt liberally salted with resentment. Another inquiry about the fate of her father had yielded nothing.

What if they never learned anything? How long would they live this way? What sort of life was it to be drifting, waiting in a hopeless cause? There was barely enough money to keep up with expenses. She had no hope of going to university. She had no friends.

And there it was.

Sanja had held out the possibility of friendship. They were bound to meet from time to time, and it was tempting to think of regaining lost happiness. But Amela had come to think of Sanja as her *used-to-be* friend—except when anger was chewing her up. Then she thought of her as *the enemy*. Thinking of her now in that way was useful because it was easy not to want to be friends with an enemy.

She shook her head briskly to clear her thoughts. She had other matters to take care of. With the money her knitting had earned, she bought some more yarn and a nice cabbage to make sarma. That would please her mother. Amela trudged home, content enough with her purchases, but tired and dissatisfied with herself.

It was nearly two o'clock when she crossed the bridge. Two o'clock when she needed to make a decision. She could avoid Sanja's street and go home or ...

Cursing her weakness, Amela walked up to Sanja's front door. She raised her arm, her hand forming a fist. Was she going to use it to knock on the door or slam it against her forehead because she was being stupid? She gave the door a timid tap. It flew open.

"I didn't think you'd come," Sanja said, clearly delighted. She reached out to take Amela's arm and drew her inside. "Before you disappear," she said, smiling broadly. "I'm so glad you're here! I hate drinking coffee alone."

As Amela removed her shoes, the familiarity of the house nearly undid her. Six years. The painting of the monastery was still hanging on the wall. She flicked a glance at the other wall that held a likeness of Saint Sava. The picture of the Serbs' revered saint disturbed her in a way it had not when she used to see it. Uneasily, she followed Sanja into the kitchen where she set her packages down beside her chair.

Guessing at Amela's discomfort, feeling awkward herself, Sanja tried to lighten the mood. "You've been in this kitchen so many times," she said. "Do you remember the water fight?"

"With your brother. Yes," said Amela.

Sanja smiled. "Goran is taking exams at university in Belgrade. When he's home, he still teases me sometimes. He also earns some money as a part-time driver for the IPTF."

"International ... ?"

"International Police Task Force."

"Oh, that's right," said Amela. "They're in Tuzla, too."

Sanja continued, "He's found out from one of the officers about a job in Austria."

Amela nodded. She was sorely aware of how many people

were finding work abroad with jobs so scarce in Bosnia.

"Aren't you going to university?" she asked Sanja.

"I wish I could, but not yet. The war. And my father's decision to resign from the army. Even though the costs are low, my parents decided that Goran should finish first. What about you?"

"We're thinking about it," Amela lied. She envied Sanja. There was simply no way either she or Sejo could afford to go. If there hadn't been a war ...

War. It may be over, but it's never far away, Amela thought as she stared at photographs pinned to a corkboard on the opposite wall. In one, a handsome guy in an army uniform posed beside a tank. It looked like Goran, a few years older than when she'd last seen him. She shivered and fought the urge to leave—if she were honest she'd say escape—but sooner or later she'd have to confront her demons.

Sanja set out a plate of cookies to go with the thick, strong coffee she was preparing. "Are you coming from the market?" she asked, using the brass coffee grinder efficiently.

"What? Oh, yes." Amela forced her eyes away from the photograph. She reached into the bag at her feet, and pulled out a skein of yarn in a soft shade of green that matched Sanja's eyes.

Sanja reached out slowly to touch it. "Oh, this is luscious!" she cried.

Amela had bought it thinking of knitting Sanja a scarf. The idea had surprised her, but it was the sort of thing she would have done if they'd never been apart.

"Do you like to knit?" asked Sanja, stroking the yarn.

"I knit to make money," Amela answered quickly. She hoped she hadn't sounded bitter, because she wasn't. She was glad, really, that she'd found a way to help her family, but she was reluctant to talk to Sanja about her family's problems.

Sanja poured hot water into a small copper pot, measured in two spoonfuls of the ground coffee, then put it over a flame to reach a frothing boil. "You knit to make money," she repeated. "Do you make a lot of money?"

"No, I make very little money," Amela admitted. "My mother and I can sell knitting and needlework in Tuzla and Sarajevo, mostly to internationals. There are organizations that help women, especially war widows. Some make carpets."

"Yes, of course," said Sanja. "I know about those organizations. I understand about people who are refugees."

Amela suspected that Sanja didn't really know about refugees, and she was about to comment sharply when the feeling of silky fur on her ankle announced the arrival of a cat.

"You still have Siva! How old is she now?"

Sanja reached down to pet the soft gray fur. "This isn't Siva," she explained. "This is her son Sivi. Go on, Sivi. Greet our visitor."

"What happened to Siva?"

"She died while I was away."

Sivi bumped his head against Amela's ankles and she obliged him by scratching behind his ears. Away? Maybe during the short visit to Tuzla, or, Amela supposed, on holiday trips after the war.

Sanja carried the coffee pot to the table where she gave it a minute to cool. She regretted her slip of the tongue. Maybe someday she'd tell Amela about her experiences in Krajina, but not now. She wasn't sure enough yet of Amela to go into that private matter. But would she ever be?

"About our six years apart," she said. "If we're going to try to be friends again, then that time needs to be filled in."

"Yes, I agree," Amela said hesitantly. "But it won't be easy, Sanja, and you'll get defensive."

"I won't."

"You will. Trust me," replied Amela.

Sanja looked off into the distance, suddenly unsure of herself and even more unsure of Amela. She didn't quite know what she'd get defensive about, but she was determined not to be.

"We can leave the subject alone forever, Sani," said Amela softly.

"No, there'll always be a barrier. Of course, filling in the blanks doesn't guarantee that there won't be a barrier. We could even be throwing up a higher one."

"I know," said Amela. "But you're right. We should try."

"Yes, but not today. Today let's just talk about trivial things."

Sanja reached for the pot and poured the dark liquid into the tiny cups. The grounds rushed into the cup with the coffee, some staying like thick cream at the surface, the rest falling to the bottom. She handed Amela a milk pitcher and bowl of sugar cubes as she turned the conversation to recollections of their school years.

"Do you remember the cherry tree at your weekend house, and that kid who …" Sanja paused, startled by the sound of the front door opening.

She had promised Amela that neither her mother nor brother would be there, but it must be one or the other. Sanja shoved her chair back to investigate, but before she could get up, Goran, tall and handsome, stood in the doorway. He was grinning wickedly, pleased with himself for having surprised his sister. But it was not herself Sanja was thinking of as she glanced warily at her visitor.

Amela's brown eyes grew dark in a face that had gone white. Otherwise, only her fingers gripping her cup betrayed her tension. She had known a couple of Serbs in Tuzla, but this was different. This was Bijeljina. She steeled herself. She would not show fear in front of this man. With disciplined calm she took in Goran's strong jaw and the dark-fringed green eyes, so like his sister's. He was, indeed, the soldier in the picture.

"Well, big brother," said Sanja, studiously keeping her tone light, "this is a surprise. I didn't think you were in town today."

"My trip to Niš was cancelled. Milan couldn't go."

"Oh? Why not? Can you go another time?" She was stalling, hoping she could avoid introducing Amela, whom Goran seemed not to recognize. Sanja didn't want him spinning things out of control just when Amela had finally made an overture.

Typically, Goran wasn't about to be put off. He slouched against the doorframe, his cocky manner a trademark of Bijeljina men. "Hello," he said, directing his greeting to Amela.

Sanja answered quickly. "We're talking about knitting. You wouldn't be interested."

"Probably not," he replied, "but I'd be happy if this pretty girl wants to spend some time with me." The girl looked familiar, but he couldn't quite place her. He thought he knew all Sanja's friends.

At his words, Amela's stomach tightened. She knew he was flirting, but all she felt was terror.

Sanja glared at her brother. "Go away!" she demanded. "We're having a nice conversation." His laugh followed him as he headed toward the stairs.

Amela gathered up her yarn. "I've got to leave now," she said. "Thank you for the coffee." She was having trouble breathing. Her hands were clammy as she picked up her bag. She hurried to the front door, flung it open, and sped down the walk.

"Amela, wait!" Sanja was right behind her, and reached for her hand. She tried to sound reasonable although she felt like screaming. "I can't tell you how miserable I am that my stupid brother ruined our day! Please tell me that this won't keep us from getting together again."

Amela shook her head, struggling to release her hand from Sanja's grip.

"Listen to me," Sanja begged. "Goran isn't the bully at the bakery. Surely you can tell the difference."

"I don't think I can do this," said Amela, her voice shaky. "There are too many reasons why we should just go our separate ways."

Sanja stared defiantly. "You always used to say I'm stubborn, and that's true. I still am. We'll find a way if we want to. Please, Amela. We must keep trying."

"Why?"

Sanja stepped back as if she'd been slapped.

"I mean it," Amela said. "You don't know even a little of my struggles. This is your town, and you're comfortable and safe here. But I'm not. Every time I walk down the street I feel like some creep is waiting to pounce on me. I can't sleep well because somebody might lob a grenade through my window."

"That might have happened in 1992," Sanja said sharply, "but this is Serbia in 1998, and things like that don't happen."

Amela was dismayed. She didn't know which part of the comment was more appalling, but she couldn't let one part of it go unchallenged. "Sanja," she replied in measured tones, "this is not Serbia. This is Bosnia."

Sanja's green eyes flashed. "This is the *Republic* of Serbia, *half* of Bosnia. We may not have our own license plates any more, but we have our own Parliament and our capital is Banja Luka. The peace agreement says so."

"All the peace agreement did was make us stop shooting one another!" Realizing that she was yelling, Amela shook her head again, frustration filling her like air in a balloon. Then suddenly, she deflated. "I'm sorry. I really am. I just can't do this."

Sanja dropped her head. She'd made all the goodwill gestures she could. If Amela didn't want to be friends, so be it. They had reached the sidewalk, and it was like reaching the boundary line that divided their country.

As Amela started for home, Sanja went back into her house. She was furious with Goran for intruding. She managed to avoid him until late afternoon when he found her watching an Argentine soap opera on television.

He glanced at her sheepishly. "Look," he said, "I'm sorry I barged in. I didn't mean to upset her. I was just kidding around."

"Yeah." Sanja gave a grudging acceptance of his apology.

Goran dropped into the fat armchair usually occupied by their father. "Milan couldn't go to Niš because he was talking to a man about work in Austria. If he gets a job there, I'll try, too. I could send you some money. I'll bet you wouldn't return it."

"You bet I wouldn't!" said Sanja. "The only money I've earned was for a few days as an election interpreter last fall."

"So what was she doing here?"

The question was abrupt. Rather than answer, Sanja shrugged as if she didn't know what he was talking about.

"C'mon, Sani. Your knitting teacher. She's very pretty."

"Mmm. Yes."

"Well?"

Feeling pressured, Sanja said, "Maybe she can teach me to knit, and then I can make money, too. And I won't have to go to Austria to do it."

Goran pursed his lips in thought. "So Amela sells knitting, does she?"

Sanja shot him a quick look. "Oh, you *did* know it was Amela."

"Not at first. It came to me after I went upstairs." He stared thoughtfully at Sanja, then said, "You know, it might not be smart to associate with a Muslim girl."

Sanja glared at him. "She used to be my friend."

"I know. I'm just saying it's not smart to associate with her. Doesn't she have any friends like her?"

"Like her? You mean thoughtful, intelligent, and pretty? And don't tell me you didn't notice."

Goran got out of the chair and sat beside his sister on the big mohair sofa. He put his hand on her shoulder. "Hey, I wasn't trying to insult her. Maybe she's intelligent, and God knows she's pretty. Or should I say Allah knows?"

"Don't make jokes about religions either! This whole stupid business of who's better, Serb or Croat, Christian or Muslim, got us into war, and I'm sick to death of it!"

"You know that's not what caused the war."

"I don't!" she raged. "But if you know what caused it, be good enough to tell me!"

Goran's temper was heating up, too. "Oh! You want me to give you a history lesson? Tell me what our grandmother did that made the Croats expel her?"

Sanja glared at him, fuming, and said abruptly, "Not one damned thing. And that's my point. What did Amela do to make her leave Bijeljina?" Then she clamped her mouth shut feeling miserable. They never fought like this.

Goran stared at Sanja, in pensive silence. It had been years since he'd thought about the departure of the Muslims. At that time, he was fifteen. He hadn't understood why they went except that bullets were flying. But that was years ago and people were still blaming the Serbs!

It wasn't fair, none of it. All he wanted to do now was finish school, make money, and enjoy a comfortable life for a change. He glanced uneasily at Sanja who was pointedly ignoring him. He knew she wanted those things, too—and certainly one more. She wanted to be friends again with Amela.

CHAPTER
16

Sanja sat up gasping. Raindrops were tapping briskly at her bedroom window, but it wasn't the rain that woke her. It was the nightmare.

She hadn't had the dream since … when? … almost three years ago. At the sports center in Banja Luka. But it was the same dream. She was wading through crimson blood trying to reach little Mirko … or was it Nikola? This time the bruised face had been blurred. But whoever it was, he was still crying, still holding out his arms to her, and still moving farther and farther out of her reach.

Sanja flung off her covers and lurched to the window, gulping in the damp air, cool for early July. Then she went into the bathroom and splashed cold water on her face. She had jerked awake that other time, too, in a cold sweat, queasy, and revolted by the blood lapping around her ankles.

So … why now? What had caused it now? Could it be the problems she and Amela were having? Were they enough to stir her subconscious, to jolt her brain cells so that they dredged up gruesome memories of war? Was it an omen? The thought made her shudder.

Sanja went back to the window and leaned her arms on the sill, soothed by the soft, moist breeze. The rooster in the yard next door crowed his early morning greeting.

It *must* be Amela, or rather not Amela herself, but the tension between them. The tension that had to do with their wartime experiences. Sanja was determined to get rid of that tension. And soon. She was tired of drifting. She had felt hopeful when Amela came for coffee and they had approached the idea of talking about the past. But then Goran came in. And Amela fled. There was no doubt that Goran's showing up unexpectedly was a setback.

Sanja wished she could roll back time. She wanted to be twelve again, lingering with Amela in the plum tree, soothed by its delicate blossoms. She wanted to play and giggle. She wanted to cancel out all the anger and confusion and violence and misery of the past years.

She'd been glad for Ivana's sister's wedding on Saturday. It had been a welcome relief. At the reception, she had laughed a lot and danced a lot. Long over her anger at Ranko for deserting her, she had flirted with him and had a wonderful time. The wedding had given her a break from daily stresses, a day off from problems. It was a shame to return to the realities of post-war Bijeljina—burned houses, difficult friendships, boredom, and unemployment.

The next morning, when the nightmare hadn't come again, Sanja began to feel better. She was making a breakfast sandwich when she heard a knock at the front door. Hope flickered that it was Amela, but it wasn't. Ivana was standing on the porch, and Sanja was pleased to see her anyway.

As Ivana watched Sanja prepare a second sandwich, she leaned her elbows on the table and cupped her chin in her hands. "So, you know that IPTF guy who's been coming on to me?" she said.

Sanja smiled. Ivana was obviously making the most of her

new job as an interpreter for the International Police Task Force. Full reports were available from Goran who, as a driver, always got an earful.

"Which one," Sanja asked, "the Italian or the Jordanian?"

"The Dutch one."

"That's a regular UN you have there," Sanja teased. "So what about the Dutch one?"

"He asked me to a party," said Ivana.

"Good."

"No, not good."

Sanja looked surprised. "But you love parties," she said.

Ivana pouted, then said, "It's in Brčko. It's at the house of a Muslim."

"So what?"

"So ... what if they poison my food?"

"Poison your food? Where did you get such an idea?"

"One of my boyfriends told me. He says he's heard it happens all the time."

"Won't you be eating the same food as everyone else?" asked Sanja.

"Oh." Ivana sat back, considering what Sanja had said. "That's true," she replied at last. "It might be fun. He's cute, the Dutchman. And tall. Maybe I'll go to the party."

Sanja walked with Ivana as far as the small neighborhood store where she bought a box of cherry juice and some pasta. On her way home, she saw Amela coming her way. Sanja braced herself. It had been just over a week since Goran had made his surprise appearance. What should she do, stop and say hello to Amela? Would Amela reply? Would they stand there in awkward confusion, not knowing what to say? Sanja decided that the choice would be Amela's.

"Hi," Amela said, her greeting hesitant. "I … uh … about the other day …"

"You don't have to explain," Sanja replied.

"I know. I just … I mean, I don't blame you for what happened. You know, with your brother and all. It's just … it's just too much for me to handle."

Sanja didn't know what to say. It was a lot for her to handle, too.

"And about meetings at the memorial," Amela went on. "Well, I'll think about it."

She hurried away, leaving Sanja to stare after her nonplussed. How could Amela treat her like that? How could she be so dismissive?

"She'll *think* about it," Sanja mumbled to herself. "*She'll* think about it! What about me? Doesn't *my* opinion count?" The more Amela's words gnawed at her, the more annoyed she became.

Resuming her walk home, Sanja was so engrossed in her thoughts she didn't hear someone approaching.

"Hey, Sani."

She looked toward the voice and scowled. She didn't feel like talking to anyone.

"Who's your friend?" he asked, watching Amela's retreating form curiously.

"Just a girl I knew in school."

"She looks familiar. That's not Amela, is it?" He touched her arm. "You wouldn't have a Muslim friend, now, would you Sani? That wouldn't be smart."

Sanja glared at him. She was exasperated with Amela, irritated with things in general, and now she was annoyed with Ranko. He had a Muslim uncle, so what was the big deal? Of course his uncle lived in Tuzla. But what kind of place had Bjeljina become if you couldn't even stand on the sidewalk talking to someone?

"I can do anything I like," she snapped, yanking her arm away.

He moved back and said, "I thought you'd gotten over being mad at me a long time ago."

Sanja knew he was referring to abandoning her in Krajina. She would always be grateful for the brilliant ways he had helped her then, but she did not like having it thrown up to her, and she certainly didn't like what he was telling his friends about their so-called romance.

"You need to be more truthful about what you tell people," she said as she walked away fuming. Maybe flirting with him at the wedding reception had been a mistake. She'd just been having fun. Was it so terrible to want to have fun?

"Just be careful which people you're friends with," Ranko called after her.

Sanja was still upset when she reached home. The sight of a Mercedes parked in front of the house aroused here curiosity and cooled her temper. It was an old model with a few dents and a bit of rust here and there.

Inside the house she found Goran, who had finished his exams at university. He was lounging at the kitchen table, sitting on one chair with his feet on another. He grinned when he saw his sister and raised his beer bottle in a salute.

"Like it?"

"The car? It's very nice," said Sanja, aware of her understatement. "Whose is it?"

"It's mine. You know I've been making good money driving for the IPTF."

"You can't have made enough money to buy a car."

"I've worked out a deal with some other guys. We all own the car, then swap or something like that. You know, Bojan over on Račanska Street gets cars all the time at good prices. The cars need some engine work, like this one did, but that's Bojan's specialty. Come on, I'll take you for a spin."

Sanja agreed. Maybe a drive would blow away the day's dark clouds and improve her mood. Goran lit a cigarette, set the Mercedes in motion, and soon they were leaving town.

"I thought you gave up smoking."

"I did," he said. "Last month. I give it up every month."

Sanja rolled down the window, letting in the warm air, fragrant with the aromas of the countryside. She saw Goran's glance, a warning that an open window would bring on pneumonia, but she had long since dismissed the myth that most people clung to. She leaned her head back and let her frustration seep away.

Goran glanced over at her. They were on the road to Granny Radmila's, passing the place where their bus hit the mine.

"I feel ghosts every time I pass that spot," said Goran.

He turned onto the road with the elementary school and memorial. The memorial where she and Amela had tried to jumpstart their friendship, Sanja thought gloomily. They probably would not be meeting there any more. Well, so be it.

In spite of her resolve, tears sprang to her eyes. Determined that Goran should not see such weakness, she pretended to study the scenery until one place caught her attention. It was a long-deserted farm. The house looked like it had been burned. Vines and shrubs were growing up inside the shattered walls. Branches poked out through holes that had been windows.

"Don't go onto that property," Goran warned. "IPTF maps don't show mines in the Bijeljina area, but you can never be sure a farmer didn't plant a couple to protect his property for his return. And along the rivers, mines break loose with spring thaw and drift. Best to be careful."

"You and I know too much about mines," said Sanja.

"But of course it's safe around the memorial," Goran went on. "That's a regular spot for couples."

"How many girls have you brought there?" she asked him.

Goran raised his eyebrows. "Me? Sani! What a question." Then he grinned. "Don't tell me you haven't been out here with a guy."

"Huh. Not the guys I know, thank you," she said. "Find me someone I can have a decent conversation with and I'll consider it. And don't say Ranko. Or even Milan, nice as he is."

"He'll be leaving next week. He got a job in Germany."

"Milan did? And what about you?" Sanja asked, feeling a tug on her heart at the idea.

"I'll have to see if my plan works out," he said.

"Oh, you have a plan now."

"Yes. I'm saving for computer classes in Belgrade. Then I'll be able to get a good job in Germany or Sweden. I could go as a carpenter tomorrow, but carpentry is seasonal and the weather is too cold or too hot. I prefer comfort." Laughing, Goran glanced at his sister. "How does that sound?"

"Well, comfort would be nice."

But, she thought, he'd live abroad. She had lived all her nineteen years in Bijeljina, sometimes happy, sometimes not. Yet lately she had been dissatisfied. She watched dark clouds rolling in from the west, from Serbia just a short way across the river. She gazed out at the countryside that was so familiar to her—the wide, swift-flowing Drina, the trees along its banks. She could not imagine what it would be like to live in a different country. Still, if her life in Bijeljina didn't improve … and if things with Amela didn't get better …

"How are your meetings with Amela?" Goran asked, as if reading her mind.

"I don't know what to do," Sanja said bleakly. "It's like we want our friendship to be the same, and yet it can't be. Besides, she challenged me."

"What?" he said. "The queen of *I dare you* challenged? How?"

"We've said we should tell each other what's happened since we've been apart, sort of compare our war experiences. We're never going to trust each other again if we can't do that. But she said I'd be defensive."

"Sure," said Goran.

"What do you mean, 'Sure'?"

"I'd expect you both to become defensive, not to mention really mad—and that's when you'd either move beyond it ... or not."

"How do you know that?"

"Because I've done it. There was a kid I knew in high school. We were both in the army ... well, different armies ... and right after the peace agreement, we happened to be in the same bar. Not in Bijeljina. Our armies had fought one another, but what the hell, the war was over, so we had a couple beers. Okay, a lot of beers. We yelled, cursed, threw insults. We blamed each other for the war, for everything. After a few hours we shook hands and wished each other a happy life."

"Why haven't you ever told me that story before?" asked Sanja.

"The subject never came up."

Sanja sat quietly, mulling over what Goran had told her. Then she asked, "How well do you remember that night back in 1992?"

Goran's eyes clouded. "Well, I remember the shooting. We snuck out of the house and some soldier threatened us. And that pharmacist, Dragan, backed him off."

"Amela's father's friend," Sanja recalled.

"Yeah. Later we heard that Amela's father was arrested.

I never thought he was political. And I remember her sister ... Dina, wasn't it? She was a looker. Her hair was blonde—Amela's is darker, more honey-colored, but she's a looker, too."

It was raining again. Sanja sighed as she rolled up her window.

She didn't feel she owed Amela an apology, but, still, if they could just talk, just share their different experiences, their different ideas ... not arguing, but trying to figure things out.

"Well," she said with an air of finality, "I've done all I can. If Amela wants to try again, she'll have to make the next move."

CHAPTER
17

Amela heard her mother's voice, but it was muted by her own conflicted thoughts. She had every right to be reluctant about friendship with a Serb, yet she regretted the way she had rebuffed Sanja. Had she destroyed any chance they had of mending their broken friendship? Had there ever *been* a chance to repair it? Did she even *want* to repair it?

"Amela, my prescription should be ready," her mother called again. "My blood pressure medicine. Would you pick it up for me?" Hanifa was at the sink, chopping tomatoes and cucumbers for a šopska salad. "You know the apoteka."

"Yes, I know it, and I know the pharmacist."

Hanifa glanced over her shoulder, smiling as her daughter came into the room. "Oh. Yes, you do. He's a nice man."

A nice man. He was a hero. Dragan had risked his life on that fearful night to help her family. The soldiers would not have hesitated to shoot their fellow Serb if they had known that. Amela's father had still been taken away, but Dragan had possibly saved the lives of the rest of the family. Oh, yes, he was a *very* nice man.

"He was at my wedding," Hanifa was saying cheerfully. "He is a very good friend of your father's."

Amela felt her usual sinking sensation at her mother's

unshakable use of *is*. Was her mother really getting more difficult, or was Amela just tired of living behind a film of unreality?

As she stepped outside, the sunshine lifted her spirits. She desperately needed something to do. Tending to the chickens they'd bought and the vegetable garden they'd planted wasn't stimulating. Neither was knitting. Although it occupied her time, it didn't occupy her mind. If *only* she could go to university! She shooed that thought away. Wanting something vague, like activity, was easier than wanting something specific, like an education.

Amela crossed over the canal and turned at the first corner where two boys were kicking a ball. They reminded her of Sejo. How she missed him! As she approached, the ball was heading her way, so she kicked it. The boys stopped running and hung back. A brief pause, then one of them booted it in her direction. She smiled and sent the ball to the smaller one who instinctively butted it with his shoulder. The taller one scrambled after it, but Amela beat him to it. Not for nothing had Sejo taught her how to play. He would have been proud! After a few minutes, she waved to the boys, grinning as she turned down their pleas to keep playing.

Soon she was at the apothecary. A sign on the door gave the hours the shop was open, and it was less than a minute before Dragan showed up.

"Ah, Amela," he greeted her as he reached to unlock the door. "How nice to see you. Your mother came yesterday to order a refill, but she didn't tell me you would be picking it up."

Amela followed him inside. She had not talked with him since she had been back in Bijeljina.

"You've grown into a lovely young woman," Dragan said. "Your father would be proud. I know you miss him."

"I do. My family is so grateful that you've never stopped trying to find out what happened to him."

He shook his head sadly. "There's not an avenue I haven't explored. But, tell me, what are you doing these days?"

Amela considered her dull life. "Not much. I've been knitting things to sell in Sarajevo."

He raised his eyebrows, looking at her with approval. "Good for you. Have you been to Sarajevo?"

"No, sir. What's it like?"

"Oh, not the city it was before the war. Back in 1984 when the Olympics were held there, it was as fine, in a small way, as any European city. Now, of course, it's recovering from siege and shelling and snipers. Ah, Yugoslavia was a good place. Our life was good." He went on dreamily. "My wife and I spent many happy days in Cavtat, a little fishing village near Dubrovnik." He shook his head briskly. "But, you're here for a prescription. Let me get it for you."

Amela glanced around the store while she waited for him to get the package from the back. When he returned, she said bluntly, "You know that our house was burned."

As Dragan handed her the medicine, he eyed her carefully. "Yes, I know," he said.

It wasn't just anybody she could be direct with, and maybe she shouldn't be with Dragan. He was a Serb, but she trusted him and decided to be bold. "Do you think the fire was set deliberately?"

His eyes clouded with concern. "I'd rather think it wasn't, but there are those who want a purely Serb town and object to any reversal. How do you feel about that?"

Amela thought it was a strange question. "How do I feel? Enraged. Scared. Suspicious of people. I don't know. Sad?

Confused? All of those?"

"Yes, probably all of those. But not defeated. Not ready to run."

"I don't know. We're here to find my father or to wait for word about him."

"Yes, for your father. I've long since accepted his death. And you may remember that I lost my son," he said.

Amela felt a tug of guilt. She had forgotten that Dragan's son had been a soldier killed in the third year of the war. Although his son had been in the Bosnian Serb army, her sympathy for Dragan was real, and she laid her hand on his arm.

The pharmacist lifted his head and straightened his shoulders. "My dear," he said, "your compassion for your family is laudable, but don't give up on yourself."

Amela left the shop with Dragan's words only somewhat easing the ache in her heart. He had asked her if she was defeated and ready to run. She had answered, "I don't know." Was that really true? Was she so tired of the day-to-day struggle that she would give up on her father and on Sanja? As for not giving up on herself … What exactly, did that mean?

Amela had not wanted to come into town, but now that she was there, she decided to walk through the park. She saw a young woman with a child in a pram, an old woman feeding pigeons, and children running and laughing. It made her feel good to watch them, their mouths smeared with gooey candy. She and Sanja had once been like that.

Yes. They had. She glanced down at the tote bag she had impulsively brought with her, and then resolutely hurried toward the canal. If she didn't act now, it would be too easy to change her mind.

As she approached Sanja's house, she struggled with

indecision. It wasn't Saturday. What if Sanja's mother or brother should answer the door? Amela shriveled at the thought. But it was Sanja who opened the door, and although she registered surprise—or maybe shock—she invited Amela in and led her to the kitchen.

Amela set her bag beside her chair and took from it a soft package wrapped in pale green tissue paper. "I brought you something," she said, handing it to Sanja.

Sanja took the package and squeezed it, her expression a mixture of astonishment and pleasure. "Oh! This is so .... I don't know what to say. It's … it's … " Sanja unfolded the scarf that Amela had knitted and held it to her cheek, her eyes moist.

"Don't get tears on it. It might shrink," Amela teased.

"Well, I'm thrilled. Thank you."

Amela smiled. It felt like old times, and she started tapping her foot to a song playing on the radio.

"That's *Red Apple*," Sanja remarked. "Aren't they cool?"

Amela nodded. "They are."

"You said once you like *White Button*," said Sanja.

"Yes, *White Button* is super. How about *U2*? Or Merlin?"

"I like Vlado. But definitely *U2*. And Madonna," Sanja replied, thinking how rare it was now to see Amela relaxed and smiling, more like the happy child she'd been.

"Listen," said Sanja, "I have to take some books to the high school for my mother. Why don't you go with me?"

Amela started to say *No way*, but then she thought again. She'd been back in Bijeljina almost three months. Maybe it was time for her to try living like a real person.

"Well, okay," she agreed hesitantly. "But I won't go in."

Sanja shrugged. It was the school she had attended until a year ago; the school Amela would have attended, too, if she had stayed in Bijeljina.

It was warm and a bit muggy after a night of rain. When they reached the street the school was on, the girls were glad for the lipa trees that lined it. In the spring, their blossoms were lusciously fragrant, their leaves a tender green. Now in early summer, the trees were welcome shade-givers. Amela waited beneath one while Sanja took the books into the building.

On a nearby tree trunk, Amela saw a death notice posted. The photograph was of a man about the age her father would be. As she gazed at it, the face of the man and the cross faded, replaced by a dim image of a Muslim crescent and her father's face. She tried so hard to keep her father's image alive, nourishing it every day with the photo beside her bed. The picture had been given to her by her Aunt Biserka when she arrived in Tuzla. It was all she had of him.

"Bijeljina *looks* the same," Amela murmured when Sanja rejoined her. "It just doesn't *feel* the same." She thought about that for a minute, then said, "No, that's not true. It *doesn't* look the same."

"What do you mean?" asked Sanja.

"Surely ... " Amela hesitated. The comment she was about to make would likely cause more conflict, but she couldn't hold back. "Surely you've noticed there are no minarets. Surely you've noticed that the mosques aren't here anymore." She couldn't control the sarcasm as she said, "What do you suppose happened to them?"

"Well, the one in the center of town—the one near the park—I heard Muslims blew it up like they blew up a lot of others in Bosnia. Like they blew up the market in Sarajevo."

Amela's jaw dropped. "Muslims? *Muslims* blew it up? How can you say such a thing?"

Sanja's face took on a dark frown. "They did it so Serbs would get blamed. There was more than one side fighting the war, you know."

"I wasn't talking about the whole war," Amela said. "I asked about the mosque." She felt desperate for truth. Truth for a change. "Why on earth would Muslims blow up their own holy site? Who told you Muslims did it?"

"It was common knowledge."

"*Your* common knowledge." She tried again. "Who told you?"

"I don't know," Sanja said "It was years ago. The space was supposed to become a park, but that hasn't happened."

"And, I ask again," Amela said with dogged determination. "Who told you what happened to it?"

"I *don't know*," Sanja said, annoyed at being pinned down. "The radio. TV. The government."

"Propaganda. And you believed it," said Amela, not bothering to hide her contempt.

"Why wouldn't I? They're reliable sources. Muslims don't have a monopoly on information and they *did* blow things up."

Amela's reply was even more sarcastic than before. "It seems that nothing else in Bijeljina got blown up. I know all you Serbs think ..."

Sanja's eyes narrowed and her voice became raspy. "Let me tell you something. You *don't* know all Serbs, and you *don't* know what we all think. I'm so tired of you saying 'The Serbs did this' and 'The Serbs did that.'" Her hands were shaking. She linked her fingers, gripping them to keep them steady. She lifted her chin and said, "I'm not *the* Serbs, I'm *a* Serb, and proud of it."

Without another word, Sanja spun on her heel and stalked away. It was over. There was nothing more to say.

CHAPTER
18

S anja didn't look back.

Neither did Amela, who chose to follow a different direction. But at the canal, Amela took a detour. She walked purposefully into the center of town, to a small grassy area where she stood as if roots had sprung from her sneakers and burrowed into the ground, holding her fast. It was not the first time she'd been there, but she had always hurried on, not wanting to dwell on what was missing.

The mosque.

She closed her eyes, remembering its slim minaret reaching gracefully toward the clouds. Now there was nothing graceful, nothing reaching, nothing soaring.

Nothing.

There was only dirt and rocks and weeds barely visible behind an ugly wooden fence. Suddenly the loss of the mosque symbolized for Amela everything that was lost in Bijeljina.

"The mosque was blown up," she said aloud, as if speaking the words could bring answers to her questions. "Leveled. Why would anyone destroy a house of worship?"

She shuddered. Not since the day at the cemetery in Tuzla had so many outrageous words sat like acid on her tongue. That day she'd hurled them at people who fostered evil. Today she swallowed them. She hated those people then. She still hated them. She stared at the wooden barricade, imagining attacking it with her bare fingers, shredding it to a pile of splinters. What a futile thought. Hadn't she learned about futility in the cemetery?

With a deep sigh, she started on up the street, meaning to head across the canal and home. Then she came to the church. She stopped beside the iron fence and stared at the path leading to the front door. Like a mindless robot, she went through the gate and up the short walk.

The door, wooden and polished to a high gloss, was carved with a figure and unfamiliar symbols. It had a strange, claw-like handle. She wouldn't have touched it, but the door stood open, inviting her in. Amela stepped inside. She was alone. She had never before set foot in a Serbian Orthodox church, and she was astounded at her audacity.

Why am I here? she wondered. Did she hope this place would yield up answers to explain the past few years? They were unexplainable. No. She shook her head in disgust. This place would give her no answers. It was dangerous for her to be there. But she was curious, and curiosity temporarily buried her uneasiness.

The interior was cool. The silence was like an invisible cloak. She took a few timid steps, pausing under the high, domed ceiling. Above were chandeliers, elaborate with crystal ornaments. There were no benches or chairs; she didn't think they used prayer rugs. Now that she was used to the quiet, Amela found it strangely calming. She wouldn't stay long, just for a few minutes. It was fascinating. There were pictures everywhere, many of people wearing colorful robes, richly decorated with gold. A table at the front was draped with a lacy white cloth and on it were a gold cross and flowers.

Amela was increasingly nervous, yet too intrigued to leave. She took the precaution of moving into a corner as she continued to study the decorations. Here and there along the walls were big chairs, like thrones. Everything was so rich, quite unlike the simplicity of a mosque. What was she supposed to feel in this place? Her family and friends would be shocked to know she was in a church.

With that realization, fear broke loose, fear both of condemnation by her own people and of those whose house of worship this was. If they found her, would they force her to say she was Muslim? Or worse, would they force her to take an oath of Orthodoxy? Would they say she was defiling their holy place by her presence? Yet, how would anyone know she was Muslim? Unless she would be expected to perform some ritual.

Amela whipped about, frantic and disoriented. Where was the door? There! She rushed outside, halting to glance to her right and left. Nobody was watching. She hurried down the path, desperate to reach the safety of the sidewalk. Just passing the gate were three young men. When they caught sight of her, they stepped through it and instantly surrounded her. Through eyes glassy with terror, she recognized one of them, and knew that he recognized her. It was the guy from her neighborhood, the one who had bullied Sejo and blocked her way in the bakery. The one who didn't want Muslims living in the Serbian town of Bijeljina.

Clutching her bag to her, she tried to dodge past them. All three grabbed her, moving so close she could feel their warm breath on her neck and cheeks. She tried to keep from shaking. It wasn't smart to show fear.

"Well," said the bully, "if it isn't our little *Turkish* girl invading our holy place. What did you leave in there, bitch? Did you crap on the floor—maybe smear it on the walls?"

"Let's take her inside, so she can show us," said the skinny one, squeezing her arm.

The third one spoke with an ominous chuckle. "No, let's take her someplace private. We've been looking for some fun, and she'll give us hours and hours of pleasure, won't you, whore?"

"Yeah," said the bully. "Even Turks like to have fun, don't they?"

Amela tried not to flinch as he lowered her hands and drew his finger across her breasts. She felt her legs go weak as they dragged her toward the gate.

"Hello, hello. How nice to see you all here."

A man's pleasant voice came from the direction of the church building. Amela caught just a glimpse of him. He was wearing a long black robe. He paused. His tone changed and became stern. "You young men come inside," he said. "I want to talk to you."

Amela felt their grip loosen, and as she did, she summoned every bit of strength she had and ran. Her heart was pounding louder than her footsteps as her sneakered feet hit the pavement, but she was away, and didn't stop running for several blocks. Then she leaned against a shop window, doubled over from the pain in her side, shaking and gasping for breath. Her legs refused to hold her up any longer. She slid to the sidewalk.

And that was how Samir found her, leaning against a wall, her hands covering her face.

"Amela! What's wrong?" He bent down and took her hands in his. "You're shaking. Are you sick?"

"No, no. It's okay, Samir. I'll be all right."

"What are you doing in my part of town?" he asked.

Amela looked around. She hadn't run in any particular direction; she had just run.

Samir sat down beside her and waited. His questions were

an invitation to talk—a request, but not a demand. She knew she could get up and leave without anything but a polite thank you, and he'd just say she was welcome. But she needed to tell the story.

She described going to the site of the mosque, of how angry she was about its destruction. Then, embarrassed, she said, "I don't know what to say about where I went next. You won't approve."

"Well, you won't know until you tell me," Samir said.

Amela picked up a pebble and rolled it between her fingers. "I went into the Orthodox church."

"Why?" He said it quietly, as if he were asking why she wore denim jeans or picked wildflowers. As if she could give him an answer.

"I don't know," she said simply.

"It's all right to be curious," he said. "What did you think of it?"

"It was ornate. And strange."

Samir waited a moment, then he said, "Did something happen there?"

"It wasn't in the church," Amela replied, "but something that happened on the path outside." She was ashamed to tell Samir about being accosted. She couldn't look at him. She told the story with her hands folded in her lap and her gaze locked on them. She was humiliated, but when she looked up, Samir's expression was kind and he shook his head sadly.

"At God's house this happened," he said. "But the priest came at the right time."

"Yes. I wasn't sure he'd help me, but he did."

"I'm glad your story ended well," Samir said. "But now? First there was the fire and now this. Are you afraid to stay in Bijeljina?"

Amela thought about what Dragan had said to her earlier. When he'd asked her whether she would give up, she had told him she didn't know. Now she was silent, reflecting on what had happened.

"Yes, I'm afraid," she said at last. "They want me to give up, to leave. But I'm not going to, Samir. I'm not going to be forced away."

Samir sat back with a satisfied smile. "That's exactly what I hoped you'd say."

CHAPTER
19

Two hours after her fight with Amela about the mosque, Sanja was still seething. When her mother left for the market, she got out her tools and started weeding the vegetable garden, using the trowel to vent her feelings. But furious digging did little to shrink her temper as she ticked off her grievances.

Amela was being dramatic. *Jab!*

Muslims *did* blow things up. *Jab!*

They blew up buses. *Jab!*

Serbs were *not* liars. *Jab! Jab! Jab!*

A shadow fell across the garden. Sanja looked up, so startled she dropped the trowel.

"I've got to talk to you," said Amela.

"I'm busy," Sanja replied coolly. "I'm weeding."

"So I see. But, Sanja, something happened today. You need to hear about it."

"Go away. You've made your opinions known."

Amela's reply was icy. "I hoped you'd care about what happened, but how like a Serb to be insensitive."

Sanja jumped to her feet. "If you came here just to badger me, you can leave," she said. "You've rejected me too many times. You'll get no comfort from me."

"Comfort?" Amela slammed her bag on the ground. "It's a little late for comfort! Serbs took everything … our home, our way of life, people we loved." Her voice sank to a whisper. "Especially …"

Sanja stared at the ground. She knew Amela was thinking of her father. Then she threw her hands in the air. "But listen to yourself. Over and over you say, 'The Serbs did it; the Serbs did it.' You never *think* that people on all sides did things and all sides had victims."

"Sanja! The Serbs were the aggressors, and they still are. This morning … "

"Aggressors?" Sanja interrupted. "*Huge* numbers of Serbs demonstrated against war. Muslims created a militia and set up barricades. So who was the aggressor?"

Amela tossed her head. "Oh, so Serbs are allowed to defend themselves, but Muslims aren't?"

"Of course Serbs defended themselves. Muslims were creating a Greater Islam."

"That's a lie," Amela shot back. "The plan was for a Greater *Serbia*. Your side did terrible things. I don't … I don't suppose it matters to you that a Serb shell killed my … my cousin Jasmina."

Sanja paused, her fists clenched. "Well, she wasn't the only cousin who was killed." She took a deep breath. She glared at Amela, then sat down again and covered her ears. "Go away. I don't want to listen to any more accusations."

Amela persisted, sitting down, too, and leaning forward for emphasis. "Listen, for every Serb killed, hundreds of thousands of Muslims were killed."

"You're exaggerating," Sanja scoffed. "Anyway, this isn't a contest."

"You just don't …"

"Listen to me!" Sanja demanded. "There's no *more* or *less*.

Losing someone is losing someone."

"Oh, *really?*" Amela countered fiercely. "As if *you* ever lost anyone. While Tuzla was being shelled, nobody shelled Bijeljina."

Sanja's temper flared again. "Let me tell you something." She closed her eyes, then opened them slowly, saying, "My cousins—you remember little Mirko—were murdered by Muslim forces in the Drina Valley."

Sanja ignored Amela's gasp and went on, "So you can delude yourself all you want that killers are innocent, but you're wrong."

"I never said killers were innocent," Amela said. "I'm saying that all the killing was horrible."

"Yes!" Sanja shouted. "It *was* horrible."

Amela responded, wringing her hands and forcing the words. "All Bosnians ever wanted was peace!"

"How can you say that?" Sanja demanded. She started to get up, then turned back to Amela, saying, "Maybe we should engrave *'All Bosnians ever wanted was peace'* on my cousins' tombstones."

"It's true! You know it's true." Amela blew out a sharp breath. She hugged herself, trying to stop shaking.

"Oh, no I don't," Sanja said, taunting. "But maybe that thought should have comforted Goran and me as we lay in a smashed bus."

Amela frowned. "Smashed bus?"

Sanja flung Amela a withering look as she said, "Our bus hit a mine. People died. And who do you think put the mine there? Some of your peace-loving radical Muslims!"

Amela shook her head. "You don't know that."

"Oh, yes I do. They left a message. Claimed credit. Revenge against Serbs."

"Revenge?" Amela repeated, her tone biting. "Well, what could you expect? You surely remember that night … that night when the Serbs attacked us."

"So that means that Goran and I deserved to get blown up?"

Amela tore out blades of grass and twisted them. "You *know* I didn't mean that," she said. "You just don't understand … "

Sanja leaped to her feet. She grabbed her soda can and heaved it with all her might at the nearby fence. It hit with a clang, and she swung back around, her eyes narrowed. "I *do* understand, damn it!"

Amela ignored her and went on bitterly, "Listen, Sanja. For years the Bosnian army didn't have weapons. We couldn't even defend ourselves."

"You got NATO to bomb our soldiers. Bombs, Amela, bombs!"

"We got …? I *wish*! Anyway, after how many miserable years? After how many innocent people died? You just don't get it."

"You are *so* condescending," Sanja yelled. Heat washed over her cheeks. "This is getting us nowhere. Come back when you're more rational. Or don't come back. I don't care." She stalked toward the house.

"I came here to tell you something," Amela called after her, "but now I don't even want to because you won't listen. You'll just yell and blame me."

Sanja paused, her shoulders rigid. "I will not!" she said defiantly. Slowly she returned.

"Yes, you will. And then I'll blame you. Sometimes I get so furious, Sanja, I … I …"

"Me, too."

Amela dropped her head into her hands. She continued, her voice quivering, "I'm just so sick of anger and violence."

"I am, too," Sanja said. She sat back down. In the silence she could hear the soft hum of a bee. "Surely we can disagree without re-fighting the war."

Amela looked up. "We can try," she said.

A bird lit nearby and started pecking at the newly turned earth. Sanja folded her arms, then unfolded them. "Is this a truce?" she asked at last. "Do we need a white flag?"

Amela picked up a handful of dirt, letting it sift through her fingers. "Let's just stop blaming each other," she said.

"All right," Sanja sighed. "That night in April, Goran and I sneaked over to your house, remember?"

Amela nodded. "After you left, Dina's boyfriend was shot."

Sanja's eyes widened. "The boy who brought her chocolates?"

"Yes. I saw him sprawled in the gutter. Dead." Amela took a deep breath. She was gratified to see Sanja's look of horror. "Arkan's militamen were banging on doors searching for Muslims, dragging us out and shooting us. The town was going crazy. We went to Dragan's."

"If you didn't trust Serbs, why did you go to Dragan's?"

"Sometimes you take a chance. You trust or you die."

"So you could trust him, but not me? That doesn't say much for our friendship," Sanja said roughly.

Amela waved off the comment. "Don't turn this into a personal thing. We went where we were safest."

She picked up her story, telling Sanja about the night at the weekend house. Then she described the journey through woods and streams and cornfields.

Sanja listened intently, her eyes showing concern, as Amela continued.

"I watched Sejo run ahead of me, ducking to keep from being a target. No seven-year-old should have to go through that. You just don't know what it's like to run for your life."

"You have no idea what I know," Sanja muttered.

Amela went on, "For several weeks we hid in a school. Soldiers had burned everything in the village." She shook as she described the night on the hillside. "It's terrible being a refugee. It made me feel worthless."

Sanja thought of her grandmother and of Vesna. "Yes, I know."

"No," Amela insisted. "You can't really know …"

"Stop it!" Sanja shouted, her patience finally shredded. "Stop saying I obviously don't know things. I've suffered panic, heat, exhaustion … been threatened … been terrified."

Amela shook her head. "What do you mean?"

"You think I was living an easy life here in Bijeljina," Sanja said. She went on before Amela could comment. "I went to Krajina and got my sick grandmother and a little boy out of that war zone. We were refugees. I drove narrow mountain roads ... and I'd never driven before. I got shot at."

Her words poured out, like liquid released from an uncorked bottle. "And checkpoints? I hid at them … quivered in fear at them. I rode with a man who used false papers and bribed guards with enough liquor to fill the Arabian Sea. I saw a good, decent man beaten to a pulp, his wife in agony. We were all terrified."

Amela listened to more of the story, her mouth open in stunned silence. Then she said, "I ... I ... Oh, Sani, I had no idea."

"So you see, I *do* understand. We Serbs have suffered, Amela, just like you have."

Amela's thoughts turned to Adnan. Trying to hold back the tears, she told Sanja about him. "He was sweet and handsome and kind. He made me smile." She broke down. "You'll never know him, my Adnan. A shell killed him … in the Kapija in Tuzla. I thought … I thought we'd have … plenty of time. I'll miss him forever." She sobbed, overwhelmed by grief.

"Do you know how many people have lost loved ones?" she went on. "How hard that is? How hard it is to know you'll never see them again? You'll never have them with you to love again? It hurts your heart and you never get over it."

"No. You never get over it." Sanja drew Amela toward her and held her. She could feel Amela's distress entwined with her own.

"I have this … dream," Sanja said, her voice breaking. "I'm wading through blood. I can feel it around my ankles, warm and sticky. Ahead of me … my cousin Mirko, his little face battered."

It took both girls a long time to stop crying. At last Sanja said, "But the war's over now."

Amela rubbed her palms over her wet cheeks. "I don't think so. I came to tell you that I was attacked at your church today by that bully and his two friends."

"What? How awful!" It wasn't at all what Sanja had expected to hear. "Are you …?"

"I'm all right. But after we talked yesterday—well, after we fought—I was curious." Amela's eyes smoldered as she told what had happened.

Sanja said, "If it hadn't been for that priest …" She left the rest unsaid as she took Amela's hand. "I'm so sorry."

"I don't blame you for all that's happened, Sani."

"And I don't blame you either. I'm just so sorry about everything. About your father, my family … Adnan." She sighed. "We're all like … like, you know, things that get washed up on a beach. The waves just picked us up."

"So … what do we do now?" Amela asked.

"We go on … as friends."

CHAPTER 20

The next day while Amela waited for the bus to Granny Radmila's farm, she thought about what she and Sanja had been through. Happily, their friendship had survived. Somehow they would work out their differences, but Amela's troubles weren't over. She still had no education or steady income. The questions about her father were still unanswered. She felt uncomfortable and threatened in Bijeljina.

When the bus came, Amela found a seat near the front. She was glad it wasn't crowded. On the country road where farmers stood beside their donkey carts waiting to sell their bundles of potatoes and onions, her thoughts took a different twist. This was where Sanja said the mine had exploded. Goran had been injured; people had died. The story had been a sobering one.

A short distance later, a large woman wearing a patterned skirt, a different-patterned blouse, and a kerchief knotted under her chin got on. She took the seat across from Amela, placing her string bag of onions, bananas, and paprikas next to her. The woman probably could feel at home as a Bosnian Serb, while Amela was an unwelcome Bosniak, yet both had been born Yugoslav. *Bosniak* was a label Amela still didn't wear easily. It must be nice to be a paprika, she thought. Nobody ever told you that you were a banana.

At her stop, Amela got off and trudged up the road. On her right, shrubs and underbrush grew on land that dipped to a creek. On her left was an abandoned farm she had always tried to ignore. Maybe she preferred not to see *Arkan,* the name of the Serb militia leader, spray-painted boastfully in bold red on the ruined house. The area around the house was choked with vines and weeds. Amela focused her attention on the road ahead, determined not to let the place upset her.

When she came to the memorial and the elementary school behind it, she wondered about the woman who lived there. Sanja said she was a refugee from the Krajina. Now, having heard Sanja's Krajina story, Amela's curiosity was aroused and she approached the school. Along a covered walkway between the main building and an annex was a doorway hung with heavy brown burlap. Outside were two rickety chairs. There was a noise from behind the curtain, and then it was swept aside by a short, stout woman wearing a black blouse and skirt.

"Hello," said Amela. "I'm a friend of Sanja's."

"Sanja's?" The woman's delighted smile displayed two missing teeth. "Well, then please sit down. I've just made coffee." Without waiting for Amela to accept the invitation, the woman ducked back through the burlap curtain, coming out a minute later with a tray.

"This is so kind of you," said Amela, taking a cup.

"My name is Mira. I don't know many people here, but I used to have lots of friends." Mira seemed eager to talk. "I'm a widow," she went on. "I owned a large farm in Krajina … near the Una River. Generations ago my ancestors were sent there to keep the western frontier safe."

Amela nodded. She knew about the Krajina. It was part of the history of Yugoslavia that she had studied in school.

Mira frowned. "Then came the war. Bah! Politicians! Guilty … every one! Three years ago … you remember? … Serbs were forced to leave Krajina. Not by choice." She shook her head. "Oh, no."

"I remember," said Amela. "I was living in Tuzla then."

"I was stupid," Mira went on, her expression sour. "Politicians told us, 'Nothing to worry about.' So I stayed. Stupid!"

Mira took a sip of coffee as she gathered her thoughts. "By the time we left, everything was chaos. I couldn't find my son. My mother fell and broke her leg. Good people took care of her." She paused and took a deep breath. "I had to get the children out. Neighbors threw stones … one hit the baby's head. She was bleeding."

"And the others?" Amela asked. "The children's parents, your mother … ?"

Mira sent a grateful look to the heavens. "Everybody survived."

"I'm so glad. What were you able to bring out with you?" Amela asked gently.

Mira leaned forward and laid her hand on Amela's knee. "Only my three grandchildren. And I'm thankful for that."

Amela had been impressed by Sanja's story of her grandmother and the little boy, and now this woman's story touched her heart. "Thank you for telling me. I'm happy your family is safe," she said, standing up and handing her cup back to Mira.

Mira stood, smoothed her black skirt, and nodded. "It's a beautiful day. Enjoy it."

It *was* a beautiful day. Sweet country fragrances floated on the summer air. Butterflies journeyed joyfully among wildflowers and roadside grasses. It was warm, but cooler than in town. Amela threw her arms wide, and spun around and around. Then she reminded herself that she had come to buy groceries. She hurried across the road to Granny Radmila's farm.

Amela bought fresh spinach, cabbage, cherries, and cheese. She was surprised when the old woman asked idly about Hanifa who, she said, she remembered from "the old days." Amela tensed. She didn't want to discuss her family with the Serb woman.

"And your father, child? I heard he went off. Why did he go off?"

Went off.

Was Granny Radmila oblivious to the war's tragedies? Was she insensitive or was she being deliberately spiteful?

Angrily, Amela grabbed her bundle of produce and hurried away. As she walked along the deserted road, she marveled at the difference between the two Serb women, Mira and Granny Radmila. Then, remembering Mira's advice to enjoy the day, she calmed herself and decided to do just that. It would be wrong to let a stupid remark ruin her earlier mood. She was perfectly content to be alone, to stretch and to feel the strength in her long legs. The morning that had been hazy had grown warm. Now the distant clouds were heavy and the breeze smelled like rain was on the way.

As Amela passed a farmhouse between Granny Radmila's and the vacant field, she heard chickens squawking. At the corner of the fenced yard, a boy of about seven and a younger girl were chasing each other, the girl squealing with delight as she whipped away from the boy's outstretched arm. Amela remembered chasing Sejo when he was little, both of them laughing until they dropped.

She glanced back. The children had come out to the road and were jumping and dancing along. Amused, she stopped to watch them. They reached the fence that divided their property from the one next to it, the place with the destroyed house.

At that moment, the little girl cried out, "Oh! I left the gate open! He got loose!"

"He," Amela guessed, was a goat that was ambling onto the deserted property. Seeing the child dart after the animal, Amela dropped her package and raced back. The boy took a step forward, then an uncertain one back.

"Don't!" Amela shouted. She grabbed his sleeve and held onto him. He stared up at her in wide-eyed fright. Amela knew that he, just as she, had been thoroughly indoctrinated at school about mines. Frantic about his sister, he was also terrified to go after her. The girl had paused, her attention on the goat.

Amela tightened her hold on the boy's shoulder. "What's her name?"

"Tatiana. I'm supposed to take care of her," he moaned.

"Tatiana!" Amela called out. For a dreadful second she was back in Tuzla, running toward the Kapija, screaming her cousin Jasmina's name. But this was not Tuzla, and she focused on the little girl. "Tatiana, you must stay right where you are. Do you understand?" The child looked bewildered.

"That's right," called Amela. "You're being very, very good. Wait there. I'm coming to get you."

Tatiana's mouth puckered as if she was about to cry, but she gave a slight nod. Her brother was crying and hugging himself.

So intense was her attention on the child that Amela hadn't heard the car drive up, and she jumped when she heard a man behind her cursing.

"How could you let her go in there?"

Angrily she replied, "Like I'd *let* her do that, Goran?"

Goran knelt and gathered the little boy to him, whispering in his ear. The child wiped his eyes and nodded his head.

"I'm going for her," said Amela.

"No," said Goran, "I am."

"Tatiana," the boy called to his sister, "this man is my friend. He will come to get you, so just stay there."

Goran studied the scene even as he, too, instructed Tatiana in a calm, but commanding voice. Then he turned and went to the trunk of his car and pulled out a rope that he tied around his waist.

"Here," he said, handing the rope to Amela. "You see where grass has been trampled? I'll follow that path."

"What's the rope for?"

"To pull me back," Goran said over his shoulder "… if … I can't make it on my own. Don't let it drag on the ground."

Amela held the coiled rope high with both hands. As Goran moved forward, she carefully allowed the rope to play out. Probably there weren't any mines; nevertheless, she called out a caution. "Be careful, Goran."

Though intent on his mission, he replied, "Nah, I thought I'd start waltzing."

Amela gritted her teeth, but stayed focused on his progress. She gasped with each step he took. When he reached Tatiana, he picked her up. She whimpered and snuggled against him. He turned slowly. Amela swallowed hard.

Goran inched closer. When he reached the road, he set the little girl safely on the pavement. The children jumped up and down and hugged each other.

Amela felt drained. "Goran, you could have been killed."

"So could she," he said simply.

"Bad goat!" Tatiana screamed. The animal, ignoring her, was wandering back toward them.

Amela and Goran exchanged alarmed looks. During the brief celebration, they had forgotten about the goat.

The air split with the crack of the explosion. Amela was thrown across the road. She lay on the pavement, her ears ringing. Everything went black, then fuzzy. A touch on her shoulder made her grimace. Someone was shaking her gently. A voice asked if she was all right. She struggled to open her eyes.

"Amela, look at me."

She moved her head slowly, trying to focus.

"Amela! Look at me!" he said again.

Children. Crying. She sat up and looked around her, her mind gradually clearing. Goran was tearing the cotton material below her knee.

"You've taken a bit of shrapnel," he said.

"The children ... the children ..." she stammered.

"They're okay."

Footsteps pounded on the road, coming closer. A woman was shrieking. Amela supposed it was the children's mother. Without a word to Amela or Goran, she shepherded her two young ones away.

Goran examined Amela's leg. "I need to bind this," he said.

Reality was fighting its way into her mind. "There was ... There really was ..."

"... a mine. Yeah. Could have been worse, though."

"Not for the goat," said Amela. She began laughing hysterically, but only for a moment before the laughter dissolved into tears.

Goran grabbed a tee shirt out of the car and tore strips. Carefully, he removed the metal piece, and then wrapped the strips of cloth around the wound. He scooped Amela up and put her onto the passenger seat of his car. In spite of the warmth of the afternoon, her teeth were chattering. Goran got a blanket from the trunk and wrapped it around her. He threw her grocery bag into the back seat, put the car in drive, and proceeded to break all speeding records.

"Where are we going?" she asked, her voice tense. "Don't take me to the hospital."

"But you ..."

"Don't!"

"All right, all right," he said. "My house first then. But you might need stitches and a tetanus shot. Sanja will clean you up and you can probably wear something of hers. You and I are both kinda messy."

For the first time, Amela noticed the dirt in Goran's hair. There was blood on his sleeve. His or hers?

When Sanja saw them, her reaction was dramatic. "Oh, my God! Come in quickly!"

After the wounds had been cleaned and treated, and the adventurers had changed their clothes, the three of them sat at the kitchen table while Sanja served tea.

"I called Dragan," she told Amela. "He'll be at your house in thirty minutes." She looked from her brother's adhesive strip to Amela's much larger bandage, and asked him, "Why is yours such a little cut and hers is a gaping wound?"

"Not gaping," said Amela.

"Not gaping," echoed Goran, "and although my wound is slight, I was heroic, wasn't I, Amela?"

She rolled her eyes and laughed. "And you're so very modest!"

Sanja looked stern. "Death traps do not belong where goats can trigger them. They don't belong anywhere! We need to tell someone to post warnings."

"I'll report it," said Goran.

Sanja refilled the cups, then said, "Goran, you were coming back from your interview. How was it?"

"Good. I'm almost sure to be hired."

"Hired?" asked Amela. "I thought you had a job with the IPTF."

"They'll give me a few days off for this. Interpreters and drivers are needed for the September elections," Goran explained. "The pay's super."

Of course! Amela's thoughts raced. She had been an interpreter in Tuzla for registration and two elections. Sanja had done registration in May and June. Why hadn't she ...? But, of course. She had been distracted with the move back, the house fire, bullies, struggles with Sanja. She hadn't been paying attention. But now maybe ...

"I'm going to apply," said Sanja. "You should, too."

Amela felt a surge of hope. Here was a chance to do real work and get well paid for it. Then her hope vanished, gone as quickly as a shooting star racing across the night sky. She jumped up, overturning her chair. She felt a jolt of pain and grabbed the edge of the table.

"Thank you for what you did, Goran," she said, limping toward the door.

"Hey!" he shouted. "What do you think you're doing? You shouldn't walk on that leg. And what's the matter with you anyway?"

"Amela," said Sanja. "Getting hired won't be a problem. Don't turn away from this chance."

Amela's good intentions about the future failed her, and she said grimly, "You forget who I am ... or *what* I am! A job isn't possible for me. Not in Bijeljina!"

"Listen, " Goran said, "there's a non-discrimination policy."

But Amela wasn't listening. She limped toward the door.

"Hang on," said Goran, grabbing his keys. "I'll drive you." He waved off her protests.

He was right. Amela knew she could never make it on her own. Sanja helped her to the car and watched them drive away.

The short drive didn't allow much time for conversation, but neither Amela nor Goran was in the mood to talk. As they neared her street, Amela mumbled stiffly, "I hope you get the election job."

"You can, too. Don't be stubborn."

"I'm being realistic," she insisted. "You don't know what it's like to be the white pebble on a brown-pebbled beach. You and I are just different."

"If you mean . . ."

"I mean everything!" she snapped. "All the things that made us kill each other. All the things that make it hard to live together. I don't know whose fault it is. That's just *how* it is, and I hate it!"

As soon as the car stopped, she got out and made her way up the walk without a backward glance. Her leg nearly gave out, but she clenched her teeth and kept going. After all, the pain in her leg was much less than the pain in her heart.

CHAPTER
21

Amela's phone call to Sanja was brief. "I've got news. Meet me at the memorial at two o'clock."

When Sanja hung up the receiver, she scooped up her cat, disturbing him as he was gymnastically poised to lick his hind leg. "News? Aren't you curious, Sivi? I hope it's good."

Amela was waiting at the memorial when Sanja arrived. She handed her a can of soda.

"Are we celebrating?" Sanja asked.

"Yes. But first I want to tell you how sorry I am for the way I acted the other day. I got my hopes up, and then ... I don't seem to handle disappointment well."

Sanja touched Amela's arm. "Goran and I talked about it," she said, "and we understand why you were upset. But, how's your leg?"

"Healing. It's better every day. Dragan's doctor friend is taking care of me."

Sanja frowned. "You don't trust the hospital, do you?" she asked.

"Not really. Trust doesn't come easily."

Sanja nodded. She remembered Ivana's worries about poisoned food. "I understand. Or ... I'm trying to. Now, quick!

Tell me your news. Unless it's bad, and then I don't want to hear it."

"No, it's good news," said Amela. She tried to look nonchalant, but a giggle gave her away. "I have a one-day job as an interpreter with the International Police Task Force."

Sanja squealed and threw her arms around her friend. "As an interpreter? How great!"

"There's a big one-day meeting in Tuzla. We'll leave very early and come back very late. There won't be time to visit my family. But I have a *job*, Sani!" Her grin faded to a look of panic. "I'm so nervous! I haven't been an interpreter since last fall. What if I mess up?"

"Don't be silly, Amela. You can do it. How did you find out about it?"

"I didn't. A man called and asked me to come in for an interview."

"Super! How did he know about *you*?"

Amela shook her head. "I don't know. I figure it was Dragan. The man just said someone had given him my name."

"Wow! I wish somebody'd give them *my* **name**. What good does it do for me to have a brother working for them if he can't even get me a job, too? But that's okay. I'm happy for you."

"But ..." Amela suddenly looked stricken. "How do I know it's safe?"

Sanja caught herself. She was about to dismiss Amela's concerns, but these days when people were suspicious of party food and hospital staffs, it shouldn't be surprising that Amela was wary of traveling with strangers.

"I'll check it out," said Sanja.

Amela was also concerned about leaving her mother, even for a day, but Dragan offered his help and so did Samir. Neither one would let her miss such an opportunity.

A few days later, she sat on her front step waiting for the police officers she was traveling with. Even at six o'clock, the end-of-July day was already promising to be hot and sticky. Amela didn't mind the early start. She had been awake since four, swinging from anticipation to anxiety. Any remaining doubts were about her ability, because both Ivana and Goran had told Sanja the job was legitimate.

The drive to Tuzla was short and pleasant. The small van was very different from the back of a vile-smelling truck. And this time, Amela thought happily, she didn't have to worry about being shot.

The two officers—Tim, an Irishman, and Sergio, from Spain—were friendly. English was the common language, and they thoughtfully included her in their conversation. She was glad for the practice. At first she had trouble with Tim's puckish humor. He would tease, then wait for her to react, and when she did, he'd burst out laughing, his eyes crinkling.

They arrived in Tuzla with time to spare, and, since they were all hungry, Tim bought sandwiches and coffee for their mid-morning breakfast. Tim joked that the coffee was like mud from the bottom of Dublin's River Liffey. Amela laughed. She liked being on a professional business trip.

Tim explained that the IPTF's mission was to train and advise the post-war police force. The meeting, which included humanitarian affairs representatives as well as police chiefs and judges, was to discuss the rule of law. They got down to business quickly, and Amela was kept busy helping Tim and Sergio understand comments made in her language as well as translating English for the female judge on her right.

She went to lunch with Tim, Sergio, and Ivan, an IPTF officer who worked in Tuzla.

"Well, luv," Tim said, "good interpreting isn't just saying words, it's being informed and understanding nuance. You're doing a great job. Brilliant."

"Thank you," she said modestly, although her heart raced with excitement.

"You know, Miss Amela," said Ivan, his English heavily accented by his native Ukrainian, "it is pity you do not live in Tuzla. My *tovarysh* ... how it is in English? Friend. My friend in OSCE office say is need for interpreters for election next month. You be very good for them."

"She can work in Bijeljina," said Tim.

"But she so more comfortable in Tuzla. Yes?"

"Yes, Ivan," said Amela. "I would be."

"You'd need to spend about a week here," said Tim.

Could she do it? If she could make sure her mother was cared for ... "I have an aunt who lives here," she said hopefully.

Tim's eyebrows went up. "Well then, why not check out this election business, luv? We can't give you any more work back in Bijeljina for at least ... what, Sergio? A couple months?"

Sergio shrugged. "Who knows? Maybe not then." He turned to Amela. "I 'splain you. Regular guy was in accident. He comes back at work next week."

"Then, Miss Amela," said Ivan, "you must speak to this aunt, and I right now speak to friend to ask for you."

Tim nodded his head enthusiastically. "I guess you already know that elections are monitored by the OSCE—the Organization for Security and Cooperation in Europe," he explained. "One of their lads is here at the conference."

Amela's phone call to her aunt Biserka confirmed that part of the plan. Sejo got on the line, stuttering with excitement. "You ... you will come here? When? When?"

"September, but only if they give me the job," she added.

When the conference ended, Amela went for the interview. It had been a year since her last interview with OSCE. She was nervous, and hoped no one noticed her wipe her sweaty palms on her skirt.

Although Amela had worked on elections before, she listened carefully to the interviewer. Maybe some things had changed.

"Election supervisors are from various countries," the woman said, "but English is the common language." She explained further that in this—the election for presidents and members of Parliament—each supervisor would be assigned to a polling station with an interpreter. Their jobs were to ensure that proper procedures were followed, advising or making suggestions when necessary.

"You should hear soon whether you've been selected," the interviewer said, "and, if so, you'll get instructions about where and when to report."

Amela left the office breathless. How much she owed to her English teachers and to television programs, but most of all to her fellow refugee in the school! That woman had run her English class as if there were no war, no hiding from military patrols, no hunger. The studying Amela had done there had paid off. Surely she would be hired.

I *will* come back in September, she insisted to herself. "I will!"

CHAPTER
22

A few days after her trip to Tuzla, Amela was offered the interpreter job. There was more good news because Sanja was chosen to work in Bijeljina. The two of them thought the time could not go by fast enough, but on a crisp and clear morning in September, Samir took Amela to the bus station.

"You make us proud," he said. Then he kissed her cheeks and put her on the bus.

Amela was happy to be back in Tuzla. She smiled when she heard the muezzins calling the faithful to prayer. She went to Jasmina's grave, placing fresh flowers there and gazing at the photo of her lovely cousin. Then she sat for a long time beside Adnan's grave. The anguish she'd felt at his loss and the fury on that June day, her birthday three years ago, would never go away entirely, but they had at last shrunk to a tender sadness and a sober regret.

The next morning, thrilled about her first day as an interpreter and determined to make a good impression, Amela dressed in her best skirt and blouse and polished her old black boots. She couldn't quite get them to shine, but they looked presentable.

In a brief meeting with her supervisor, Trevor, a fifty-ish, balding professor from England, she tried to settle her nerves.

She supposed Trevor had an advantage over the supervisors who came from Sweden, Germany, or Poland in that English was his native language, but he said that was not necessarily so.

"You see, I'm from Cornwall—and some of my countrymen think that's outside the Realm. They accuse us of not speaking proper English, but you have only to listen to our American cousins here to wonder what *proper* English really is." He laughed, then said, "Yesterday I heard an American chap say he spoke Dixie."

"You know from your previous experience that your job is very important," Trevor told Amela. "Our driver is a lad named Senad. Drivers aren't required to know English, so you'll translate between us and also at the polling station." Amela was thrilled. She liked meeting interesting people and doing something worthwhile. And getting paid besides! She silently blessed her IPTF friends and whoever had recommended her for the job with them.

In the afternoon, she and Trevor rode to a village almost an hour away to inspect the polling station, a small theater that was burned during the war and now abandoned. The station's Committee Chairman was there, checking out the space. Amela and Trevor introduced themselves, and then she translated as the men discussed arrangements for the two days of voting.

The lobby was dingy, showing the effects of fire, but once it was cleaned a bit and tables set up, the space was adequate to move voters both in and out through the wide double doors. There would be room inside for about twenty voters at a time. Each voter would move along, sign the register, receive a blank ballot, vote behind one of four cardboard screens, then deposit the marked ballot in a box before exiting.

Trevor nodded. "I see one of the political parties has put up a poster on the wall outside. It's inside the fifty-metre limit."

"Yes, I saw it, too," said the Chairman. "It will be down within the hour."

Later Trevor invited Amela, Senad, and members of another team to join him at a lake outside town. It was dark, but too early for the musicians in the many new, post-war nightspots. The air was still summer-mild, and the group sat at a table overlooking the water. Unruffled by breezes, the lake wore the smooth sheen of patent leather. Circles of light cast by lamps along the shore looked like giant gold buttons.

"Was there shelling here?" asked Daniela, a supervisor from Romania who had brought her interpreter, Zufer. Amela had met him at orientation.

"Yes," said Zufer. "Here and in town. And ... Amela, you know."

"Yes. The twenty-fifth of May in 1995," she said. "An evening like this. People were sitting at an outdoor café in the city."

"The Kapija. Where you saw the memorial earlier," Zufer told the supervisors.

Amela nodded. "Serbs shelled Tuzla throughout the war, but less than in some other places. But that evening ..." Growing pressure in her chest made her pause.

Zufer glanced at her and took up the story. "Seventy-one young people were killed including a child not yet three. Sons, daughters, brothers, sisters."

And boyfriends, thought Amela.

Zufer swallowed hard, then said, "There's no one in Tuzla who didn't know someone."

Daniela drew her jacket more closely about her.

Trevor shook his head and gazed out at the tranquil water. "How does one get past it?" he murmured. "How do you move on after something so terrible?"

How *had* she moved on? Amela wondered. Maybe by taking small steps and then, eventually, bigger ones.

The next morning well before six, everyone gathered at the center to pick up the ballots and sensitive election materials. The polling stations were to open at seven sharp; however, some voter registers had not been delivered.

"We can't open without them, can we?" Amela asked.

"No, we can't," said Trevor. Nevertheless, they set out for the run-down theater.

Senad carried the boxes from the car into the lobby where the committee's tables had been set up. Charred and broken furniture had been shoved against the back wall. Amela introduced Trevor to the five members of the committee, all people from the local community. With the committee busily going about their setting-up duties, Amela joined Trevor at the front door of the bullet-riddled building. A large crowd, mostly women with children, was gathering. People were getting noisy, obviously impatient to vote. How upset would they be if the station didn't open on time? Two policemen paced with slow, tense steps, keeping watchful eyes on the crowd. Glances from the Chairman and his committee showed their concern.

Trevor toyed with a button on his jacket, rubbing it like a worry stone. "My station last year had a 98 percent turnout of registered voters," he told Amela. "You people take voting seriously. Maybe too seriously," he added as a woman began shouting.

The committee's Crowd Controller joined them, frowning, obviously not happy at the prospect of controlling a big, unruly crowd. By seven thirty, the crowd was still passive, but building to a potential tidal wave. A Humvee with SFOR emblazoned on its side stopped across the road—NATO's peacekeepers, the Stabilization Force. One of them spoke into his radio.

Amela could feel waves of anger and distrust. She moved closer to Trevor and the Crowd Controller. There was no way the three of them could hold the crowd back if they decided to storm the building, but the materials behind them had to be protected.

Trevor pulled out his radio and spoke into it. "Two policemen are trying to control at least two hundred people on the road," he said. "What do you advise? Over."

"Registers are coming. Hang on. Out."

"Bloody hell," Trevor swore.

Amela had been able to overhear some talk. "They are mostly refugees from Srebrenica," she told him. "There was a terrible massacre there."

"Yes, yes, I know." Moisture was forming on his upper lip and forehead.

"They're suspicious and angry, Trevor. They think this is a plot to keep them from voting." Amela could understand their feelings. Imagining their agony made her feel miserable.

Trevor glanced at his watch. "Nearly eight o'clock," he mumbled as a large group of women moved toward them, heads down like riled Spanish bulls. One woman planted herself directly in front of Amela. She was a head shorter, but fierce. She gestured wildly and as she yelled, spit flew. Amela jerked back, wiped her chin and held up her hand, trying to reason with the woman.

Trevor grabbed Amela's elbow. "You'd best get back inside. I'll ..."

He broke off in mid-sentence. Some of the women shoved past, pouring into the lobby. The Crowd Controller was swept along. Beside Trevor, Amela flattened herself against a wall. She felt helpless, but determined to stay with him and do what she could. Then a policeman pushed through, pulling along an anxious-looking man who was carrying a package.

Trevor reached out to the man to help him get through. "Well, it's about bloody time!" he growled. Amela followed him inside where he, the Committee Chairman, and the Crowd Controller gradually herded the howling women out, making it clear that voting would begin as soon as an orderly line had formed. Amela took deep breaths. Trevor wiped his brow. The committee whipped things into shape with amazing speed, and not long after eight o'clock, they were handling a long line of voters.

With order restored, the Crowd Controller found time to demonstrate to a few children the "magic wand" he used. Once sprayed with a "magic liquid," he told them, the voter's index finger would shine purple under his ultra-violet light. "That way no one can vote again, and it helps to make the elections fair." The children nodded, intrigued.

The rest of the day passed with only one incident, an argument between the Chairman and a young woman on the committee over a procedural matter. A man had a registration receipt, but his name was not on the register. They brought the matter to Trevor who, through Amela's translation, advised them to use a tendered ballot, one that would be sealed, sent to Sarajevo for authentication, then inclusion in the final counting.

At seven that evening, the Crowd Controller announced to a long line of people that everyone would have a chance to vote the next day. The car was loaded with materials to be taken to the headquarters, then Amela dropped wearily onto the back seat, glad to relax. The day's events had been fascinating, but strenuous, and now her head was aching.

It was dark in the hills. The narrow road was deserted. Trevor, in the front, had turned his radio off, but there was an occasional report from one of the supervisors over the car radio that was tuned to the official channel. Suddenly a man's voice came through, a voice so creepy, so sinister, it made Amela sit up and gasp.

The voice drawled out the hated name in English.

"*Tu-u-r-r-kish.*"

Amela cringed, feeling it drip like slime.

"*Tu-u-r-r-kish,*" he repeated, and then another man answered with a stream of words in Serbian.

"They're on our frequency!" Trevor protested. "They're not supposed to be on our frequency! Amela! What is he saying?" When she didn't answer, he said again, "What's he saying?"

"I can't ..." She drew a ragged breath and tried again. "I can't say those words. They're filthy ... disgusting!"

The voice stopped at that point. "But ... try to tell me," said Trevor, turning to look at her. "What's it about?"

"He said ... oh! ... he said terrible things. That they will do to us Muslim girls what they did to our m-mothers. Please. I can't ..." She broke down, unable to repeat the rest.

"It's okay," Trevor reassured her. "They're just bullies on a radio, and you're safe with us."

Later at a café where people gathered, everyone was talking about the verbal assault. The women were shaken, humiliated and frightened; the men were like tightly coiled springs, angry and ready to fight.

"That is exactly the reaction the sleazy men wanted," Trevor told them.

With the support of their foreign colleagues, the local people began to calm down. They could put the incident behind them, they agreed, because early the next morning they would resume their duties as professional election workers. It was their way of overcoming the indecencies of the war that seemed still to remain.

The next day before dawn, the voting materials, secured the night before for safekeeping, were picked up. The interpreters renewed their vow to deliver a successful election.

To Amela's relief, the set-up went well. Voting began promptly at seven o'clock. People waited patiently in long lines, exchanging information about children and complaining about unemployment.

At mid-morning, the chairman's wife brought coffee and pastry. At lunchtime, she brought bureks, prosciutto, apples. Amela doubted that they could afford such generosity, but it was what her own mother would have done. She had already decided to donate most of her earnings to household expenses with a little to Sejo for anything he wanted.

In the middle of the afternoon, the line was still forming outside. Amela was amazed and touched, as she had been before, by the very old people, stooped and hobbling, who shuffled in and waited patiently, determined to cast their ballots.

"Have you noticed," Trevor remarked, "the husbands and wives who share eyeglasses? Even the chairman has lent his a few times. And many of the old women are wearing the traditional full trousers gathered at the ankles. What are they called?"

"Dimije," said Amela. She had worn them once. When her little group of refugees arrived at the school, dirty and disheveled, people sheltering there had shared things rescued from the deserted village. At the time it had been, for Amela, a convenient necessity. Now, seeing these women who had trekked long distances to vote, she felt proud to have dressed like them.

Shortly after Trevor's comments about eyeglasses, an old couple came in, signed the register, and each took a ballet. The woman stepped behind the cardboard screen, her husband close behind. In a flash, her voice could be heard clear across the room as she staunchly proclaimed, "I can do it myself!"

There was a moment of stunned silence, and then the people in the polling station erupted in cheers. The Chairman strutted to the middle of the room, raised his arms, and declared, "*That is democracy!*"

By seven that evening, everyone was tired. The door was locked, and they gathered around a long table to sort, count, and record.

The figures tallied on the first count, bringing the second loud cheer of the day. Then a weary, but satisfied group headed for homes and beds. After turning in the ballots, Amela, Trevor, and Senad joined a few others celebrating at a café that was still open at two in the morning.

"Amela," said Trevor, "you are a remarkable young lady. Your abilities have exceeded my expectations. I don't know what your future plans are, but you'll have a letter of recommendation from me."

He raised his glass, and said "A toast to our Bosnian friends. We wish all of Bosnia success."

CHAPTER 23

While Amela was working in Tuzla, Sanja and Goran were preparing for general elections in and near Bijeljina. Sanja had greatly improved her English in the weeks since she had been chosen. Now it was mid-September and she felt confident. Two days before the elections, interpreters and drivers were called together to learn about procedures and to meet their supervisors. As they waited in a crowded reception hall, they were an animated group.

"Sanja?" She turned to see a stocky man of about forty. "I'm Felip, your driver. We met briefly when I was on a construction job in your neighborhood. Have you seen Ivana?" he asked.

"She's an alternate," Sanja answered. "I don't think she's here."

"I'm here," squeaked a female voice. Ivana, obviously out of breath, joined them. "They just called me because somebody dropped out."

"There's our answer," said Sanja, giving Ivana a big hug.

Felip had met both Sanja's and Ivana's supers, as he called them. "Look for a Dutchman and a Finn," he said.

Sanja gave him a look. "Oh, that narrows it right down."

When the supervisors came out of their meeting, everyone gravitated to their teams, delayed sometimes by laughter and hugs as people recognized each other from previous elections. Ivana's supervisor, Joop, from The Netherlands, was a large, hearty man with a goatee. Standing behind him was a gracious, brown-haired woman in her late forties who introduced herself as Hanna from Helsinki. Felip introduced Sanja and Ivana.

"Pleased to meet you, Sanja," Hanna said. "Interpreters and drivers have a meeting now, so why don't we visit our polling station early tomorrow morning?"

Joop winked at Sanja. "She says in her no-nonsense way. I've worked with this woman before. She's a slave-driver."

"And he's a lazy clod," teased Hanna.

Joop invited some of the supervisors and interpreters to gather at a restaurant for dinner that evening, and Sanja was glad to be included. At home she prepared for the evening. Her hair was still wet when the phone rang. She wasn't surprised that it was Ivana.

"Aren't you excited?" Ivana asked.

"Excited and a bit nervous. I don't have as much experience as you do with people from other countries."

"Oh, don't worry. They're great," Ivana assured her. "And there's a really good-looking American guy. Goran's his driver. I wonder if he's single."

"Goran? Last time I heard he was," Sanja teased.

"No silly, the American. So what are you wearing tonight? I've got that new blue dress."

Sanja hadn't really thought about it. "Probably my green one," she said. She didn't begin to have the wardrobe Ivana had.

Hanna was ordering a taxi to drive to the restaurant outside town and had asked Sanja to join her. As Sanja was leaving the house, she passed Goran.

"I wish drivers were invited tonight," she said.

"That's okay. I have plans, but I did offer to give my supervisor a ride. I'm sure I'll like him."

"Is he married?" she asked her brother.

"Scott? I don't know. Why?" He grinned. "Are you interested?"

"Not me. Ivana. You know her radar for men."

Goran thought about it. "I don't think Ivana's his type. He's fun, but I think he also likes serious conversation."

"Really," said Sanja, her interest stirred.

Everyone gathered at the restaurant. Ivana looked lovely in her blue dress and her newly colored pale blonde hair.

"My favorite color so far," Sanja told her.

Ivana swept her fingers through the casual cut, saying, "I'll keep it till I get tired of it. I like that dress. Green suits you. It matches . . . "

". . . my eyes. I know," said Sanja with a laugh. "So where's this dreamy guy you want to get your claws into?"

Ivana looked around, frowning. "I don't see him. Oh, he just walked in. What d'you think?"

Sanja was surprised and impressed. Ivana thought most guys were good-looking, but this one really was. However, Sanja decided not to fan Ivana's flames, so she said simply, "He looks nice."

She didn't want to stare at him, but she was curious. Scott was tall. His hair was the color of sand on a Montenegro beach. He had a pleasant smile and moved with easy confidence. People seemed to like him, judging by the way they greeted him. He glanced her way, and Sanja hoped he hadn't caught her staring.

Ivana had wandered over to talk to her supervisor as Joop got people seated around a long table and waiters began taking orders. Hanna chose a chair next to the end of the table and Sanja sat across from her. She put her purse on the floor beside her chair and when she straightened, she was looking into the brown eyes of the American. He had taken the seat to her left at the end of the table.

"Nice to see you, Hanna," he said, glancing at her, before turning back to Sanja. "I'll bet you're Goran's sister."

"I'll bet you're right," Sanja answered. "How did you know?"

"Goran described you," said Scott.

"My brother seems pleased to be working for you."

"Not so much *for* me as *with* me. We're teammates. I'm Scott Brennan." He held out his hand and Sanja took it. His grip was firm, but firmness didn't quite explain the delight that left her feeling short of breath. She was glad the waiter arrived. Sanja was not used to being flustered. She took advantage of the waiter's taking orders to study Scott more closely. She liked what she saw.

He looked at Sanja and cocked his head toward Hanna. "She's an old timer. Registration supervisor in '96 and '98 and polling station supervisor for two elections in '97, right?"

Hanna smiled. "You have a good memory, Scott."

"And you?" Sanja asked him. "Have you been to Bosnia before?"

"Sanski Most and Banja Luka, both in '97," he said.

Sanja recognized both those places. They had been part of her Krajina trip. "How have you managed to come so often? Don't you work?" She could have bitten her tongue. She hadn't meant to be rude.

Hanna laughed and patted Scott's arm. "Americans consider this a vacation."

Scott must have seen that Sanja was embarrassed because he

smiled and said jokingly, "My boss did seem eager to get rid of me." Then he laughed and explained, "Actually, I'm a lawyer. I did my first trips in law school as part of my international studies, and now my firm has a generous leave policy for good causes."

"And they think Bosnia is a good cause?" asked Sanja.

"Yeah, they do. And so do I."

As dinner continued, Sanja learned that Scott was twenty-four, lived in Washington, D.C., and had an older brother, Peter.

"That's my father's name," she said. "Well, Petar it is here."

Hanna spoke of her husband and their teenaged daughter. She said they all liked ice fishing.

In response to Sanja's question, Scott said, "I like horses to ride, onion rings to eat, jazz and Cajun blues music to listen to, and big band music to dance to."

Sanja said, "Goran and I … Oh, never mind."

"What? Tell me," Scott urged.

"Well, because of the war we had a lot of free time, so we learned English and dancing by watching television. I guess that sounds silly."

"It doesn't at all," said Hanna, and Scott agreed with a shake of his head.

Sanja smiled at them both. "I didn't expect to feel comfortable here," she said. "I thought election people would be serious all the time. But this is such a fun group."

Hanna let out a hearty laugh. "Believe me, a sense of humor is an asset in this job."

The party ended—too soon, Sanja thought—but everyone had planned an early start the next morning to check out their polling stations.

"So, Hanna," said Scott, placing his hand over Sanja's as they got ready to leave, "have you decided to keep her or can I make a bid for her?"

"You may not. She's mine," Hanna told him.

"Too bad," said Scott, winking at Sanja. She knew he was flirting, but she was breathless all the same.

The next day, Sanja told herself that one night of dreaming about Scott would have to do. She threw herself into the election work, which she found interesting and stimulating. She felt more useful and capable than she had since she had worked on registration in June.

The weather was sunny and she liked getting out of town. The polling station was at the far side of a village at the end of a mountain road. It was in one large room, a combination town hall, café, and bar. Over the weekend, there would be no liquor served inside. Neither the Chairman nor Hanna would put up with any nonsense.

"Voters will enter through the front," Sanja translated for the Chairman as they walked the path they would take, "get their ballots, drop their marked ballots in the box next to the bar, and then exit out the back. Then, if they want, they can walk a short distance from the building and sit at the tables outside where a lamb will be roasting on a spit ... and they can order drinks." He concluded with a flourish.

"That might bring a record number of voters," Hanna told Sanja.

Back in Bijelina that evening, Sanja joined Hanna and others for an early supper. She was surprised and pleased to see Scott there. She took the seat he'd saved for her and they talked easily. She was eager to know everything about him. He liked sports, he liked to travel, to read, to play practical jokes on his brother, and he hated Brussels sprouts.

"That's not possible!" came a shocked cry from the Belgian supervisor sitting across from him. She grinned at him, then said, "I must object on behalf of my hometown."

"But I like Belgian waffles," said Scott in an attempt to salvage her national pride.

"And I'm fond of American cheese," she said, continuing the good-natured banter. That comment prompted an argument about national foods that a Scotsman brought to a close by declaring, "How can anyone not like haggis?" Two people hooted while others groaned.

The next morning Sanja and her team left early for the polling station. The Chairman and his committee all had been affected by the war. One was a refugee from Sarajevo, another was an army widow, another a former soldier who had lost a leg, another unemployed because his company had gone out of business.

At the end of a busy first day, Hanna, Sanja, and Felip were offered a late-night supper, but they had to pick up another team and get the ballots and sensitive materials back to the center. There were, however, two other diners, and Sanja stopped to talk with them. They were locals who had not been among the day's voters. She reminded them they still had another day.

"Oh, all right," said the man, "I'll be there tomorrow morning."

"Good," said Sanja. "I'll look forward to seeing you both."

The woman glanced at her husband. "Well, I . . ."

"She doesn't vote," he said.

"Aren't you registered?" Sanja asked the woman.

"Oh, yes," said his wife, "I registered, but my husband doesn't approve."

Sanja was livid. "Don't you realize that voting is both a duty and a privilege? The next time you have a complaint about the way things are run, remember that half your household didn't vote."

Hanna waited until they were out of earshot before she asked Sanja about the conversation. Told of the exchange, Hanna howled with laughter. "You gave them plenty to think about. I'm proud of you!"

The next morning, both husband and wife arrived at the polling station shortly after it opened.

"Good day," Sanja greeted them. As the woman took her ballot, Sanja was careful to keep a straight face. After the couple had voted and left, however, she and Hanna exchanged high fives.

It was well past midnight when counting and paperwork were finished, everything was packed up, and they all congratulated each other. After the ballot boxes and other materials had been delivered to Bijeljina, Hanna announced, "It's pivo time! My treat!" She turned to Sanja and said, "You've earned a beer … and more. I've heard there are jobs in Sarajevo, and I'm going to give you a letter of recommendation."

It was icing on the cake — or foam on the beer! — thought Sanja. Now there were two things that gave her hope for the future … a best friend back and the possibility of a job!

CHAPTER
24

Sanja's good luck had not run out, as she found out the next day when she was putting away some freshly ironed clothes in her wardrobe. She heard Goran's heavy footsteps pounding on the stairs just before she heard him call out, "Sanja, you wearin' jeans?"

"What?" She started into the hall and was nearly knocked down. "What do you care what I'm wearing?"

"Go put on a skirt."

"My, you're bossy."

"Okay, listen. We're invited to dinner. Scott's mentioned trying to get me to the States to work and to get my degree."

"The *United* States?"

"*Of course* the United States … America!" Goran was flushed with excitement.

"But, wait …" It suddenly hit Sanja that Scott was inviting her to dinner. "*We*? I mean, he wants to take *us* to dinner? Now?"

"He asked me to ask you," Goran flung over his shoulder as he disappeared into his room.

"Goran!" Sanja called to him, laughter bubbling up. "Go put on a skirt." She ducked the pillow her brother threw at her.

Scott met Sanja and Goran at a small restaurant near his hotel. His face lit up when he saw Sanja, and when he took her hand it wasn't to shake it, but to hold it for a minute. She'd thought about him through the two election days and wondered if he could really be as thoughtful and funny and smart as he had seemed. As they settled down for drinks before dinner, she decided he was all of those and more.

He and Goran got along as if they had been life-long buddies. They joked and laughed and had no hesitation kidding, although they obviously respected each other.

"Goran thinks the election went well," said Scott. "How about you, Sanja?"

"I guess so. There was a good turnout, but people voted along party lines and the same old politicians won."

"Nothing ever changes in the Balkans, except boundaries," said Goran.

Scott nodded agreement. "Bosnia's got to find a new direction. You need new faces, new blood."

"Not mine," said Goran. "Politics isn't my thing."

"Mine either," said Sanja. "I don't want to make laws or run for office, but I would like to help people, help them recover."

Goran picked up the thread. "Recovery is a big problem. We can't even count on having water and electricity. We need to get back to real life. Jobs, education, travel." He threw Sanja a smile as he said to Scott, "One time early in the war Sani and I made plans to travel. First we said to Portugal—you know, just picking a country out of thin air. And then we said anywhere. Egypt. America."

"America?"

"Well, I was sixteen," said Goran, "and I was just thinking any place. But I really would like to see America someday, and not just in films."

Over dinner Scott said to Sanja, "Goran told me he

recommended your friend for a job with the IPTF, and that led to her working on the election, too. I think that's great."

Sanja shot a look at Goran. "Uh … that would be Amela?"

"Caught," he said as he registered her startled gaze. He might never have blushed in his life, but he was blushing now.

"Did I say something I shouldn't?" asked Scott.

"No, not at all," Sanja assured him. Looking directly at her brother, she said, "I'm just surprised *someone* failed to tell *me*."

Goran shrugged. "I just dropped her name. More wine, Scott?" he asked, obviously eager to change the subject.

After dinner Scott ordered coffee. He leaned toward Sanja and said, "Goran's told me a bit of the story about your … what do you call her? The word for grandmother. Baka?" When Sanja nodded, he went on, "Well, I'd like to hear more. If you don't mind telling me."

Sanja had told the story only to Goran and Amela, and Scott would be a different sort of audience. She hesitated, but, still, he seemed genuinely interested. She took a deep breath and began.

"It started when we got a ham radio message from Baka who lived in the Bosnian Krajina. You've been to Sanski Most, so you must know where that is." Scott nodded, and she went on. "The message was that Baka was very ill and someone must come get her."

Scott was a good listener, paying close attention and only inserting an occasional question. When Sanja paused after telling about leaving with the doctor, he was silent. She bit her lip. She'd said too much. Or he thought she'd been crazy to do such a thing. She vowed never to tell the story again.

Then he reached across the table and took her hand. "What you did took a lot of courage. It's an amazing story. I'd like to hear more of it."

"Why don't you come have coffee at our house?" Goran suggested. "You can meet our parents—if they're not already asleep." Scott accepted the invitation.

The heat of the day had lessened, and there was a soft breeze. As they walked through the park, Scott linked his fingers with Sanja's. She smiled and thought how *right* it felt. Sanja steered the men to the front porch and started inside to make coffee.

"I'll help," said Scott. He followed her to the kitchen. Sanja was nervous, her hands so unsteady she wasn't sure she could carry the serving tray, but Scott took it from her. She had wanted so much to spend more time with him. Now that he was actually at her home, she didn't know what to say to him. She wanted to know everything about him, but would he think she was prying if she asked too many questions? Did he really want to hear more of her story or was he just being polite?

She went to get the cookies she'd forgotten, and when she returned she heard Scott saying to Goran, "My roommate got married last month, so I'm alone in my apartment now."

"You have your own place?" Goran said. "That would be awesome." He looked envious, and Sanja knew he was comparing his life with Scott's.

"What about your parents?" Sanja asked him. "Where do they live?"

"Washington, D.C., not far from me. My dad's with the State Department and my mother's a college history teacher." He took the coffee cup she handed him with one of the smiles that made her heart spin. "My folks are great. Some people expect my dad to be stuffy because he's a diplomat, but you should see him handle a basketball and hear his lousy jokes."

"He sounds nice," said Sanja. "But you didn't become a diplomat like him. Do you like being a lawyer?"

"So far. I've only been with the firm three months, but I've known the senior partner since I was a kid."

"Why did you want to be a lawyer?" asked Goran.

Scott considered the question. "I'm an idealist," he said with a shrug. "Things like fairness and honesty and equal treatment are important to me."

"What about justice?" Sanja asked.

"What's just?" Scott countered. "Justice for one person or group might mean oppression for another. It's a matter of perspective, of how you see things because of where you're coming from—your point of view based on knowledge and experience."

Sanja looked puzzled. "But shouldn't justice be for everybody, not a particular person or group? Doesn't it mean fairness and for everybody to be equal?"

"I don't know about *being* equal," said Scott, "but everybody should have equal treatment under the law. At least that's the theory."

"And they should have rights," she insisted, "and their rights should be respected."

Goran jumped into the discussion. "You mean like our grandmother? Tell me her rights were respected!"

"Well, she …"

"So to protect our rights, we had to go to war," Goran insisted.

"No, we didn't!" Sanja said vehemently.

"We had to defend ourselves—defend our rights. Serbs' rights weren't respected!"

"Of course they weren't," said Scott. "And neither were those of Muslims and Croats."

Sanja shot him a wilting look. "How is shooting and killing and blowing things up respecting *anybody's* rights?"

"Hey, don't ask me! You're the one who brought up justice."

"I did, didn't I?" said Sanja, giving him a wry smile. "But how can there be justice when people are afraid of somebody with more power?"

"Ah, power," said Goran, shaking his head. "That's what it all boils down to."

"There can be power for good as well as power to dominate," Sanja argued . She leaned forward, excited by the discussion. "Is that what justice is about, Scott?"

He smiled at her. "You're asking me?"

She smiled back. "Of course. You're the lawyer."

He shrugged. "What reason do people have to fight if they know they'll get fair and equal treatment from whoever is governing them?"

"So they want justice from their government?"

"Sure," said Scott.

"But ..." Goran frowned and rubbed his ear lobe. "Sometimes fighting is caused by people who want power ... or want to keep it."

Sanja was surprised to hear that comment coming from her brother; it sounded like something their father might say.

Scott answered, "To me, justice means taking power away from those who abuse it. And that can't succeed unless people promote it."

"By having elections and making laws," Goran put in eagerly.

"By electing *decent* politicians and making *good* laws," Sanja corrected.

Scott chuckled. "You're more of an idealist than I am," he told her. "But I'm also a realist. I know that no system is perfect, and the best any of us can do is to keep trying to make it better. That's why I come to Bosnia to help with elections."

"And we're glad you're here," said Goran.

"Well, actually I ... all of us ... get more out of it than we give. We meet such terrific people. Tonight for instance and being with you two." Scott may have meant both of them, but his eyes were on Sanja.

Goran noticed the look. It was apparent that the conversation wasn't going to end soon, and it was also apparent they didn't need him. He stood up and said, "That's it for me. Sani, are you seeing Hanna off tomorrow morning?"

"No, she says she'll sleep till the very last minute, so we've said our goodbyes." It was disappointing knowing that Scott, too, would be boarding the bus to return home.

But Goran said, "Scott's going to spend a few extra days traveling around."

Sanja's pounding heart told her she wished he would stay in Bijeljina, but she knew that would never happen. "Oh, where?" she said lightly.

He tilted his head and looked at her thoughtfully. "I'm ... not sure. How about meeting me in my hotel lobby tomorrow, and we'll talk about it over breakfast."

After Goran left, Scott and Sanja moved inside. As he settled himself on the sofa, he asked, "Why was Goran uncomfortable when I mentioned Amela and the IPTF job?"

"Oh, that." Sanja explained about the childhood friendship, the wartime separation, Amela's return, and their reconciliation. "She's in Tuzla now."

"You'll have a lot to talk about when she gets back." Scott was referring to the election jobs, but Sanja knew they'd spend a lot of time talking about *him*.

As they talked, their words tumbled over one another.

Scott described his country—Cape Cod's fishing villages; San Francisco's Chinatown; Washington's monuments; and the Mississippi River with his special favorite, jazz. Sanja talked about her country—its ancient bridges, glorious mountains, the 1984 Olympics, folk music and dance. They confessed to childhood mischief—she to tormenting Dina with bugs; he to carelessly setting a shed on fire. Sanja felt that at last she'd found a man she could share her special thoughts with, who considered her ideas and laughed with her.

The hall clock chimed midnight, and someone could be heard moving around upstairs.

"Probably my mother," Sanja explained, as she saw Scott glance toward the entry stairs. "She's a light sleeper."

"Well, this isn't the best time to meet your parents—although I'd like to."

"Yes, I'd like that, too," said Sanja as she got up and followed him to the entry where he bent to put on his shoes. When he straightened, he moved toward her and took her in his arms. She pressed against him and returned his kiss.

"Tomorrow?" he asked.

"Tomorrow."

CHAPTER
25

When Sanja arrived at Scott's hotel the next morning, he was in the lobby waiting for her. He was dressed in black—jeans and tee shirt—and holding a black leather jacket.

"Well! Don't *you* look cool," she said.

"What, you didn't think a lawyer could be cool? We can also be hungry. Let's get something to eat."

Over breakfast he said, "There are so many places for me to see. Where would you go?"

"Me? I don't go anywhere. Well, I have wanted to go down the Drina Valley to visit my cousin Miroslava. Her husband was killed early in the war, and she got married again last month."

"The Drina Valley," he mused. "I'd like to see the bridge at Višegrad, the one in the novel by Ivo Andrić. Great book."

"Oh, you've read it," Sanja said, pleased.

After breakfast, they walked to the central market, which was thriving as usual early in the day. Sanja took Scott's hand to lead him along the crowded aisles. After a few minutes, they came to a stall full of hats … straw hats, felt hats, black berets, hats with flowers, caps with metal studs. Sanja picked out a bright purple hat with a swooping pink feather and settled it on her dark hair, tilting it at a rakish angle. Scott took down a hot pink boa, laughing as he draped it around her shoulders. Giggling, she returned the favor with a wide-brimmed straw hat whose loads of flowers drooped over the brim and tickled his nose.

"You look silly," she told him.

"And whose fault is that?" he teased.

Sanja removed the hat and smoothed his sand-brown hair.

He took the hat and perched it on Sanja's head. "It suits you better than me," he said.

She laughed. "How sweet of you to say so! But what I really need is a pair of sunglasses."

She finally decided on a sedate pair of glasses, which Scott bought for her, and then he bought her a second pair with wide, swooping cats-eye frames splashed with multi-colored sequins. He bought himself a pair of leather gloves.

"What are those for?" asked Sanja.

"Ah, that's my surprise. If my conversation with Goran this morning worked out, it should be waiting at your house when we get back there."

"It?" Sanja prodded, but Scott wouldn't say any more. A half hour later, they arrived at Sanja's.

"What's that?" she asked as they approached the house. "Is that the mysterious *it*? It has wheels and it's ... um ... orange ... or is that rust?"

"Hey, it's a beauty," said Scott. The small motorcycle Goran's mechanic friend had rented him was parked in front of the house. "Let's take her around the block to see how she handles."

Sanja looked dubious. She gave one of the tires a trial kick. "Do you want to push it or should I?"

Scott tossed his jacket aside, got on the bike, and waved to Sanja. "Where's your sense of adventure? C'mon," he said, revving the engine.

Sanja's sense of adventure was never in short supply. She

swung her leg over the seat and settled behind Scott. In spite of its questionable appearance, the bike roared its way around the block. As they cruised the neighborhood, Sanja wrapped her arms around Scott's waist and rested her cheek against his shoulder. She had never felt so contented.

"This is super," she said when they returned to her house. "Where are you planning to go?"

Scott grinned. "Make me some coffee and you can help me decide."

Over coffee at the kitchen table, Sanja studied a map, drawing her finger across the area west of Bijeljina. "Well, here are Doboj and Banja Luka and Prijedor ... but you don't want to go there," she said, repeating the words Rasim had used during the Krajina trip. "But you know what?" She drew her finger south along the Drina River valley. "This is where my cousin Miroslava lives. And here's Višegrad where the bridge is."

"Okay," Scott said. "We should be able to get there by suppertime."

"We?"

"Certainly. I need a tour guide, you know."

Sanja's head was spinning as she cleaned up the kitchen and waited anxiously for her mother to return from shopping. When Stefana came in, Sanja introduced Scott, expecting her mother's reaction to be cool appraisal followed by cold rejection. To her surprise, Stefana's attitude was pleasant. She agreed to the trip when Sanja said she had phoned Miroslava, and her cousin was excited about the visit.

"I'm envious as hell, but have a great time," said Goran, who was on his way to Belgrade.

Sanja named the motorcycle *Narandžasti Đavo*, christening

it with a few drops of tap water. "That means Orange Demon," she told Scott.

They rode south, arriving at dusk, and were greeted by Miroslava and her new husband, who had also been married before. His two small daughters immediately vied for Scott's attention. During the two-day visit, he took them each for short rides on the bike, and he and Sanja played what Scott called "tag" and "keep-away" with them.

The second afternoon, Sanja and Scott found a picnic spot in a small grassy area that Miroslava said was safe. They spread a blanket and enjoyed the food Sanja's cousin had prepared.

"What will you tell your American friends about this trip?" Sanja asked.

"I'll say I was spirited away by a wood nymph."

"Oh, good!" she said. "One who could weave spells and who adored frogs and turned you into one."

"And then kissed me, and turned me back into a prince," said Scott. "Try it and see if it works."

That evening, Miroslava's husband played music—Serbian, American, and a variety of others. Scott danced the fast songs with the girls and the slow, romantic ones with Sanja. The girls and Miroslava said they were heartbroken that their visitors had to leave. Sanja, too, would have liked the visit to be longer.

Scott got his wish to go to Višegrad where they had lunch and then held hands as they leaned on the wall of the arched sixteenth–century bridge.

"I didn't think it was my place to mention Miroslava's husband and sons," Scott said.

Sanja nodded. "Yes, I couldn't stop thinking about them. They were slaughtered early in the war. Miroslava and I did talk about them. She still has nightmares—like I've had about

Mirko. She'll always be sad and miss them, but her new life is very satisfying. She'll never trust Muslims, though. She knows about my friendship with Amela and accepts it … for me. But she doesn't ever want to meet her."

Sanja gazed at the swift-flowing water of the Drina River for a few minutes, then she said, "Well! We'd better be going. Do you think the *Orange Demon* will get us back to Bijeljina?"

"If it doesn't start, it's fate," Scott replied, squeezing her hand. "We were meant to spend the rest of our lives on Andrić's bridge."

Sanja grimaced. "Oh, please!"

But the *Orange Demon* did start, and they headed north again, returning to Bijeljina in the evening.

Scott dropped Sanja off and went to his hotel to bathe and change clothes. Although he had to leave at dawn the next morning, he eagerly agreed to spend the evening at the house, where Sanja's parents had prepared a barbecue on the front porch. She grinned at her father and Scott as they exchanged traditional, but limited, plum brandy toasts. It helped that her father could manage English fairly well. For her mother, she translated. It was past midnight when Stefana and Petar went upstairs. Sanja was glad they had all gotten along well, but she was happy to have Scott to herself.

She made coffee, and they sat comfortably in the parlor and talked. He never seemed to tire of hearing about her life.

"Sorry I couldn't meet Amela," he said.

"Me, too. She's spending a few days in Tuzla with her family. You'd like her," Sanja told him. "She's clever and pretty. She's not like me. I'm impulsive, Amela's careful; I can be impatient, Amela never is; when I get mad, everybody knows it, but if Amela gets mad, she simmers. Well, except one time." Sanja told Scott about the day Amela had come to the house and forced a showdown.

"That settled it. Now she's my best friend forever. There's no one I admire more than Amela," she said. "Is there somebody you admire ... somebody famous or in history?"

A person he admired? He searched for a name.

"I don't know … uh … Aristotle? King Arthur? Okay. Maybe Hank Aaron."

"Who's that?"

"Homerun king. Baseball. Then there's Thomas Jefferson," Scott said. "There's a quote of his I like. It's inscribed inside his memorial in Washington."

"What is it? Tell me," Sanja urged.

"It goes: *I have sworn upon the altar of God eternal hostility against every form of tyranny over the mind of man.*"

Sanja ran the English words carefully through her mind. "I like that," she said.

"And you, Sanja; somebody you admire?"

She smiled. "I suppose many Serbs would say Prince Lazar. But, I think Joan of Arc," she admitted, "not because she was a saint, but because she was bold and was faithful to what she believed in."

"That doesn't surprise me. You were bold and faithful when you went to Krajina. You told me some of the story over dinner and a little more on our trip, but I'd like to hear the rest."

"Sometimes I get upset thinking about it, so I don't very often ... think about it."

Scott shook his head. "Then you don't have to …"

"No, I want to tell you," she assured him. "I told you the story up to when the truck broke down and we were hopelessly stranded by the side of the road."

Sanja went on to tell Scott about Miloš and Vesna who'd found them there. As she described the driving, the soldiers, Miloš being beaten, women being raped, children spouting hateful words—she began pacing. Reliving the tension was even more emotional than she expected. Scott, who had been on Bosnia's mountain roads, could understand the panic an inexperienced driver would feel, but there was no way Sanja could convey the rest, the misery and horror. She went on to describe her grandmother's courage, Vesna's devastation, Rasim's compassion. She dropped onto the sofa and started to cry.

"I'm sorry," she said, her voice wobbly.

Scott moved over to her and took her in his arms. "Hey, don't be, Sani," he said, stroking her hair. "It's okay. Go ahead and cry."

Always before, she had stopped herself when her feelings of sadness or anger had threatened to overwhelm her. This time she just let go.

Scott continued to hold her, murmuring soothing words and stroking her cheek. He gently pushed aside a lock of her hair and kissed her tenderly. Then he was holding her tighter, and kissing her neck, her throat, her mouth. His touch sent rivers of fire through her, and she clung to him, returning his kisses, reveling in an explosion of feelings.

He slipped his hand under her shirt and felt the smooth skin of her back. "I want more," he murmured.

"So do I," she responded.

The clock chimed four, and they drew apart. "Good Lord!" said Scott. "We've been talking all night!"

"Talking?"

He laughed. "Well, I think I remember talking, but that wasn't the best part."

Sanja ran her fingers through her hair and swiped at her mascara-smudged eyes. "I must look like a sewer rat," she moaned.

Scott held her at arm's length and studied her. "Nonsense. You're a stunning creature."

It was Sanja's turn to laugh. "And you said you believe in honesty. When does your bus leave?"

"At six. I've got to go," Scott said. At the front door, he pulled on his shoes.

"Scott." Sanja paused. She needed to find the right words. "Tonight when I was sad, you were so caring and you comforted me."

He straightened and moved toward her, drawing her close and kissing her as if he never wanted to stop. But they both knew he had to go to the hotel … to the bus … to the airplane … home, to America.

"Sani, I don't want to leave you, but I have to," he whispered. "But something special has happened to me, and I'm not going to let go of it. I'll call you as soon as I get home."

She stroked his cheek. "I'll wait for your call."

They exchanged a desperate look. There was so much to say and no time to say it.

"You will write to me, won't you?" Scott asked.

"Of course I will," she promised.

He turned and went out into the morning.

How could he leave her! This was what she'd been missing, someone she could share her dreams with.

Sanja started to gather the coffee cups, then stopped and smiled. In the last few days so many doors had opened. She'd found the beginnings of a life. Was it too much to hope that she'd also found a future?

CHAPTER
26

When Sanja woke at noon, she immediately called Amela. "I'm glad you're back. We need to meet. There's so much to talk about."

"Come to my house," said Amela. "It's a nice day and we can sit outside. I'm tired of trips to the memorial."

A half hour later, Sanja joined Amela on her front step.

"Oh-oh," Amela said as soon as she saw her friend. "You met someone. The glow's blinding me. So give. An interpreter? Do I know him?"

"A supervisor. An American," Sanja replied. Just saying it out loud was exhilarating.

When Sanja finished telling about Scott, Amela's response was immediate and enthusiastic. "You're in love!"

Sanja hadn't put her feelings into words, certainly not those words. Was she? She had never been in love, so how would she know? When she closed her eyes, the memories were so clear—Scott's smile, how good he smelled, the strength of his shoulders as she clung to him on the motorcycle. She had been sublimely happy in his arms. She thought of his kisses, sometimes gentle, sometimes urgent, and she trembled remembering. But it was more than that. Just as fiercely she longed for his thoughtfulness, his intelligence, his humor. He had brought her joy, but he hadn't said he loved her.

Amela couldn't keep her amusement to herself. "All this ecstasy from ... uh ..."

"Talking," said Sanja sternly. "We talked about *everything!*" Sanja felt her face grow warm. "Well, there might have been a kiss or two," she added grinning.

"And you tried desperately to fight him off, but failing, accepted a passionate romance as your fate." Amela was enjoying Sanja's giddiness. "So how was it? The kissing."

Sanja closed her eyes, remembering. "Divine."

"It sounds like he loves you, too," Amela said gently. Then she grabbed Sanja's hands and danced her around the yard. They giggled like twelve-year-olds, as if all the intervening years of misery had never been. At last they settled back down on the step to share their election experiences.

"I've gotten a lot more out of the last week than just stories," said Sanja.

Amela shot her a grin. "I guess so," she said. "The love of your life."

"Well ..." Sanja said, smiling, "but I mean even more than that. Like more confidence."

"And helping our country," Amela added. "And making new friends. I can't wait to hear about Scott's call."

Sanja tried to still her jitters. She knew it took many hours to travel by bus to Croatia, and then many more hours to fly across a continent and an ocean, plus there was the time difference between Washington and Bijeljina. Scott had said it might be as late as ten o'clock before he could call. Even so, for the next two days, Sanja went out of her way to pass the phone, giving it a pat, coaxing it to ring.

After a dozen or so pats, she had a sudden, terrible thought.

If he called! Maybe he … maybe … She swallowed hard, wanting to purge her mind of the worry. Oh, he'd call. He *said* he'd call. She'd just have to be patient. "Or not be patient," she mumbled impatiently.

The second night, Sanja sat on the sofa with a book, staring at the pages, paying no attention to the words. Ten o'clock came, then eleven. At midnight Sanja had visions of lost glass slippers. Doubts began to pester her, stronger than before. Why would a handsome American lawyer be interested in her? Oh, maybe he'd enjoyed spending time with her, but once he was home, his life would go back to what it had been, and she would be forgotten. Maybe there was even a girl there he liked. Maybe he liked her a lot.

Stefana came downstairs and started into the kitchen just as the phone rang. Sanja's book hit the floor as she leaped up and raced to the entry, but Stefana got there first.

"It's for you," she said. "Your American friend," she added, tossing Sanja a curious look as she handed over the receiver and then went up the stairs. Sanja caught her breath. She was grateful that her mother's sense of honor didn't allow her to listen. With a shaking hand, she gripped the receiver. Scott's voice made her heart beat fast again.

"I miss being with you," he said.

During the next four weeks, they talked often and sent long letters. She wished they could email, but Sanja was seldom able to get to an internet café in Belgrade. Scott's call in mid-October brought news. The senior partner of his law firm belonged to a group that was interested in Bosnia. After Scott had given a talk about his experiences there, the group made a decision. They wanted to sponsor several Bosnian young people either in Bosnia or in the United States. Scott was so excited when he told Sanja about it, she could hardly understand him.

"Just slow down and tell me again. They want to sponsor somebody? What does that mean exactly?"

"It means they'll help get visas … and help with college enrollment, jobs. They'll pay school expenses and living expenses and find housing. Everything! Isn't that terrific?"

"Yes, it's terrific," said Sanja, trying to sound enthusiastic, yet casual. She couldn't imagine such a chance for herself or Goran, but she didn't want to say so.

"Sanja, you're not getting it. This is for you! They asked for names of qualified people. I recommended you and Goran and Amela. Somebody else who's been there knows another person. Now you'll need to write about your experience and why you'd want to do this, but it looks very promising! Then there's applying for school and visas … my dad can probably help with those. You'll need passports and…" Scott scarcely paused for a breath, "… I'll be a reference for Goran, and you have Hanna's recommendation letter."

"Scott, slow down. I can't believe this. I'm in shock!"

"I'm sending you an email tomorrow. Can you pick it up?"

"Yes! Yes! We'll go to Belgrade and definitely pick it up!"

After the phone call, it took Sanja days to come back down to earth. As soon as she, Goran, and Amela could manage it, they followed Scott's instructions and started the necessary paperwork, which they faxed to him.

"I've passed along the information you sent," Scott told Sanja a few days later. "I'm leaving tomorrow for two conferences, so I may not get a chance to call you for a couple weeks."

Sanja missed Scott's calls. His two letters were disappointingly short, but on an overcast day an envelope arrived with his law firm's return address. Sanja stared at it as if she'd found it at the bottom of a rabbit hole. What, exactly, did the envelope contain?

Goran wasn't around and Sanja needed somebody to talk to. Showing up unexpectedly on Amela's doorstep was not something she'd ordinarily do, but there was little lately that was ordinary.

Thinking of Scott, Sanja's mind was a continent and an ocean away. As she approached Amela's house, she didn't notice the bully until they were almost face-to-face. He played a hip-hop game, trying to force her to one side of the walk or the other. Remembering how he had threatened Amela at the church, she said, her voice low and menacing, "Get lost, you pervert."

He looked surprised, then with a pathetic laugh and a rude gesture, he walked on by. *Blast him*, she thought. Another time she'd have yelled at him, but not today. She had something much more important to do. Still fuming, she crossed the street, and as she reached Amela's walk, her thoughts returned to the reason she was there. She was tapping her foot impatiently when Amela opened the door.

"Oh, my goodness!" Amela said in surprise. She ushered Sanja inside, took her jacket, and waited while she slipped off her shoes and put on the slippers Amela held out to her.

"I'm happy to see you," said Amela, "but what's urgent enough to have you dancing on my doorstep?"

"I've got to talk to you," said Sanja, waving the large white envelope in Amela's face.

"Sure. I'll make coffee."

Sanja knew better than to circumvent established custom, but she fretted while Amela got the coffee grinder and set the liquid to heat.

"I got this envelope," Sanja announced, placing it on the table. "Did you get one?"

"No. Is it from Scott?" Amela asked.

"It has the law firm's return address," Sanja replied, twisting her hands nervously. "I don't know what's inside."

"And you want *me* to open it?" said Amela. "If Scott wrote you a love letter, should I read it? And answer it, too? And be as sappy as you would be?" she teased.

"Of course not."

"Well, Sani, he's called you often enough, and set a pretty amazing plan in motion. So why is this letter a big deal all of a sudden?"

"Because he's been away and I haven't talked to him for over a week. Because it's an envelope with the law firm's address. Because what if they've changed their mind? Or he has. What if he's writing to say it's not going to happen or he doesn't want me … us … to come? I'll have heart failure."

Amela sighed. "And if he's writing to say he wants you to come?"

Sanja took a deep breath. "I'll have heart failure."

Amela took the little coffee pot off the stove. "And I thought I was the skittish one," she mumbled.

"But this is different," Sanja protested. "He's from a foreign country thousands of miles away and he's amazing and what if he doesn't still like me?"

Amela had never seen Sanja, the brave one, the strong one, the unflusterable one, so . . . well, flustered. She just couldn't hold back a broad grin.

Amela set the coffee cups and the sugar bowl and a plate of cookies on the table, sat down, and reached out her hand. "Give me that," she said. She reached for a knife, slit the envelope, took out a letter, then handed it to Sanja. "Will you *please* just read the letter?" Then she added with an impish grin, "I dare you!"

"You're not allowed to dare me," Sanja pouted. With shaking hands, she took the letter. It was written on the stationery of Scott's law firm with an impressive logo at the top. She laid the letter, face down, on the table and took a sip of coffee as she tried to steady her nerves.

"Sanja ..." Amela prompted gently.

The letter wasn't from Scott, but from someone in the firm on behalf of the sponsoring group. It was full of information about the business group's agreement. Sanja gave a whoop of joy. She read aloud details about the sponsorship, including when and where Scott would meet the three of them in December. The three of them! That meant that Goran and Amela would receive similar information. With a broad smile, Sanja passed the letter to her.

Inside the envelope was a smaller one with a personal note from Scott that read, *Hurray! It's definite! I'm excited! You remember I'm going to conferences out west—Will call you when I get back. Can't wait to see you!* It was signed, *Love, Scott.*

"Oh!" cried Sanja, clutching the note to her heart. She read it to Amela.

"Oh, Sani! No matter how much I'll miss you, I want you to go."

"You've been accepted, too."

Amela shook her head. "I know, but I'm not going anywhere till I know something about my father. But you can't pass this up. You'll have a life at last."

"I understand about your father, really I do," Sanja said, "but I want you to have a life, too." Suddenly, they were presented with more opportunities and challenges than either of them knew how to handle.

Amela was thoughtful for a moment, then said, dreamily, "America. Imagine."

"My nerves get jiggly just thinking about it," said Sanja.

Amela had avoided asking one question. "Sani, have you told your parents?"

The glow went out of Sanja's eyes. "No, not yet. We—Goran and I—thought we should wait until we were pretty sure it was going to happen."

"What will they do?"

"Our father will be happy we've gotten such a lucky break. Our mother will freak." Sanja was sure of it. "But I'm going, Amela. Just like I went to Krajina."

"You'll do it, Sani, because you're strong and because you deserve the best."

"Well, the next person I'll tell is Ivana when we go to the disco tonight. She'd never leave here, but she'll think my going is a wonderful adventure. Are you sure you don't want to go to the disco? I know it isn't really your style, but you could use some fun."

"Thanks for the offer, but no. I'm not brave enough or foolish enough to go clubbing in this town. Besides, I don't mind staying home with a good book."

"Okay," Sanja said. "So, have you heard any more about jobs since our election work?"

"Not a regular job, but I did get two days of work with the IPTF next week. Tim's so nice. Now if *he* weren't married … Anyway," she said, "Tim's trying to get me a long-term job in Sarajevo. He says I might convince Mama it's easier to get missing person information there than here. I'll have him to thank if my life takes another turn for the better."

Sanja stared at the ceiling, wondering whether she should

break a promise. She decided if there was ever a time, this was it. "Do you know who gave Tim your name and recommended you?"

"It must have been Dragan. He's legend. He's done so much for my family."

"Well, no, it wasn't Dragan." Sanja hesitated.

"Really? Wait! Do you know who it was? How do you know? I owe him … or her? Ivana?"

"It wasn't Ivana. It was Goran."

Amela felt as if the wind had been knocked out of her. "Are you *sure*?"

Sanja stood up to leave, giving her stunned friend a hug. "Yes, I'm sure," she said, pleased. "And thanks for being a friend when I need one."

On her way home she glanced at the precious envelope from the law firm and smiled. It wasn't the letter and the packet of information in it—marvelous though it was—that made her heart race. It was Scott's note inside, the note signed, "Love, Scott."

CHAPTER
27

Later that night, Sanja met Ivana on the corner. "Ready to party?" she asked her friend as they walked into the disco.

Ivana grinned. "Always."

It was predictably noisy and crowded. As they worked their way to a small table at the back, Sanja peered through the cloud of smoke to see whom she knew there. Seated, and with their orders placed, Ivana took out a cigarette and ceremoniously lit it.

"I know you don't want one, Sani. You're so different." She laughed and blew smoke across the table.

Sanja laughed, too. "It's my fate. I've never been like everyone else."

"And that's exactly why I like hanging out with you."

"Your new dress is *très chic*, Ivana."

"Something to spend my IPTF pay on. I also got the latest Madonna video."

"Oh, I want to see it," Sanja exclaimed. "Maybe I can squeeze a little out of what I saved from my interpreter job to buy a video by Vlado."

"You're pretty secretive about your earnings. Just what are you saving for?"

Sanja had saved money for university and maybe a little travel. Somewhere. Now somewhere was America, and it would be for whatever she needed now that Scott's plan was working out.

"Has Goran heard about the job in Austria?" Ivana asked. "So many friends are sending money from abroad to their families."

"No," said Sanja. "Nothing about Austria."

"There's plenty of money in Bijeljina, you know."

"If you're in the right business," Sanja acknowledged. "Or know the right people. But prices are sky high."

"I'm lucky," said Ivana. "My IPTF guys keep me in cigarettes."

"Any special guy?"

"Are you kidding? I'm playing the field. What about you? Is Scott still calling?"

"Oh, yes." Sanja was sure her face would give away her feelings, so she told Ivana about Scott and his plan.

By the time she'd finished, Ivana was wide-eyed and speechless. "He's so good-looking!" she exclaimed. Education and work opportunities were fine, but for Ivana, nothing was better than a good-looking man. "And you could go to university in America?" Ivana asked.

"Yes, and Goran, too."

"I just can't believe how lucky you are! But I wish you'd leave Goran here."

"Don't tell anybody, please," Sanja said. "This may not work out. But what do you think?"

"Sani, you surely don't need to ask! It's fantastic! An adventure!" She reached for the ashtray and rested her cigarette. "Hey, Sani, isn't that Ranko in the corner?"

Sanja glanced behind her. "You mean the one crawling all over that girl? Yes, I think it is."

A friend of Sanja's came to lead her onto the jammed dance floor, and she easily slipped into the pleasure of laughing, joking, and dancing. She was standing near the bar when she heard her name.

"Sanja, my lovely."

She turned her head, recognizing Ranko's smooth voice. She was sure he'd had too much to drink.

"Go away, Rado."

He looked at her with bloodshot puppy-dog eyes, and begged, "Be nice to me, Sani."

She swallowed the words she wanted to say. Because he'd always been a friend, she tried not to be too smart with him, but he did irritate her sometimes. When he had driven her to Krajina three years earlier, he had been more fun and less annoying. Lately he seemed always to be moody and too often drunk.

"Don't you have a girlfriend?" she asked.

He dismissed his girlfriend with a jerk of his head. "She's out there. How about a turn, Sani?"

"Thanks, but I've nearly worn out my shoes. I'll pass this time."

"Nah, you won't." He grabbed her arm and pulled her along with him, threading his way to the middle of the square. "Ah, beautiful lady, you smell so good."

Sanja huffed her annoyance, but decided it was better to go along with it than cause a scene. He wasn't yet so drunk he was unsteady, but he was on the way. Even so, she was tempted to walk away and leave him. Then an arm reached past her to tap Ranko on the shoulder.

"I'll take over from here, Sani," her brother said.

"Super. I'm your damsel in distress."

"I'm your knight in shining armor," Goran called over his

shoulder as he steered Ranko toward a table.

"A scary thought," she murmured. She returned to the bar where she joined Ivana who had a sour look.

"He's here," she said. "That idiot from work who I dumped last week. The one who's got a wife and three kids back in Pizza or wherever he's from. He wanted me to dance with him and I said no."

"Good for you."

Sanja's attention was caught by a man's voice. He was behind her, but speaking close to her ear. "... too many Turks in this town and some people are cozy with them. Traitors had better watch out."

Sanja turned and saw a man not much taller than she. He had a florid complexion and heavy features. Beside him, leering, was the bully from Amela's neighborhood. Another guy who Sanja didn't know completed the odious trio.

Ivana nudged Sanja to get her attention. "The idiot just winked at me," she said. "Let's leave. I don't like the men here."

After what she'd just overheard, Sanja had to agree.

"Do you want to troll for a bit?" asked Ivana. "A couple of the girls said they might."

"You go with them. I think I'll just go home." She waved goodnight to a friend who had bought her a beer, and said to Ivana, "Will you tell Goran I've left? He's over there with Ranko."

Sanja picked up her jacket and walked to the door.

"She'd better listen. I meant what I said," the man told his friends. "Bad things can happen to Turk lovers."

Sanja didn't hear the comment, but Ivana did. The man set his drink on the bar and headed for the door. Ivana was alarmed. She started to follow, accidentally bumping the arm of the bully as he reached for his beer. He grabbed her arm and gave her a dirty look before turning back to the girl next to him. But it was not the bully Ivana was concerned about. The man whose remark had frightened her was gone.

She didn't know what to do. If the man meant trouble, she should warn her friend, but Sanja had already left. Ivana spun around to get Goran. He was gone. So was Ranko. It wasn't a big place, but it was crowded. Ivana set out to find them.

Sanja had left the disco steaming over the man's nasty remarks. What an insufferable jerk! As if she was going to let some hate-spewing fool pick her friends for her. It wasn't late, not yet midnight, when she crossed the bridge over the canal. Walking briskly in the cold November night, her anger was gradually soothed. She thought, as she had before, how ironic it was that Bosnia had suffered a war and ethnic violence, yet the nighttime streets were still safe and free of street crime.

Sanja approached the corner of her street. She had always liked her neighborhood with its mix of homes and small shops. She was about to cross the street when she felt a presence behind her. Strong arms grabbed her from behind, spun her away from the street and shoved her against a building, pressing her face against the wall. Her assailant was not much taller than she, but he was much, much stronger. Every nerve in her body throbbed. Sanja felt like a trapped insect.

The prick of a knife on her neck made her grow rigid. It wouldn't take more than a flick of his wrist to pierce her neck. She wanted to scream, but her throat had closed up.

"So, Turk lover." The malice in the man's voice was like the sting of a snake bite. "You betray your people. You choose to play with a barbarian Muslim. A bad choice," he hissed.

He moved the knife down, sliding it under her jacket where she could feel its sharp edge pressing against her side. "Maybe I'll hurt you or maybe I'll just let you deliver a message to that Balija slut. Or maybe I'll do both."

Sanja was desperate. She lifted her heel and slammed it down on his foot. His knife arm slackened. She pulled her arm free and swung with all her might. She felt the vibration shimmy up her arm as her fist made contact with his nose. He loosened his grip, howling in pain. She twisted away and turned to run, but she wasn't quick enough. His hand closed around her arm. He slammed her back against the building. She looked into eyes that glittered with hatred.

"You'll pay for that," he snarled. He turned his head slightly, saying, "Get us inside this shop."

When he spoke, Sanja realized that someone else was there. She got a quick glimpse of the guy from the disco—not the bully, but the other one. She heard glass break. Her attacker gave her arm a painful twist as he dragged her inside. When he backed her up against a display case, she saw that his nose was bleeding. Her flash of satisfaction was brief. His backhand stung her cheek. Her teeth cut into her lip and she tasted blood. A second blow with his fist snapped her head sideways. Sanja was still reeling when she felt again the cold blade against her neck.

The other man was by the open door. He said, "When you finish with her, I get a turn."

"Shut up!" the man holding Sanja growled. "That's not what we're here for." Putting his face close, he said to her, "Now about your loyalties ..."

A noise by the door made him turn his head. Sanja heard thumps, grunts.

She stumbled as her attacker was wrenched away from her. The knife dropped at her feet with a clatter. She watched as the man was dragged outside, past his partner who lay motionless on the floor. A shadowy figure flung him, face down, then gave him a savage kick. He rolled and lay still on the pavement. Sanja's rescuer slammed his boot again into the man's ribs. The man cried out. His cheek rested on the pavement, and in the dim light Sanja could see the fear in his eyes. Now *he* was the trapped insect.

The face of the man who had rescued her was still in deep shadow. Then he spoke.

"Go home, Sani."

"Ranko?"

"Go."

CHAPTER 28

Somehow Sanja managed to get her legs going. When she got to her house, she fumbled to open the front door, then collapsed on the floor of the entry. She huddled against the wall, shaking violently and trying to quiet her moans.

She had no idea how long she was there, curled into a ball in the silent dark. Then Goran came in and started up the stairs. He'd reached the third step when he stopped.

"Sivi?" he called softly. "Do you want out?" He went back down to the entry and switched on the light.

"Turn it off," Sanja said, her hands covering her face.

"Sani? What are you doing there?"

"Turn the damned light off, Goran!"

He was used to ignoring Sanja's orders, but this time he obeyed. He sat down on the floor beside her and cradled her in his arms.

"Hey, you're shivering. And your hands are like ice. Sani, what's wrong?"

She leaned against his shoulder and shook her head. She expected him to demand answers, but instead he waited patiently for her to speak. He hadn't yet seen her face, which throbbed painfully. She finally began her story, but before she'd finished it, he got to his feet and turned on the light. When he looked down at her she heard his sharp intake of breath. She could feel fury radiating from him like heat.

"No, wait," she pleaded, pulling him back down beside her. "There's more. Ranko came." Her mouth was swollen; it was hard for her to get the words out. "He saved me. If he hadn't … shown up, I don't know what … would have happened." She shuddered. The foul scent of her attacker lingered on her clothes. "Don't leave me," she begged.

Gently Goran touched his sister's bloody lip and bruised cheek. He was silent for a few minutes, then said, "You're sure about what the man said? About Turks?"

She gave an emphatic nod.

He leaned back, rubbing his earlobe, thinking. "So it was retaliation for your being friends with Amela and a warning," he said. "Word's gotten around … to the wrong people."

"Wrong people?" Sanja spoke slowly. "Goran, this is the town we grew up in. What's changed?"

"Bullies have more power to be bullies."

Sanja slumped against him. She felt heavy, like her blood was thick.

He gently wiped away a tear that trickled down her cheek. "Don't cry, baby sister," he said. "Somehow it'll all work out."

"Do we have to tell Papa? Or worse, Mama?"

Goran wrapped his arms tighter around her. "I'm not even sure we should tell Papa," he said softly, "but one look at you …"

It was a useless worry because their mother was already on her way down the stairs.

"What's going on here?" Stefana demanded. She hovered above them, growing more and more rigid as the story was told.

"Sanja, you know the Muslims can't be trusted, yet you

deliberately sought that girl's company. How can you blame Serbs for protecting their community and their loved ones? You've brought this on yourself."

"Mama!" Sanja said, shocked.

And then her father spoke. He had come down the stairs so quietly no one had heard him.

"Stefana, Sanja is not to blame," he said wearily. "A violent person attacked our daughter. He's the one to blame. And in a way, you and I are, too. We've given our children a rotten world to live in. I only hope they can sort out the mess."

He reached out and helped Sanja to her feet, then kissed her cheeks and said, "Goran, fix an ice pack. Sanja, get some sleep. We'll deal with this in the morning." Then he turned and went back upstairs.

Stefana shook her head. "Bijeljina used to be so nice," she said. Then she glared at her daughter and said tightly, "You're not to leave this house." Then she stormed back up the stairs.

Sanja and Goran exchanged looks.

"Cover your eyes and don't solve the problem," Goran muttered. "You and I will be leaving, Sani. Soon."

"No." She put her fingers on his lips to stop him from speaking. He'd try to cheer her up, convince her that life was the same today as it had been yesterday. But it wasn't. Hopes and dreams had been swept away in a few terrifying minutes. She hadn't wanted to cry, but couldn't choke back the tears.

"Don't you understand?" she asked. "It's over. Scott will never … He'll think … Scott will think we're savages." She covered her tear-stained cheeks with her hands. "And … you know something? Maybe we are."

CHAPTER 29

Amela had been up barely a half hour the next morning when she heard a knock at her front door. She was amazed to see Goran there. He looked troubled.

"Sanja needs you," he said.

"Why? What's happened?"

"Do we have to stand here in your doorway?"

Amela was astounded. Goran, usually confident almost to the point of arrogance, was fidgeting. "Come in then," she said.

He stepped into the entry, but still seemed uncomfortable. "My car's out front. Can we go for a drive? There's something I need to tell you."

"About Sanja?" Now *she* was getting nervous.

"Sanja was attacked last night. She's okay," he added quickly.

Amela's eyes grew wide. "What happened?" She shivered, remembering her experience at the church.

"Amela?" Hanifa called. "Would you bring me my knitting?"

"Right away," Amela replied. In her shock, she had forgotten that her mother was upstairs. Goran was right. His car would be a better place to talk. "Let me get my mother's knitting," she said, "and then I'll be right out."

Goran drove toward the outskirts of town in silence. Amela waited for him to speak. Finally her patience snapped, and she said, "Are you going to tell me what happened?"

He told the story, his voice strained, as he struggled to stay calm. When he said the man had called Sanja a Turk lover, Amela buried her face in her hands.

"It's my fault!" she cried. "I've been stupid … and selfish."

Goran looked grim. "It's *not* your fault. And not Sanja's either. There are a few rotten bastards in town. You can't blame yourselves for what they do."

"Maybe not, but there are more than a few, and it only takes one to kill you!"

"Look, I'm not trying to make light of what happened. It shook me up, too. Our father's talking to the police today."

Goran and his father might believe the police would help, but Amela didn't. The so-called investigation into the house fire had gone nowhere.

"Sanja's in danger," Amela moaned, "because we wanted to be friends again. Since when is friendship threatening to people?"

It was a question Goran didn't want to answer.

Halfway to the Majevica Range, he turned off onto a dirt track. Amela suddenly realized where they were.

"This is the way to the weekend house we used to have," she said. "We stayed out here that night, you know. The night …"

Goran cursed. "I know which night you mean. God! Can't we ever get past the war! All I want to do is have a decent life, and the damned war keeps getting in the way!"

"I know," she agreed. "Goran, the house … It's just past the village. Could we stop there? Please?"

"That's why we came this way. Sani said you wanted to go there sometime. I didn't think you'd been yet."

Amela didn't reply. She was intent on watching for her house. Thoughts of the past temporarily overrode those of the present. She ached as she thought of the fruit trees her father had tended and the vegetable garden her mother had nursed along. She remembered playing cards with Dina and tag with Sejo. She and Sanja had picked wildflowers and even weeds, honoring them with flower-like names. Some of her happiest childhood memories were of this place—and some of the worst when her childhood ended abruptly at twelve.

"There," she said, pointing. "That's it on the ... Oh!" She gaped at the building, or what was left of it. It looked like it had been burned. Only stubs of walls remained. Weeds and scrubby growth had overrun the yard.

They got out of the car. Dazed, Amela started to move toward the shell of her former home. Goran grabbed her arm. "Let's not repeat that scene with the mine," he begged.

"Oh. Right," she said. Her voice sounded far off. She stood as if turned to stone, looking with horror at the remains of her house. "It's ... it's ... gone," she finished lamely. "Just like ... just like ..." She sank to the ground, swallowing her tears.

"... just like your father," Goran finished for her, frowning.

Amela said, "Yes." She drew a long breath and stood up. She shuddered, then forced herself to speak briskly as she turned toward the car. "Let's go."

Back on the road, she determined to put the destroyed house out of her mind. There were more immediate problems to deal with. She said, "We need to talk about Sanja. What's she going to do? She isn't safe in town. That is, if your mother ever lets her out of the house again."

Goran's frown deepened. "One incident can't rule your life," he said. "But, that's not the real problem. This has made her feel guilty or ... I don't know ... humiliated. She says she won't ever talk to Scott again, and she won't let me tell him what happened. She's mortified; she thinks she's not ... not worthy ... or something."

"Not ...? Oh, Goran! That's ridiculous!"

"She says he'll think we're all savages."

Amela ran her hand through her hair in utter frustration. "Tell me we aren't," she groaned. "Tell me the war was just a civilized way of settling our differences."

"War brings out the best and the worst in people," said Goran. "And Sanja knows that, she's just all twisted up."

"So, we need to get her untwisted."

"Yeah, but she's also a prisoner. Mama plans to ship her off to relatives in Belgrade."

"No! She can't go to Belgrade! You realize that Scott's expecting her in America in just over four weeks."

Goran nodded. "I knew I'd have to maneuver Mama into letting us go then. Now I have to maneuver Sanja out sooner. Amela, I need your help with Sanja."

"Glad you didn't ask me to help with your mother."

"Well, Mama's gonna have to give in on this one," he said, sounding resolute. "Anyway, Sanja's had practice leaving. She took off for our grandmother while our mother was sputtering, 'Get back in here.'"

"Yeah, that's the spirit she needs to get back. Just when we thought life was getting better, all this new trouble," Amela said, disgusted. "You're still going to America, right?"

"Definitely. If Scott can get me into college and a job, it'll turn my life around. Sarajevo ... America. Anywhere. I love my sister, but I'm not about to give up this chance."

"You can't give it up," Amela urged him. "At least one of you will get a better life."

"And you, Amela. You can still go."

"I don't know. My family has been suspended for so long

waiting for news about my father, it's like I'm stalled." And now, she thought, what if Sanja didn't go? But she must!

"Don't just throw away the chance, Amela," Goran continued. "Are you worried about your mother? How would you tell her?"

"Oh, I could say that it's the only way I can save my soul—to get out of this wretched place where memories are sour and thoughts of the future are bitter. I could tell her I'm only going for a little while, that I'll be able to get work and send money home so she can fix up a house for me to come back to."

"You'd come back?" asked Goran.

"I don't know. Certainly not to Bijeljina." She was silent for a moment, then said, "Right now we have to focus on Sanja."

They drove the rest of the way in silence. When she got out of the car, she turned to Goran with a worried look. "Scott will be calling soon—maybe tomorrow."

"I know," said Goran, sounding dismal. "If she'll just talk to him. There's no doubt he's crazy about her."

Amela agreed. "She's being completely ridiculous. She's unreasonable and stubborn. She just won't listen!"

"Who? Sani?" was Goran's mocking response. "Ridiculous, unreasonable, stubborn? You can't mean *my* sister!"

Amela was at her wit's end. "So Scott doesn't know about the attack."

"No."

"What are you going to tell him when he calls?" she asked.

"I'm going to be in complete defiance of Sanja's orders and tell him everything. Then it's up to him. Listen," he said, "I'll get my sister out of the house if I have to wrap her in a rug and carry her out over my shoulder. I'll bring her here tonight … or sooner if I can."

"I'll try to reason with her," said Amela without conviction.

She couldn't relax. She paced from the kitchen to the parlor and back again. She was staring out the front window when Goran's car drove up. Sanja got out. Amela raced to meet her.

"Oh, Sani! Your face," she cried.

"I brought heavy makeup," Sanja said, sounding shaky.

They held each other close as Sanja gave way to a storm of tears. It seemed to Amela that their lives, which had recently shown such hope, were falling apart again. Goran watched with deep concern, then turned to leave.

"I'd better get back to the house and deal with our mother," he said, managing a resigned smile. "That won't be easy once she finds out her prisoner's escaped. Anyway, you two have a lot to talk about."

Amela led Sanja inside, wincing at her battered face. First she offered words of comfort, then she chided Sanja for her rejection of Scott.

"Amela, you of all people should understand," Sanja begged. "Our world is barbaric. It's completely alien to Scott's world. I'm convinced he'll be better off without me."

Amela was dismayed at what she heard. It was as if all Sanja's usual courage and composure had seeped away like rainwater into a filthy sewer.

Two hours later, while Sanja was getting settled upstairs, Amela's phone rang. The call was from Scott.

"I just got back home and talked to Goran," he said, his words clipped. "He gave me your number. Sorry to be so abrupt, Amela. I'm looking forward to meeting you. Listen, I'd like to talk to Sanja. Is she all right?"

"Yes, but ... Goran told you there's a problem?"

"Yes." Scott sounded grim. "Before I called you I yelled and swore and ... Well, never mind. Goran said it's been reported to the police."

Amela said, "Sanja fought back, you know. This isn't about courage."

"I understand that. She thinks I'll judge her and reject her. I won't do either, Amela. I just need to talk to her."

The genuine concern in his voice was like a shaft of sunlight breaking through dark clouds. He was the strong ally Amela and Goran needed.

She said, "Sanja's upstairs. I *will* get her to the phone. Can you call back in ten minutes?"

"Yes. Thanks. Ten minutes."

As she climbed the stairs, Amela rehearsed her arguments.

Sanja! You didn't create the situation. You were attacked because of me. It would never have happened if we weren't friends again.

No, that would only foster guilt.

Sanja! Don't you know how guilty I'll feel if I've ruined your life?

Wrong. More guilt with an added dose of self-interest.

Sanja! You're the one who never gives up! Here you are about to achieve everything we've talked about wanting—everything you deserve—and you're throwing it away for what? Now go talk to Scott. I dare you!

As Amela had expected, it took every bit of threat and coercion, but she finally got Sanja to the phone exactly ten minutes later. Then she busied herself in the kitchen. She washed dishes. She folded and refolded towels. She poured tea, so nervous she dropped the cup. She anxiously counted off the minutes. Ten, twenty, forty-five.

When Sanja got off the phone and joined Amela, she was a butterfly, emerged at last. She was radiant. She was ecstatic.

Amela gave a triumphant yelp and flopped into a chair.

Sanja sat down next to her. She couldn't stop grinning. "It's okay now," she said. "I'm okay now. Everything's okay now."

"Well, let me be the first to welcome you back," said Amela, weak with relief. "So tell me, what did he say?"

"He said ... " Sanja paused. She was ecstatic. "He's furious about the attack, and he wants me to be safe, but what happened doesn't affect the two of us. And the sooner I'm with him, the better he'll feel."

"Oh! Oh! I'm so happy for you! So, tell me the rest," Amela said. "About you. About him. About the plan."

Sanja looked at her, dazed. "He said two colleges have accepted us as late registrants for the spring semester." She took a deep breath and plunged on. "He'll meet us at an airport near Washington. Can you believe it, Amela? We're going to America!"

"If you weren't such a great person, I'd say you don't deserve him."

"Of course I don't," Sanja agreed. "And I'll never shut him out like that again. He's wonderful! And by the time I see him ..." She winced as she touched her cheek, still tender. "By the time I see him, I should look normal."

"The bruises and swelling will be gone," Amela said. She still felt like crying over what Sanja had gone through. "But," she continued, "what will your parents say about your leaving?"

"Good question. Goran's been preparing them for his departure for some time, but mine will come as a shock. Papa will accept it. He wants what's best for me." Sanja paused with a pained expression. "Oh, I think my mother does, too, in her own way. I just hope telling her doesn't start the next Balkan war."

CHAPTER
30

The next morning, Sanja went home and Amela made a quick trip to the nearby market. When she returned, she was surprised to see Dragan at the front door. He was a friend, but not the kind who stopped by for tea. Her heart beat like a wild bird trying to escape from a cage. Did Dragan's visit have to do with her father?

"I knocked," he said, "but no one answered."

"My mother is at a friend's house today."

Dragan was fidgeting, much as Goran had earlier. Was this more bad news?

"You haven't seen the television," he said.

Amela clenched her hands, nails biting into her palms. She understood instantly. He had heard one of the announcements that missing persons had been found and relatives were being sought to confirm the identities. In Tuzla, Amela, Dina, and Sejo had given DNA samples—including cheek scrapings and blood. They were told that samples had to come from a subject's maternal side or from his or her children. They had also given ante-mortem data about the clothes he was last seen in, any items he might have been carrying, and other personal characteristics. The information was put into a missing persons database. The first time there was a television appeal. Hanifa had responded and was staggered by the experience. Amela had responded after that, and the emotional impact, even without positive results, had left her feeling battered. It was impossible to know how they would feel if the identification was positive.

"My dear," Dragan was saying, "graves were found near the Drina, near Janja. Those who may be able to make an identification are being asked to visit the assistance center. I can't go *for* you, but at least I can go *with* you."

Amela was glad that her mother was out. She might never need to know about this latest possibility if the results were once again negative.

No matter how many times Amela had gone through the identification process, she could not escape the tension that gripped her as she entered the building. Which was worse—to keep hopelessly hoping that someone you loved was alive or to learn that he was dead?

But this time the results were not negative. Dental records had already been checked as had DNA. A medical medallion that Sejo had scratched his initials into left Amela no doubt that the remains were those of her father.

She was told of the location of the exhumed. *Exhumed!* As if that was his profession. *No!* she wanted to shout. *He wasn't an exhumed—he was a doctor!*

The process of identification didn't take long. For the remaining questions, she sat across the desk from a woman who was brisk and businesslike. That was helpful. Amela was having trouble breathing. Sympathy could unravel her.

"His …" Amela closed her eyes, then opened them and tried again. "His ring …?" she asked, her voice sounding hollow.

"I'm sorry. There was no ring," said the woman.

"But he always … Never mind. But you did find the medallion."

"Perhaps he found a way to hide it. We'll let you know if there's anything more we need from you," said the woman. "You'll receive a death certificate, and if you'll give us instructions, we'll transport your father to whatever location you request." There was nothing more, she told Amela, but could she get her some juice or water?

Amela declined the offer, took the papers and the medallion they gave her, and returned to the waiting room where Dragan sat looking haggard, shoulders hunched, hands clasped between his knees. As she started toward him, the room began to spin. She swayed and gripped the back of a chair. He hurried to help her sit down. After the fainting spell passed, she told him about the interview. Dragan kept wiping his eyes, but Amela could not let her emotions take charge. She had to be strong for her mother.

Dragan walked Amela home and stopped outside the front door. "Do you think your mother's home now?" he asked.

Amela shook her head. "She'll stay at her friend's house for supper."

"There's some good in this, Amela," he said gently. "Women with missing husbands have to declare them dead in order to get a pension. Your mother would never trade hope for money, but now she doesn't have to."

"Yes," she said, feeling weak and exhausted, "but it's not much of a silver lining, is it?"

He lowered his head, took off his glasses, and wiped his eyes. "I won't be going back to the apothecary today. I need to compose myself."

Dragan took a long white envelope from his coat pocket. "Your father gave this to me two days before they took him away. His instructions were that if he didn't survive, I was to give this to his children for college or, in Dina's case, marriage." When Amela smiled, he said, "Your father understood his children well. He also correctly read the situation in Bosnia. However, he had no way of knowing how much time would pass before I could give this to you."

Dragan put the envelope in Amela's hand. "He opened a Swiss bank account and this is the documentation," he said. "He was being prudent in the days before the war. There may be a letter inside as well. I don't know. He regretted that the funds weren't much. They were to be shared equally among the three of you."

Amela took the envelope and clasped it to her.

"Here's a sedative for your mother." Dragan said. He handed her a small bottle. "Get a little rest before she comes home."

Dragan turned to leave, then turned back with a heavy sigh. "I'm so tired," he said softly. "You know, you and I were born Yugoslavian, but our country became ill. Now, as we try to recover from our national schizophrenia, we find that we're no longer Yugoslavs."

He sank down onto the porch step and stared off into the distance. "What am I?" he asked. "Serbian? I don't live in Serbia, but in the Serbian Republic of Bosnia, so the world calls me a Bosnian Serb. Does that make me Bosnian? And for you, Amela, you were once called a Bosnian Muslim—now you're a Bosniak, a new label."

"Here's the thing," he said, folding his hands. "If we were art— we former Yugoslavs—we would no longer be the lovely mosaic we once were. We became fragmented, then were reassembled into large patches of different colors. A quite different design."

Amela gazed at him wistfully. "I'd like to be a mosaic tile again, Dragan. I'd like to be a tile in a *Bosnia* mosaic."

CHAPTER
31

After Dragan left, Amela went into the house. Although the rooms were warm, she felt cold. She couldn't cry, no matter how awful she felt. Her father was dead. But ... hadn't she known that ... really ... for a long, long time?

Should she call Tuzla? No, not yet. Soon enough she would need to tell her family. But first, her mother. She wished her mother would come home soon; then she wished her mother wouldn't come home for weeks. How she dreaded the next few hours!

Amela had a fierce headache. She tried to lie down, but it was impossible to be still. She got up and paced from the kitchen to the parlor and back again. She was glad when Sanja called asking if she could spend the night.

"We heard the TV announcement," Sanja said as soon as she arrived. "It could be about your father. I'll go with you if you like. Nothing that's ever happened to me could be as hard as this is for you."

Amela led the way into the parlor and sat on the sofa. "Thanks," she said, "but I've already talked to somebody. Dragan went with me." She went on, her voice choked, "My ... my ... father has ... He's been—" she refused to say exhumed—"found."

Sanja hugged her friend and then drew back, wiping her own wet cheeks. "You're so pale," she said. "Is there anything I can do?"

"No. Nothing. Dragan was ..."

The ringing of the phone interrupted her. It was Samir.

"The identification was positive," Amela told him. "And you?"

"Yes, for us, too. Amela, something else has come up. Is your mother home? Is it all right if I come by with a visitor?"

"You may certainly come by, Samir," said Amela, "but my mother is at a friend's."

After the briefest pause, he said, "That may be better. We'll see you in about ten minutes."

When the knock came, Sanja started to go upstairs, but Amela caught her wrist. "No. Stay. I need you."

Amela recognized the man who came with Samir, a former neighbor. She served coffee in the parlor, and then the man, Hussein, explained his visit.

"I was living in Bijeljina in 1992," he said, his expression flat and toneless. "I have lived in Germany for the past seven years."

Amela was starting to figure out why he had come. "Did you know my father?" she asked.

"Yes, I did. I, too, was taken away that night in April."

Sanja said nothing, but took her friend's hand as they waited for him to go on.

"I was there when ... It was close to the river, where we were taken. We were crowded into a shed and for a while, they badgered us with questions. Who had weapons? Who was working for Alija? What could we say? It was none of us, and all ... all I ..." Hussein's voice cracked and he took some time to blow his nose. Then he went on, "You see, they killed my brother ... the others. They thought they'd killed me, too. I was wounded ... losing blood, but I wasn't dead. After ... after they left, I crawled away and hid. I was the only one who survived." Hussein rested his elbows on his knees and buried his face in his hands. It was a while before he could continue.

"I had no family. I set off on foot for Hungary." He paused, remembering. "Eventually I found a way to get to Germany. A few weeks ago I came back … here to Bijeljina. It will never be home again, but I … I wanted to visit the grave of my brother."

Amela's hands were shaking as she refilled Hussein's coffee cup. Samir picked up his story.

"When Hussein could not locate a grave, he came to see me. I told him that the men who were taken had never been found. He contacted people who help find missing persons, and what he told them led to a search."

Hussein turned to Amela. "I want to tell you about your father. In the truck that took us away … on the road, in the woods … he was so strong. He gave us strength, too—and courage." Hussein leaned forward and stretched out his hand to Amela as if to send out a wave of comfort. "Your father was the finest man I ever knew."

When at last she was able to speak, Amela said, "Thank you for telling me. My mother … my family … we needed to know."

"I only wish …"

"No, please. After all this time, it's enough."

The men got up to leave, and Samir lingered at the door. "It's good that we know, Amela … about your father and my brother." He bowed his head for a second, then lifted it. His eyes were dull, his skin gray and stretched tight across his cheeks. There were dark circles under his eyes that she hadn't noticed before.

"I don't know how to tell my mother," she murmured.

"I'll come by in the morning. We can tell her together." Samir took hold of her icy hands. "It's over, Amela. At least the wait is over."

After the men left, Sanja helped Amela make up the spare bed.

Amela couldn't stop trembling, and Sanja put her arms around her as they sat down together.

"I wish there were something I could do for you," Sanja said softly.

"You're doing it," Amela said, returning the hug. "You're here."

"I can't believe all that's happened," Sanja said, her eyes showing the sorrow she was feeling. "I hate the horror you heard about today. And it makes me think of my ... of my cousins." Her voice was awash in her tears. She searched in her pocket for a tissue, and went on. "There are thousands and thousands of families like yours and mine ... all over this destroyed land. I don't have enough tears to cry for them all."

Amela glanced up as she heard the front door open. She stood up, overwhelmed by panic. She took a few rough breaths, gathered her courage, and started downstairs. Hanifa had hung up her coat and traded her shoes for slippers. She had gone into the kitchen where Amela found her hunched over the sink. Amela took her arm. Gently she led her to the sofa.

"Mama." She knelt by her mother, stroking the thinning hair, more gray now than black. She closed her eyes, trying to collect her thoughts, trying to find the right words, trying to keep her heart from splintering into a million pieces. She must make her mother face the truth that her husband was never coming back. Amela was afraid it would kill her.

Hanifa leaned forward, her hands covering her face. "I know," she said, her voice a mere whisper. "At my friend's. A man came."

"Hussein?"

"Yes. Her husband was ... was also one they took. He told us."

"About ...?" How could she tell her mother about the

identification? Her throat was so tight she could barely speak.

"Yes. About the rest," said Hanifa. She leaned her head back. Her lips trembled, her face was chalky.

Even so, Hanifa's reaction was not at all as Amela had expected. There were no screams or sobs. She didn't faint. She didn't wail. She merely sat very still, the only noticeable movement her index finger tapping rhythmically against the finger where once there had been a wedding ring. Was she in shock? Amela brought a glass of water, but was ignored when she offered it.

"They found him, Amela. Kemal. He won't be coming home." A deep sigh, then, "He was so brave. He helped others all his life. He was helping them still … at the end."

Amela slumped against the arm of the sofa. She wasn't sure how to behave with her mother so calm. Was it true—what she had thought earlier? Had they really known and been mourning for a long time?

If that was so, how did it change her own life? A door had closed. Would she ever be able to open a new one? She leaned her head against her mother's knee and finally let the tears come.

CHAPTER
32

Amela went with her mother to Tuzla for her father's burial. Dina, Sejo, and other members of Kemal's family were also there to honor him. A hodza was present to offer prayers. Amela hugged her mother, sharing the bits of strength they were both holding onto. They both breathed a sigh when he was finally laid to rest.

The next day, Amela went with her mother, Dina, and Sejo to the cemetery where Jasmina and Adnan were buried, and then they all went again to her father's grave. After placing their flowers and comforting each other, they sat on a bench above the town and talked. Sejo sat between Hanifa and Amela, with Dina beside their mother.

Amela put her arm around her brother. He stiffened, the response of a young man about to be fourteen, but she held fast. "There's something Mama and I think you should have," she said, giving him the silver medallion with his childish initials scratched on the back. "Papa would want you to have it."

He took the medallion reverently, turning it over, rubbing his thumb across the initials. "I remember the day I put these here," he said almost to himself. "Papa came in and found me doing it. I'd ruined this and one of his best knives." He swallowed hard. "Just when I thought he'd yell, he took the knife away from me and then the medallion and said, 'Now I have you next to my heart when I wear this.'" Sejo kissed it, then slipped the chain over his head, saying, "Now I have you next to mine, Papa." One arm went around Amela, the other around his mother. Dina reached over and clasped his hand.

Later, Amela and her mother returned to the room they shared. It had been Jasmina's. Amela remembered searching for cigarettes through piles of clothes on the bed, and felt sad. When they were getting ready for bed that night, Hanifa said, "My dear, about your going away to university …"

"Oh, Mama, I don't …" Amela began.

"Hush, child. It's all right. You've been my strength for so many years. I'm settled now, and it's time for you to spread your wings ... even if it means you'll fly away."

"Well, flying away could mean a hundred kilometers or seven thousand kilometers."

"Yes," said Hanifa with a sigh. "I would miss you terribly, but wherever your future lies, then that's where you must go. I have confidence in your good judgment."

"Oh, Mama," Amela said again, "I don't regret a minute spent with you."

Amela had always believed that knowing the truth about her father would release her to make plans for her future. But now, in November, almost three years after the end of the war and with her mother getting ready to move back to Tuzla, she was unsure; nevertheless, she prepared for the trip to Sarajevo the next day for passports.

Sanja and Goran had taken the earliest bus, and Amela

met them at the station. In spite of her occasional doubts, their happiness was contagious as they continued the trip to Sarajevo together. The three of them were excited when they looked at their new passports. *Unimaginable freedom*, Sanja called it.

"With passports we could go to Portugal, Goran! Like we said all those years ago."

Amela smiled to herself as she flipped through the empty pages, wondering what might someday be in them. She remembered her election supervisor, Trevor, and their talk about taking small steps. She wished he could know about this step and her joy in achieving something that had once seemed beyond her reach.

On the way back to Bijeljina, they stopped briefly in Tuzla. Sanja visited her grandmother in her small room. When Sanja tried to explain her decisions for her life, Baka was bewildered.

"You will be a displaced person? Why do this? I do not understand."

"Not displaced, Baka," Sanja told her. "It's my choice and a good one." Though Sanja still wasn't sure her grandmother understood, she knew her baka supported her anyway.

Shortly after Sanja returned home, she received a package from Scott. She was on her way to Amela's and took it, unopened, with her. Inside the large package was a small box, and inside the box, Sanja found a jade butterfly on a gold chain. There was also a note.

In a Chinese legend, a young man follows a beautiful butterfly into the garden of a wealthy mandarin. Instead of being punished for trespassing, the young man is given the mandarin's precious daughter in marriage.

Amela's mouth dropped open. "Now *that* sounds promising.

Although I don't know about the *precious* part."

Sanja sighed and slipped the chain over her head. Although she was no longer restricted to the house when she was in Bijeljina, at least during the day, her mother was still making tentative inquiries about her living in Belgrade.

⟶

Whenever Sanja visited Amela, she was pleased to see her toy Siva on the windowsill. The kitten was special to both girls and they peppered it with questions about their future. No matter what they asked, Siva remained mute. They, on the contrary, chattered constantly. Amela found herself eager one minute, then agonizing the next over the mysteries that lay ahead. Sanja had an advantage, buoyed by phone calls from Scott.

Hanifa and Amela disposed of the house and gave the contents to another returning family the Norwegians were helping. Hanifa would relocate to Tuzla. Sejo would move in with his mother; Dina had announced her engagement, and she would be married soon. Amela would stay with her aunt and Sanja would stay with her grandmother until Goran joined them for the trip to America. Maybe, at long last, things were falling into place.

For Amela, it was time for a decision, one she realized she had been coming to for quite a while. The hard part would be telling Sanja. For that, she suggested they return to their old meeting place, the memorial. Goran drove them there, but left, saying he'd be back for them in an hour.

"So, what's this all about?" Sanja asked when they had laid out their snack on a cloth.

Amela used the kitchen knife she had packed to spread jam

on a piece of bread. Then she said slowly, "Sani, I've thought really, really hard about this."

Sanja stiffened and laid down the banana she had started to peel. "It sounds like something I don't want to hear."

"I don't know any easy way to say it, so ... I'm going to university and I want to study law, but in Bosnia. In Sarajevo."

Sanja clutched her throat. "Wh ... what do you mean? How can you?"

Amela understood all too well how Sanja was feeling. She bit her lip, then said, "You know ..." She tried to go on, to explain, but the words lodged in her throat. She sighed and tried again. "You remember that IPTF conference, the one where they talked about the rule of law?"

Sanja held back, rigid, then gave a quick nod.

"Well," Amela went on, excited, "it means that laws the people agree to are put into writing and made definite. They keep people in government from having too much power."

Sanja could almost hear Scott saying those same words.

"Think about our country," Amela begged. "It's new with all kinds of promise. There's nothing to hold us back." As Amela talked, she was reminded of the arguments that she had made to herself. She leaned forward, needing for Sanja to understand. But why wouldn't she? She had lived through a war, too. "Our country is free now. And, at last, so am I. Our country can decide what it wants to be, what it wants to do. And ..."

"And so can you." Sanja had listened with her head down. "But," she said, looking up and wiping away a tear, "why didn't you tell me? I thought you wanted to go to America. I thought we were doing it together."

"I did want to go. And I do. And I will someday. That's what's made it so hard to choose! I didn't tell you because ... well, first of all, you'd have tried to talk me out of it and … and just like going is right for you …"

"I know," Sanja whispered. "Staying is right for you."

"Yes. I hate to disappoint you. But we can phone each other and email and, someday, visit. And you'll have Scott and Goran."

"Scott knew, didn't he? You and he have discussed this."

"Yes," said Amela, "Scott's been very helpful getting me information about sponsorship for university in Sarajevo. But don't be mad at him. He never tried to talk me into one way or the other."

Amela looked up at Mira's door, then across the road to Granny Radmila's farm. She looked along the road to the farm where Tatiana had let the goat out. This was the place where she and Sanja had first started trying to repair their friendship.

"I'll miss you," Amela said, her eyes filling with tears. "I will miss you so, so much!"

She leaned forward and held out her hand. After a brief moment, Sanja took it. She drew in a sharp breath, then laid her head on Amela's shoulder.

They held each other for a few minutes until Amela sat back. "And, Sani," she said, reaching into her backpack and pulling out a little gray toy kitten, "I want you to take Siva with you to America."

Sanja took the pet and nestled it under her chin. "Oooh …" Her voice faded away, her disappointment at Amela's decision was so great.

"Don't look like that, Sani. It's not the end of our friendship. Breaking us up has already been tried, and it was a complete failure."

Sanja thought about it and smiled. "You're right," she said.

Amela picked up her knife, wiped it clean, and then took

Sanja's hand. "There's this blood ritual I saw once on TV."

Sanja threw her head back and laughed. "No, thanks. Don't you know it's not something friends-for-life need to do?"

For Sanja, the crisis with Amela passed. The sadness of separation lingered, but the prospect of being with Scott cheered her. As for her mother ... well, informing Stefana of her plans hadn't quite launched the fierce battle Sanja had anticipated, but the matter still was not completely resolved.

On the morning of her departure for Tuzla, Sanja finished packing, then dragged her large suitcase into the hall.

"Goran," she called, "come help me."

"I'll help you, beautiful lady," Ranko said as he came up the stairs. He gave Sanja a mysterious smile before he hoisted her bag and carried it downstairs.

Sanja gathered up the rest of her things and went down. Ranko was sitting on the sofa next to Ivana, her father was in his favorite chair, and her mother was standing with Goran's arm around her. The dining table was loaded with food, and in the center was a lovely floral arrangement.

"What's going on here?" asked Sanja.

Her father stood up and kissed her cheeks. "Your mother prepared the food and I bought the flowers," he said. "It's not every day our children leave for a new life."

Sanja glanced at her mother, who was tight-lipped but obviously making an effort to be agreeable.

"Come," said Stefana. "Let's have something to eat."

They sat around the table, their plates filled with bureks, sirnica, and sarma. Sanja glanced at the father she adored, disturbed that she couldn't tell how he felt. Then he rose slowly, glass in hand, nodding first toward Sanja, then toward Goran. They got up and went to stand beside him.

"I want to make a speech," he said.

"A short one, please, Petar," begged Stefana.

"A short one," he assured them with a smile rare for him these days. "I've watched my country tear itself apart, leaving a legacy of conflict and hopelessness. What the two of you are doing gives me hope ... for your future ... and ours." His look included all of them. As Goran and Sanja hugged him, he said, "Go find your dreams."

Sanja couldn't have been more surprised and pleased with the farewell. She hadn't expected her mother to relent even a little, and she knew that for Stefana, this was a lot.

Ivana helped clear the table after the meal. Sanja said, "You've kept the short, blonde style."

"Ranko says he likes it this way," Ivana replied.

Ranko winked at Sanja, who raised her eyebrows and said, "Ah, I see."

Shooed out of the kitchen, Sanja maneuvered him to a place where they could speak privately. "Rado, about that night. I haven't told you ... " she began.

"Hush, now. There's nothing you need to tell me, Sani, except that we won't lose you forever. I hope your American knows how lucky he is."

Sanja leaned her head against his chest and said, "I'll come back, at least to visit, and maybe you can come to visit us in America."

"I'll try," he promised, kissing the top of her head.

It was a short party. Sanja had a bus to catch, and Goran was waiting to drive her to the station.

"Mama," she began as they stood at the door.

"Just go." Stefana looked tense, but she spoke more with

resignation than with rancor. Her eyes filled with tears. She ran a hand through Sanja's dark hair and said, "Be happy."

As Goran drove his sister to the bus station he said, "I'll be taking this trip in a few days. I can hardly wait!"

Amela and her mother arrived ten minutes before the bus was to leave. Hanifa went to buy tickets while Amela joined Sanja and Goran at their table by the street door.

Sanja was tapping her foot impatiently. "You're late," she scolded Amela. Then, her lips grimly pressed together, she nodded toward a table next to the other door.

Amela recognized the bully who had made her return to Bijeljina miserable. He was talking to an older man, but glanced her way and winked. She felt chilled, as if her blood had drained away. Then hot defiance flowed through her. He had mistreated her for the last time. She lifted her chin and stared back as if he were a crumb on the tablecloth. He turned away.

"My luck," Amela said, taking a seat. "He's probably here to make sure I leave his town, and good riddance."

However, the bully apparently had other plans. He loudly boasted to his friend that he was there to meet a girl who, he said, would do anything for him. When her bus arrived, the two of them were driving to a special place he knew by the river. As he talked, he kept glancing at Amela, as if wondering what final indignity he could pull off. Then he reached into his pocket. Staring at her steadily, he took out a cigarette lighter, flicked the flint, and waved the flame suggestively back and forth.

Amela looked away from him, disgusted. If his taunting gesture wasn't a clear admission of guilt about the fire, it was at least an attempt at further intimidation.

Sanja had her back to the bully, but Goran watched what he'd done and looked warily at Amela. He could tell she was more contemptuous than frightened.

The girls had a bus to catch, and they needed to leave immediately. Hanifa had the tickets and was waving to them from the door.

"Sanja's suitcase is in the car," Goran told them. "Go on out to the platform and I'll bring it."

Amela picked up her suitcase and backpack and headed for the door with Sanja following. As Amela passed the bully's table, he flicked the lighter again. She casually picked up the bottle in front of him and poured the contents over him, soaking him and extinguishing the flame. She left him sputtering as she sauntered toward the door and neatly dropped the bottle into a trash bin before stepping out onto the platform.

Sanja followed, her mouth open in astonishment. She looked back inside and saw the bully push back his chair. Then, restrained by his friend, he sat back down. Sanja burst out laughing.

The attendant was sliding Amela's luggage into the space under the bus when Goran joined them. He handed over Sanja's bag, and then gave Amela an object wrapped in a napkin.

"What's this?" she asked.

"A farewell present. Distributor cap from a car. His." He jerked his head toward the bully. "His girlfriend won't be doing anything for him for a while."

Amela grinned and Sanja threw her arms around her brother. "Justice!" she cried.

"Have a good trip," he told them. "I'll see you in Tuzla, and then it's on to America!"

Amela helped her mother aboard. Hanifa gave her the tickets for the double seat near the back, as she herself took the single one nearer the front. Amela was starting down the aisle when she heard Sanja gasp.

"Go ahead. I'll be back in *one minute!*" She cast a pleading look at the attendant who pursed his lips, looked at his watch, and glared at her retreating back.

True to her word, Sanja was aboard the bus in seconds. The door closed as she found her seat next to Amela, who was grinning broadly.

"You forgot something, didn't you?"

Sanja gave her a haughty look. "If you can be late, I can forget something. It's tradition. Here. I almost left this on the bench back there." She thrust a gift-wrapped package at her friend. Amela tore off the wrapping.

"Oh," she sighed. Inside were carved wooden picture frames.

"I got us two, one for you and one for me," said Sanja.

"How perfect," Amela said, squeezing Sanja's hand. Then she stared out the window, watching the people, the buildings, the canal. It was impossible for her to ignore the town. It was a place she had both loved and hated.

The girls were quiet as Bijeljina disappeared behind them.

"Won't you miss it," Amela asked, "just a little?"

Sanja turned her moist eyes away from the window. "Yes. Bijeljina is where I was born, where I grew up, where I learned a lot and had a lot of fun. Yes," she repeated softly, "I'll miss it. And I'll come back someday, but just to visit."

Amela looked again at the frames, imagining herself and Sanja smiling out, each at the other. "I know we'll meet whenever we can," she said, "but let's send new photos every few months. That way it'll be like growing up together."

"And growing old together," Sanja added.

Amela smiled at her. "Yes," she said. "Friends for life."

Acknowledgments

Hvala! —thank you—to the people of Bosnia, whose kindness and generosity are legend to those of us fortunate enough to have worked there. Thanks also to friends in Serbia and Croatia who have opened their hearts and homes to me in my dozen visits.

To my interpreters and drivers: Azra, Hasan, Jelena, Felip, Dijana, Sasha, Mersiha, Hussein, Amra, Edin, Amela, Sadmir, Aleksandra, and Gagi, my deep gratitude for their friendship and assistance from 1997 to 2001 and for story advice in the present.

Special gratitude to Dalibor, who grew up in Bijeljina and was a great resource as my gracious host in 2005. His grandmother's sarma is yummy!

I owe so much to others in Bosnia and Serbia: Sead (Sejo), Halisa, Vida—to name just a few—and also to friends in the United States: Biserka, Sanda, Milan, Ranka, Tanja, and Lejla.

To my daughter Denise: special thanks. Her research experience in Kosovo, Bosnia, and Montenegro; her sessions as a facilitator with Seeds of Peace; her mediation skills; her education in grief counseling; and her knowledge of disaster relief services were of tremendous benefit. I have welcomed her support, nagging, insights, and (yes, even!) "bleeding" red ink all over my draft pages.

Thanks to other family members who have supported me over the years: Duane, Doug, and Lisa.

My appreciation to the Tuesday Night Writing Group could fill another book!

My colleagues who also worked for the OSCE in the Balkans are extraordinary. To name a few: Suzanne, who accompanied me on my 2005 research trip and reviewed, with her granddaughter Natalie, the first draft; Susanne and Gordon, who both have incredible knowledge of Bosnia; Stephen, Nan, Bruce, John, and Harry whose experiences sparked my imagination. Others have helped in various ways: Tony, Robert, Scott, Bob, and the entire BozBunch, who have given advice and boosted my morale at annual reunions and many other times.

I am indebted to those whose expert advice has added greatly to the accuracy of the story: Dr. Adi Rizvić and Doune Porter of the International Commission on Missing Persons (ICMP) and Kathleen Salanik, American Red Cross, and to George Brown and Marlous van Gils for information about house fires and election monitoring, respectively. Special thanks to Peggy Bjarno, whose experience and talent with production were invaluable and whose invitation to speak to her Rotary Club about my Bosnian experiences was early encouragement.

I have relied on many invaluable sources for history and background information. A few that were especially helpful are Silber and Little's *Yugoslavia: Death of a Nation*; Loyd's *My War Gone By: I Miss It So*; Glenny's *The Fall of Yugoslavia: The Third Balkan War*; Lynne Jones', *Then They Started Shooting: Growing Up in Wartime Bosnia*; Andric's, *The Bridge on the Drina*; Filipovic's, *Zlata's Diary*; Cohen's *Hearts Grown Brutal*, Sudetic's *Blood and Vengeance*, Maass's *Love Thy Neighbor*, Kroll's dictionary and phrasebook, and several films, among them *Pretty Village, Pretty Flame*.

How I love the land of "Boz"—its mountains and valleys, stunning green rivers—a country of awesome natural beauty. It has been heartbreaking to see miles of shattered buildings and wasted farms; heartbreaking to hear the personal stories of wartime tragedies. But more impressive to me is the strength and resilience of the people; their rebounding spirits; their towering wills; and their determination to build a solid future.

ABOUT THE AUTHOR

The author has worked at the American Embassy in Paris, France and with the Citizens' Development Corps as a volunteer advisor at the Zvezdny Hotel in Sochi on the Black Sea in Russia. Her interest in international affairs culminated in seven trips to Bosnia and Serbia beginning in 1997 as an election monitor with the Organization for Security and Cooperation in Europe (OSCE) and to Kosovo in 2002 with Council of Europe. She has maintained many of her Balkan friendships.

The author is a volunteer tutor with the Montgomery County Literacy Council and a disaster relief volunteer with the American Red Cross. She currently resides in Rockville, Maryland, and enjoys visiting her three grown children in Maryland, Florida, and Louisiana.

Author with her interpreter, Mersiha
Bonavici, Bosnia, September 1998